THE BISHOP'S RECUSAL

AN ALEX HAYES LEGAL THRILLER

BOOK 4

L.T. RYAN

LAURA CHASE

Copyright © 2025 by L.T. Ryan, Laura Chase & Liquid Mind Media. All rights reserved. No part of this publication may be copied, reproduced in any format, by any means, electronic or otherwise, without prior consent from the copyright owner and publisher of this book. This is a work of fiction. All characters, names, places and events are the product of the author's imagination or used fictitiously. For information contact:

contact@ltryan.com

http://LTRyan.com

https://www.facebook.com/JackNobleBooks

THE ALEX HAYES SERIES

Trial By Fire (Prequel Novella)
Fractured Verdict
11th Hour Witness
Buried Testimony
The Bishop's Recusal
The Silent Gavel

CHAPTER ONE

BRYCE COULTER WAS GOING down for wire fraud, and everyone knew it.

The jury foreman cleared his throat, the paper trembling between his fingers. "On count one of the indictment, wire fraud in violation of Title 18, United States Code, Section 1343, we find the defendant, Bryce Coulter ... guilty."

I kept my expression neutral even as satisfaction surged through me. The gallery behind me remained silent, but I could feel the collective exhale from the victims–dozens of retirees who'd entrusted their life savings to Coulter's investment firm only to see it vanish into his personal offshore accounts.

"On count two of the indictment, wire fraud in violation of Title 18, United States Code, Section 1343, we find the defendant guilty."

Coulter's face drained of color. He tugged at his collar as if it were suddenly too tight, his $3,000 suit no longer armor but a costume that could no longer hide the fraudulent man beneath.

"On count three of the indictment, wire fraud in violation of Title 18, United States Code, Section 1343, we find the defendant guilty."

The judge thanked the jury for their service as Coulter turned to whisper frantically to his attorney. I packed my notes into my bag, savoring the moment without showing it. Federal court demanded decorum, after all. No triumphant fist pumps are allowed, no matter how satisfying the verdict.

Judge Henderson denied bail pending sentencing. When the U.S. Marshals approached with handcuffs, Coulter finally lost his composure.

"This is ridiculous!" he protested, voice cracking. "I have rights! They can't—"

The cuffs clicked into place, and reality caught up with him. This was no longer a negotiation. This wasn't a boardroom where he could charm his way out of trouble. This was federal prison, coming for him with cold metal and bureaucratic certainty.

As they led him away, one of the victims–an elderly woman who'd lost all her retirement savings to him–caught my eye and mouthed "thank you." That moment meant more than the verdict itself.

White-collar crime didn't have the same visceral impact as violent offenses, but watching a man who'd stolen millions from retirees face justice still gave me a rush of satisfaction.

The feeling lasted about fifteen minutes.

Now, back at my desk in the U.S. Attorney's Office, the victory felt hollow. Another pre-packaged win for the government's newest golden child. Another case slotted into my lane because it was a sure thing.

My phone buzzed. I glanced at the screen: James Holloway.

Heard about the Coulter verdict. Nice work, Hayes.

Despite myself, I smiled, typing back: *He cried when they cuffed him.*

Three dots pulsed before his response: *The expensive suit types always do.*

My office was different now. After the Ortega case, after exposing the public defender, Gregory Bard's corruption and bringing down Judge Leland, I'd been moved from my cramped starter office to something with an actual window. The view wasn't spectacular–just the federal building across the street and a slice of Houston skyline–but it was symbolic. A promotion without the actual promotion.

I swiveled my chair toward the wall where I'd hidden my own personal case board behind a large, framed print of the Constitution. I slid the frame aside, revealing my notes, photos, and a printed copy of the chessboard I'd discovered among Leland's papers.

Two names stared back at me: LELAND and THATCHER.

Two white bishops on one side of the board, part of something much larger–a network that had reached into the highest levels of our judicial system. I'd spent three months searching for more information on Thatcher with little success.

The name "Thatcher" had turned into a research rabbit hole of judicial proportions. Four federal judges, seven state court judges, three administrative law judges, and one Supreme Court clerk all shared the surname. I'd investigated each one, looking for connections to Leland, to trafficking, to anything suspicious. Dead ends, all of them. Either I had the wrong Thatcher entirely, or whoever it was had covered their tracks with professional precision.

A knock startled me. I quickly slid the frame back into place as Nathan Callahan peered in.

"Hell of a job on Coulter," he said, leaning against the doorframe, sleeves rolled up to his elbows in his perpetual "working prosecutor" style. "Judge Henderson mentioned you specifically. Said you presented evidence 'with remarkable clarity.'"

Swiveling in my chair to face him, I crossed my legs. "Turns out financial crime isn't that complicated when the defendant emails his co-conspirators using phrases like 'totally illegal but worth it.'"

Callahan chuckled. "Still requires the right prosecutor to package it for a jury."

I offered a thin smile in return. "Thanks, Nathan."

"You've impressed a lot of people around here, Hayes. Built some serious momentum." He stepped further into my office. "Beckett's noticed."

The U.S. Attorney himself. The big boss. Great.

"Appreciate the update," I said, trying to match his enthusiasm and falling pathetically short.

Callahan tilted his head, studying me with the shrewd assessment that made him an effective supervisor. "Most attorneys would be ecstatic about catching Beckett's attention."

"I am." I forced another smile. "Really."

"Look, I know the Leland case hit a wall. The FBI's still working it, but these things take time."

"Three months," I said, unable to keep the edge from my voice.

"And we're no closer to understanding who was pulling Leland's strings."

"These investigations move slowly. You know that."

"Meanwhile, I'm being handed slam-dunk cases."

Callahan straightened, his expression hardening. "Those 'slam-dunks' are putting criminals behind bars. That's the job, Alex."

I nodded, knowing he was right but feeling the frustration bubble under my skin anyway. "I know. I'm grateful for the opportunities." The words sounded flat, even to me.

His expression softened. "Good. And there's more coming your way. You've earned it."

"More slam-dunk cases? Can't wait."

"That's the spirit," he said, tapping the door frame twice. With that, he turned and left, leaving my door open–a subtle suggestion for me to rejoin the office ecosystem instead of brooding alone.

I stared at the space where he'd stood, wondering if this was what victory was supposed to feel like–being rewarded with cases just challenging enough to keep me busy but not significant enough to rock any boats.

A flash of movement caught my eye as Erin Mitchell appeared in my doorway, arms crossed, looking suspiciously pleased with herself.

"Your trophy case getting full yet?" she asked, strolling in without waiting for an invitation.

I crossed my own arms. "Funny."

Settling into the chair across from me, she stretched her legs out. "Three for three. The golden girl of the Houston office."

I rolled my eyes. "Sure, my batting average is perfect, but they're lobbing me beach balls underhand."

Erin deadpanned. "Alex. We're attorneys. Please don't try and talk sports. It makes it seem like you're trying too hard."

Erin and I had mostly moved past the rough patches, the tension and distrust that had nearly fractured our friendship. We'd found our rhythm again, falling back into the easy banter that had characterized our relationship during law school. But there were still moments when a shadow would cross her face, when I'd catch her watching me with something like concern or calculation. Times when her answers came a beat too quickly, too practiced, like she was holding something back. But I never pushed.

After all, I hadn't told her everything either.

"I'll have you know that I was on the softball team in high school."

"Please just stop," Erin fake pleaded.

"So, other than insulting me, why are you here?"

"I'm here to take you to lunch. You look like you need it." She glanced around my office. "Nice digs, by the way. Updated view, and the extra square footage probably makes your anxious pacing more comfortable."

"Oh yes, I'm very comfortable," I said sarcastically.

"And busy." Erin's voice lowered, her expression turning serious. "Word around the office is that Beckett's impressed with you."

"So Callahan just informed me."

"That's a big deal, Alex."

I leaned back in my chair, exhaling. "You know what would impress *me*? Finding out who the hell Thatcher is and what connection he has to Leland."

Erin glanced toward the door before leaning in. "What have you found?"

"Nothing concrete." I lowered my voice. "The FBI has Leland locked down tight. He's not talking, and his lawyer's making sure he never will. Bard's case is proceeding at a glacial pace, with continuance after continuance. And every time I try to get updates on either investigation, I hit a wall of 'not your department anymore, Hayes.'"

"Maybe that's for the best." Erin's eyes held a warning. "You took down a federal judge, Alex. That's enough excitement for one career."

"A federal judge who was just one piece on the board," I countered. "Whoever orchestrated all of this is still out there. And they know I was getting close."

The image of Ortega's execution flashed through my mind—the cold precision of the gunshot, the blood pooling on the table, and the shooter's chilling words about my mother.

You're just as smart as your mother was. But that's what got her killed.

Three months hadn't dimmed the memory or the fear it inspired.

"That's exactly my point," Erin said, her voice edged with concern. "You saw what happened to Ortega. These people don't mess around."

I dropped my eyes to my desk, fingers tracing the edge of Coulter's case file. "My mother got too close to something. Ortega knew what it was. Now he's dead, and I'm being kept busy with wire fraud cases." I looked up at her. "You don't find that suspicious?"

"What I find is that you survived a situation that would have broken most people. Now you've got a window office and Beckett's attention." Erin frowned. "Maybe the universe is giving you a chance to build a normal career."

I let out a short, humorless laugh. "Normal was never in the cards for me."

"You know what your problem is?" Erin leaned back in her chair. "You have a way of telling the universe to go to hell."

I blinked. "I don't know what that means."

"Good things are being handed to you—a promotion, recognition, cases that could actually advance your career—and you're telling the universe that's not what you want. Or at least, not the way you want it." She gestured toward my office door. "Most people would kill for what you have right now."

I shifted in my seat. "I didn't ask for any of this."

"Exactly my point." She studied me for a long moment. "Have you told Holloway about your … concerns?"

"Some," I admitted. "But he's back in D.C. Our conversations mostly center around how terrible airport food is and whether long-distance relationships can survive on monthly visits and daily phone calls."

"Sounds healthy."

"It's something." I stood, grabbing my jacket from the back of my chair. "Come on. You mentioned lunch, and I'm suddenly starving."

Erin eyed me as she rose. "You're changing the subject."

"Brilliantly observed, Counselor. They teach you those deductive skills in law school?"

She rolled her eyes but followed me to the door. As we walked through the office, I nodded to colleagues–faces that had become familiar over the past three months. Some offered congratulatory smiles for the Coulter verdict. Others simply acknowledged me with a professional nod. Still, something about their gazes made me feel like I was being watched, assessed, contained.

"You know," Erin said as we stepped into the elevator, "most people would be thrilled with your trajectory. Federal prosecutor on the fast track, prestigious cases, dating a sexy DOJ attorney from Washington."

"I am thrilled," I insisted as the elevator doors closed.

"Liar."

"I just can't shake the feeling that I'm being managed. Given enough to keep me satisfied but not enough to dig deeper."

"Did it ever occur to you that maybe you're being protected?"

I scoffed. "From what?"

The elevator slowed, and Erin's expression turned grave. "People in robes aren't the only ones with power, Alex. Sometimes the most dangerous players are the ones you never see coming."

The doors slid open to the lobby, bathed in midday sunlight streaming through tall windows. The security guards nodded as we passed, but I couldn't shake the chill Erin's words had sent down my spine.

Outside, Houston's heat made me instantly regret putting on my blazer, the humidity coating my skin as we stepped onto the sidewalk. Downtown bustled with its usual midday energy–lawyers rushing between courts, office workers grabbing quick lunches, tourists mapping out their next destinations.

"What did you mean by that?" I asked as we waited for a crosswalk signal. "About the most dangerous players?"

Erin's gaze swept the street, an unconscious security check I recognized from years working together. "Just that you might want to consider the possibility that your fast track isn't about keeping you busy. It could be about keeping you visible."

"Visible?"

"Harder to make someone disappear when they're in the spotlight." The light changed, and she stepped forward. "Come on. There's a new Thai place around the corner that doesn't water down the spice."

I followed, mind racing with the implications of her words. Was my rising profile a form of protection? A way to ensure that if anything happened to me, people would notice?

Or was it simply the easiest way to keep me distracted from what really mattered–finding out who killed my mother and why?

CHAPTER TWO

AFTER GETTING BACK FROM LUNCH, the summons came through Callahan's assistant, Cynthia, delivered with the kind of professional gravity that meant either someone important was dead, or someone important was about to make my life significantly more complicated.

"Callahan wants to see you," she said, hovering in my doorway with a manila folder clutched against her chest like a shield. The fluorescent lights overhead cast harsh shadows across her face, emphasizing the tension around her eyes. "Conference room B. Now."

I glanced at the clock, its red digital numbers glowing from my desk like an accusation. Three-thirty on a Friday afternoon–prime time for career-altering conversations. The kind of timing that made seasoned prosecutors check their retirement accounts and junior associates update their résumés.

"Did he say what about?" I asked.

"High-profile case. That's all I know." She shifted her weight from one foot to the other, her heels clicking against the linoleum in a nervous rhythm. The folder crinkled as she adjusted her grip. "But there are FBI agents in there with him."

My pulse quickened. FBI meant federal jurisdiction, which usually meant either terrorism, organized crime, or political corruption. Given my recent track record with cases that had a habit of exploding in my face, any of those options could spell trouble. The taste of stale coffee turned bitter in my mouth.

I grabbed my legal pad and followed Cynthia down the hall, my footsteps echoing off the sterile walls. The familiar scent of industrial carpet cleaner filled my nostrils. I tried to appear calm, but my heartbeat accelerated, hammering against my ribs. Through the conference room's glass walls, I could see Callahan speaking animatedly with two people I didn't recognize–a woman in a crisp navy suit, and a man whose posture screamed federal law enforcement from his squared shoulders to his regulation haircut.

The woman's gestures were precise, controlled, each movement calculated for maximum impact. The man sat perfectly still, his dark eyes scanning the room with the methodical attention of someone trained to notice everything. They both wore that brand of intensity that came from years of dealing with the worst humanity had to offer.

Callahan looked up as I knocked, his usually ruddy complexion pale under the conference room's lighting. "Come in, Alex."

The woman turned first, extending her hand with the kind of firm grip that suggested she'd fought for every promotion she'd ever received. Her palm was dry, her handshake lasting exactly three seconds–textbook professional contact. "Special Agent Sarah Chen, FBI. This is Agent Rodrick."

Rodrick nodded, studying me with the detached assessment of someone trying to determine if I was competent enough to handle whatever they were about to dump in my lap. His suit jacket hung open, revealing a glimpse of his shoulder holster, and I caught the faint scent of gun oil and aftershave.

"Have a seat," Callahan said, gesturing to the chair across from him. The leather creaked as I settled into it, the sound jarring against the silence. "We've got a situation."

I positioned my pen over my notepad, the familiar weight of it steadying my nerves. The paper was blank, pristine, waiting to be filled with details that would either make or break someone's life. "What kind of situation?"

Agent Chen opened a thick file, the pages rustling beneath her fingertips. Each document bore the official FBI seal. Crime scene photographs peeked out from between witness statements and forensic reports. "Yesterday evening, twenty-two-year-old Melissa Thatcher was found dead in her apartment near Rice University. Blunt force trauma to the head."

I kept my expression neutral, years of courtroom training taking over. My pen trembled slightly against the paper as I wrote down the basic facts, but I managed to keep my voice steady. "Any witnesses?"

"None. But we have a suspect." Rodrick leaned forward, his chair groaning under his weight. The movement brought him into my peripheral vision, and I could see the way his eyes never stopped moving, cataloging every detail of my reaction. "Blake Costello, her on-and-off boyfriend for the past two years. Engineering student, no criminal record, but neighbors reported them arguing frequently."

The conference room closed in around me. I could hear the distant sounds of traffic outside, the muffled noise of the city continuing its business while we sat here, discussing death and justice.

I looked up from my notes. "What makes him a suspect besides proximity?"

Agent Chen slid a photograph across the table, the glossy surface reflecting the overhead lights. "Security camera caught him leaving her building around the estimated time of death. His prints are on what we believe to be the murder weapon—a heavy glass paperweight found at the scene."

I studied the photo. A young man with dark hair and a nervous expression looking over his shoulder as he hurried down a hallway. The image was grainy, captured by a security camera that had seen better days, but the timestamp was clear. The hallway looked institutional, with beige walls and worn carpeting that had probably been installed sometime in the previous decade.

"But there are inconsistencies?" I asked.

Rodrick shifted forward. "The autopsy shows blunt force trauma consistent with multiple impacts, but the crime scene only shows evidence of a single blow. And the blood spatter patterns don't match what we'd expect from the positioning of the body."

"Has he been arrested?"

"This morning. He's claiming innocence, says he was there earlier, and that Melissa was alive when he left." Callahan's voice carried the weight of skepticism earned through years of hearing similar protests from guilty defendants. He tapped his fingers against the table in a steady rhythm, a nervous habit I'd noticed during particularly stressful cases. "But the forensic evidence is raising questions."

I nodded and asked, "Where's the federal angle?"

The agents exchanged a glance, one of those wordless communications that spoke of years of partnership and shared secrets. Chen's jaw tightened almost imperceptibly, and Rodrick's shoulders tensed.

The silence stretched for three heartbeats before Chen answered, her voice carefully neutral. "Melissa Thatcher was the daughter of Judge Henry Thatcher, Fifth Circuit Court of Appeals."

Time slowed down. The AC unit turned on, but the sound was muffled in my ears. My pen slipped from cold, numb fingers, clattering against the conference table. *Judge Henry Thatcher.*

The name brought sudden dizziness, driving the air from my lungs. My vision narrowed, everything beyond the conference table fading to gray. The taste of copper filled my mouth. I'd bitten my tongue without noticing.

I thought about all the Thatchers I'd researched over the past three months, late nights spent poring over judicial records and news articles, trying to connect dots that seemed to shift every time I thought I had a pattern. Judge Henry Thatcher, Fifth Circuit, appointed twelve years ago, confirmed by a narrow Senate margin after some controversy over his previous rulings on immigration cases. His judicial record was conservative but unremarkable–nothing that had set off alarm bells when I'd investigated him months ago.

But maybe I'd been looking at the wrong things. Maybe the answer wasn't in his judicial opinions or his political connections. Maybe it was in his family, the people closest to him who could be used as leverage or eliminated as threats.

The chessboard flashed in my mind, those carefully arranged pieces, bishops and knights in exacting positions. Was he the missing bishop?

"Alex?" Callahan's voice cut through my mental fog like a blade. "You with us?"

I blinked, forcing myself back to the present. The conference room snapped back into focus, colors returning to normal intensity. My notepad showed a jagged line where my pen had skittered across the paper before landing on the desk. "Sorry. Federal jurisdiction because she's a judge's daughter?"

"Partly," Agent Chen said, watching me with the sharp attention of a predator studying prey. "Under 18 U.S.C. 1114, killing a federal official or their immediate family member with intent to interfere with their official duties is a federal crime. But we also have interstate elements–Blake made several trips to Louisiana in the weeks before the murder, and some of the forensic evidence suggests the crime scene may have been staged."

"And you think that interstate travel was connected somehow?"

Chen shrugged. "It's enough to give us probable cause."

She pulled out another photograph. Melissa Thatcher's apartment, pristine except for the chalk outline on the living room floor. The image was clinical, sterile, capturing the scene with the dispassionate eye of forensic photography. Hardwood floors gleamed under crime scene lighting, expensive furniture arranged with the casual precision of someone who had both taste and money. A bookshelf lined one wall, filled with what looked like law texts and classic literature. A coffee mug sat on the kitchen counter, half-full and abandoned.

"Plus," Chen continued, "some of the evidence suggests this might have been targeted rather than random. Nothing was stolen. No signs of forced entry. Whoever did this had a key or was let in. But the medical examiner's findings don't align perfectly with what we're seeing at the scene."

I grabbed my pen and jotted down a new line of notes. This wasn't a burglary gone wrong or a random act of violence. Someone had walked into Melissa's apartment, someone she trusted enough to open the door for, and killed her. But the inconsistencies between the autopsy and crime scene suggested something more complex than a simple domestic dispute.

"What's the prosecution angle then?" I asked. "Why am I the only one hearing about this?"

"That's where it gets complicated." Callahan rubbed his jaw, the gesture revealing the stress lines that had deepened around his eyes over the past year. "Judge Thatcher has been on the Fifth Circuit for fifteen years. Half the senior AUSAs in this office have appeared before him at some point. The other half have personal or professional relationships that create conflicts of interest."

Rodrick's words carried the gravelly undertone of someone who'd spent years interrogating suspects in windowless rooms. "We need someone clean. Someone without ties to the judge or his family."

I looked around the table, understanding dawning. The manila folders, the careful way they'd presented the evidence, the fact that they'd called me in on a Friday afternoon when most of the senior staff had already left for the weekend. This wasn't just about finding a prosecutor. This was about finding someone expendable. "And I'm the only one who fits that description."

"You'd be first chair," Callahan said, his attempt at encouragement falling flat. "High-profile case, lots of media attention. It's a big opportunity."

An opportunity. Right. The kind of opportunity that either made careers or destroyed them, with very little middle ground between the two outcomes.

"What's the timeline?" I asked, buying myself a moment to think. My mind raced through the implications, weighing the risks against the potential rewards.

"Costello's arraignment is Monday morning. We need someone ready to hit the ground running." Agent Chen gathered the photographs with practiced efficiency, sliding them back into their respective folders. "The family wants justice, and they want it fast."

I stared at the case file, Melissa Thatcher's name printed in block letters on the tab. The folder was thick, bulging with evidence and witness statements, but I knew from experience that the real story was always more complicated than what fit in an FBI file. This could be coincidence–tragic timing that had nothing to do with chess pieces or conspiracy theories. Or it could be exactly the break I'd been looking for, a chance to get close to one of the bishops on that board.

"Judge Thatcher will obviously recuse himself from any related proceedings," Callahan continued, his fingers drumming against the table with increasing frequency. "But his influence in legal circles means this case will be under intense scrutiny."

"Have you spoken with him directly?"

"Briefly. He's devastated, as you'd expect. But he's also determined to see this handled through the proper channels." Callahan's expression hardened, the politician in him recognizing the potential for a public relations disaster. "Which means no mistakes, no procedural errors, nothing that could give the defense ammunition for appeal."

The weight of expectation settled over the room. I could feel the agents watching me, measuring my response, probably already forming opinions about whether I was up to the task. The clock on the wall ticked steadily, each second bringing Monday morning closer.

"I'll need complete access to all evidence," I said, my decision crystallizing. "Crime scene reports, forensics, witness statements, everything."

Agent Chen nodded, approval flickering in her dark eyes. "You'll have it by end of business today."

Callahan leaned back in his chair, studying me with the calculating gaze of someone who'd spent decades reading people for weakness. The leather creaked under his weight, and I caught a whiff of his cologne mixing with the room's stale air. "You sure you're ready for this? High-profile murder cases are different from financial fraud. The pressure's intense, and the stakes are higher."

I met his gaze directly, drawing on every lesson I'd learned about projecting confidence in the face of uncertainty. "I can handle it."

The lie came easily, probably because part of it was true. I could handle the legal aspects—building a case, presenting evidence, arguing before a jury. What I was more worried about was my own conflict of interest as far as the name "Thatcher" was concerned, and the possibility that accepting this case would put me directly in the crosshairs of whatever had killed Luis Ortega. And quite possibly, my mother.

"Good." Callahan stood, signaling the end of the meeting. His chair scraped against the floor as he pushed it back. "Agents, thank you for your time. Alex, I'll need regular updates on your progress."

Agent Chen paused at the door, her hand resting on the frame. The gesture seemed casual, but I caught the way her eyes swept the room one final time, cataloging details with the thoroughness of someone who'd learned never to take anything for granted. "For what it's worth, the physical evidence against Costello is solid, even with the inconsistencies. This should be straightforward."

I looked up at her, noting the careful way she'd phrased the statement. When federal agents used words like "should be," they were usually trying to convince themselves as much as anyone else.

"In my experience," I said, "nothing involving federal judges is ever straightforward."

She smiled grimly, the expression more human than her professional mask. "You're probably right about that."

As everyone filed out, I remained seated, staring at the case file. The conference room felt larger now, empty except for the lingering scent of aftershave and the weight of unanswered questions. Melissa Thatcher smiled up at me from her driver's license photo–young, bright-eyed, completely unaware that her death would become a chess move in a game I was still trying to understand.

The photo was recent, probably taken within the last year. She had her father's eyes, intelligent and direct. According to the preliminary report, she was twenty-two years old, a senior at Rice studying international relations with plans to attend law school. She volunteered at a local legal aid clinic and had spent the previous summer interning at the Federal Public Defender's office.

Following in her father's footsteps, building a career in public service. The kind of idealistic young person who believed the system could be changed from within, who thought justice was more than just a word carved into courthouse facades.

Now she was dead, and her boyfriend was the prime suspect in what appeared to be a textbook case of domestic violence escalated to murder.

But the timing nagged at me. Three months after I'd discovered that chessboard, Thatcher's daughter turns up dead, and I'm the only prosecutor available to handle the case. The coincidence felt too perfect, too convenient, pieces falling into place according to someone else's design.

Either this was the universe's idea of ironic coincidence, or someone was making moves I couldn't see yet. Someone who knew about my investigation, who understood exactly how to draw me deeper into the game.

I closed the file and headed back to my office. The hallway stretched before me, each footstep a reminder of how isolated I was in this building full of people who knew nothing about chess pieces or conspiracies.

CHAPTER
THREE

I FOUND Erin in her office at seven-thirty the next morning, already nursing what appeared to be her second cup of coffee while reviewing a stack of depositions. Saturday mornings at the AUSA's office were usually quiet, a peaceful silence that allowed prosecutors to catch up on paperwork without the constant interruptions of ringing phones and urgent meetings.

But Erin had always been an early riser, especially when a case demanded her attention, and the scattered files across her desk suggested she'd been here for at least an hour.

The federal building felt different on weekends—less formal, with most of the support staff gone and business attire replaced by casual clothes and sneakers. Security was lighter, the marble corridors echoed more, and the almost academic atmosphere reminded me why I'd been drawn to prosecution in the first place. The pursuit of justice without the political theater that often dominated weekday operations.

She looked up as I knocked on her doorframe, her dark hair pulled back in a ponytail. "Let me guess. You couldn't sleep either."

"Something like that." I stepped inside and closed the door behind me, noting the way she cleared space on her desk—a habit born from years of handling sensitive material that couldn't be left visible to casual observers. "Got a minute?"

"For you? Always." She gestured to the chair across from her desk.

"Though if you're here to complain about your new high-profile case, I'm not sure I want to hear it."

The comment carried the easy familiarity of a friendship that had survived law school, bar exams, and the transition from state to federal prosecution.

"Actually," I said, taking the seat, "I'm here to ask you to join it."

Erin paused mid-sip, coffee cup hovering inches from her lips. Steam rose from the mug, carrying the rich aroma of the dark roast she preferred—always black, never with sugar, a habit she'd developed during the sleep-deprived years of law school and never abandoned.

"Come again?"

"I need a second chair. Someone I trust, someone who knows how to handle complex cases without letting politics get in the way." I settled into the chair, noting how the morning light from her window highlighted the concern already forming in her expression. "Someone who understands that high-profile cases require more than just good legal skills—they require someone who can navigate media attention and political pressure without losing sight of what really matters."

She set her cup down carefully, the ceramic making a soft click against the wooden desk. "Alex, this is the daughter of a Fifth Circuit judge. Every move you make will be scrutinized by the defense bar, the media, and probably half of Washington. You sure you want to complicate things by bringing me into it?"

I waved a hand at her statement, a gesture that encompassed the magnitude of what we'd already be facing. "The case is already complicated. Between the victim's identity and myself as first chair, we're already maxed out on the complications scale. Adding your name to the roster won't change much."

The truth was, having Erin as second chair would simplify things. She had a reputation for meticulous preparation and unflappable courtroom presence, qualities that would serve us well when defense attorneys started looking for procedural errors or prosecutorial misconduct. More importantly, she had the political instincts to navigate the treacherous waters of a case involving federal judiciary, something I'd learned was crucial after watching other prosecutors destroy their careers by underestimating the political dimensions of high-profile cases.

Erin leaned back in her chair; arms crossed in the defensive posture she adopted when processing unexpected information. "How complicated?"

I glanced toward the door, then lowered my voice to a conspiratorial tone even though the building was next to empty. "Remember the chessboard from Leland's papers? The one with the bishop positions marked?"

"The Thatcher name you've been chasing for months."

"Judge Henry Thatcher. Melissa's father."

Understanding dawned in her eyes like sunrise breaking through clouds. "Alex, please tell me you're not suggesting—"

"I'm not suggesting anything yet. But this case gives us legitimate access to Thatcher's life, his connections, his background. If he's clean, we rule him out and focus on getting justice for Melissa. If he's not …"

"If he's not, then you're prosecuting the murder of a corrupt judge's daughter while investigating whether he's part of a criminal conspiracy." Erin rubbed her temples, the practiced motion of someone who'd dealt with too many late nights and complex cases. "Do you hear how insane that sounds?"

"I hear how it sounds. I also remember watching Ortega get executed in front of me, and the shooter mentioning my mother."

That stopped her cold, the way it always did when I brought up the moment that had changed everything about how I viewed the justice system. Erin had been there for the aftermath, had seen me shaking in the holding cell, had helped piece together the evidence that brought down Leland. She knew better than anyone how deep this conspiracy ran, how many lives it had claimed, how many more it might claim if left unchecked.

The silence stretched between us, filled with the weight of shared experiences and the understanding that some cases transcended normal prosecutorial work. This wasn't just about seeking justice for one victim—it was about confronting a network of corruption that had operated with impunity for decades.

"What does the evidence look like?" she asked finally, her voice carrying the careful neutrality of a prosecutor evaluating a potential case.

I pulled out the case file, spreading crime scene photos across her desk with the methodical precision I'd learned from years of case preparation. Each photograph told part of the story—Melissa's apartment, the positioning of furniture, the blood patterns that would become crucial evidence in establishing what had really happened that night.

"Blake Costello, the boyfriend. Murder weapon has his prints, security footage places him at the scene around the time of death, and neighbors heard them arguing."

"Sounds open and shut." But Erin's tone suggested she was already looking for the complications, the inconsistencies that turned straightforward cases into prosecutorial nightmares.

"Maybe."

Erin studied the photographs with the trained eye of someone who'd reviewed hundreds of crime scenes, looking for the story beneath the obvious narrative. "Could be that he planned it. Premeditated rather than heat of the moment."

"Could be," I said. "Or could be someone wanted it to look like Costello did it."

"You think he was framed?"

The question carried implications that extended far beyond this single case. If Blake Costello was being framed, it suggested a level of sophistication and planning that pointed to something much larger than a domestic dispute gone wrong.

"I need to investigate all possibilities. And I can't do that alone."

Erin was quiet for a long moment, fingers drumming against her desk as she weighed the implications. Outside her window, downtown Houston was slowly coming to life—early risers grabbing coffee from street vendors, joggers making their way through the streets, delivery trucks beginning their routes. The normal rhythm of a Saturday morning, peaceful and predictable. So different from the dangerous territory we were contemplating entering.

"If I agree to this," she said finally, her voice carrying the careful precision of someone laying down non-negotiable terms, "we do it by the book. Every procedure followed, every piece of evidence properly documented. We can't give the defense any ammunition for appeal."

"Agreed."

"And if we find evidence that Thatcher is involved in something illegal, we turn it over to the appropriate authorities immediately. We don't go rogue, we don't try to handle it ourselves."

"Also agreed."

She picked up one of the crime scene photos, studying Melissa's apartment with the attention to detail that had made her one of the most respected prosecutors in the office. "She was twenty-two years old. Pre-law student, clean record, no known enemies besides an occasionally volatile boyfriend."

"Which makes this either a straightforward case of domestic violence, or someone using that as cover for something else."

Erin looked back up at me. "And you think the 'something else' might connect to your mother's case."

I met her gaze directly, seeing in her eyes the understanding that this conversation was about more than just case assignment. "I think it's worth finding out."

Erin set the photo down slowly, her expression thoughtful. "You know, when I convinced you to come to the federal side, I thought you might get interested in white-collar crime. Maybe some nice, clean financial fraud cases."

"Sorry to disappoint."

"You're not disappointing me. You're terrifying me." She stood, grabbing her jacket from the back of her chair. "But you're also right. If there's a connection, we need to find it."

"Does that mean you're in?" I asked, a little too eagerly.

"I'm in," she said. "But we're going to need more help. This case is going to generate massive media attention, and Judge Thatcher will have every legal heavy-hitter in the state watching our every move."

"What kind of help?"

"The kind that can handle forensics, witness interviews, and background investigations without tipping our hand about what we're really looking for." She pulled out her phone, scrolling through contacts with practiced efficiency. "I know someone who might be perfect for this."

"Who?"

"Special Agent Logan Elliott. Remember him?"

"Remember him? He interviewed me after I watched Ortega get executed. Sort of hard to forget."

Erin shrugged, a gesture that acknowledged the potential awkwardness while dismissing it as irrelevant to the current situation. "Sorry if it triggers you, but he's thorough, discreet, and he owes me a favor."

"Thanks, but I'm not worried about that. What I want to know is whether we can trust him?"

She eyed me. "With this? Yes. Elliott's been chasing corruption cases for years. If there's something dirty about Judge Thatcher, he'll find it."

"And if there isn't?"

"Then we prosecute Blake Costello for murdering his girlfriend and put a killer behind bars. Either way, Melissa Thatcher gets justice."

I nodded, but something in Erin's tone made me pause. There was a finality to her words, as if she was trying to convince herself as much as me that justice *could* be that straightforward, that we could pursue this case without getting caught up in the larger implications of what we might find.

"You think I'm chasing ghosts, don't you?" I asked.

Erin gathered the crime scene photos, stacking them neatly before sliding them back into the file with the careful attention to organization that characterized all her work. "I think you've been through hell, and you're looking for patterns that might not exist. But I also think your instincts have been right more often than wrong. So we'll follow the evidence wherever it leads, even if it takes us somewhere we don't want to go."

"And if it leads us back to the conspiracy?"

"Then we'll deal with that when we get there. But Alex, promise me something."

"What?"

"If this gets dangerous—if we start getting too close to something that could get us killed—you won't try to protect me by keeping me in the dark. We're partners on this, which means we share the risks."

After everything that had happened with the Ortega case, after the times I'd charged ahead without fully considering the consequences for those around me, she was asking for honesty. Complete transparency, even when it might put her in danger. It was a reasonable request from someone who'd seen firsthand how investigations like this could spiral beyond anyone's control.

"I promise," I said, meaning it.

"Good." She pressed her thumb against her phone's screen and placed the device to her ear. "Then let's get started."

CHAPTER FOUR

THE FEDERAL COURTHOUSE felt different at eight in the morning. Empty corridors stretched ahead of us, our footsteps creating the only sound against polished marble. Erin walked beside me, a stack of files tucked under her arm, both of us moving with the efficient pace of prosecutors who'd done this dance too many times to count.

"Remind me why we agreed to such an early hearing?" she asked, adjusting her grip on the files.

"Because Judge Morrison wanted to handle scheduling before the media circus gets worse." I pushed through the heavy courtroom doors. "And because I wanted to get a feel for how this is going to play out."

The courtroom was nearly empty—just us, the defense team huddled near their table, and a handful of court personnel making final preparations. Judge Morrison sat behind the bench, reviewing paperwork with the methodical attention of someone who'd been doing this for decades. The American flag hung motionless in the corner of the room.

"Ms. Hayes, Ms. Mitchell." Morrison looked up as we approached the prosecution table. "I trust you're both prepared to discuss our timeline?"

"Yes, Your Honor." I set my briefcase down and pulled out my calendar. "The state is ready to proceed at your convenience."

Defense counsel—a silver-haired man named Lawrence Richardson who'd made his reputation defending white-collar criminals—stood at his table. "Your Honor, given the media attention this case has generated, we'd like to request additional time for jury selection. The defendant's right to a fair trial—"

"Mr. Richardson," Morrison interrupted, "this is a scheduling conference, not opening arguments. We'll address jury concerns when we get there."

I was reviewing my notes when movement in the gallery caught my attention. A man had entered through the back doors, moving with the confident stride of someone accustomed to being noticed. He was tall, impeccably dressed in a charcoal suit. His hair was silver white, perfectly styled, and his face held the kind of authority that came from decades of wielding power.

My pen stopped moving across the page. Erin noticed my sudden stillness and followed my gaze.

"Judge Thatcher," she whispered.

Thatcher chose a seat in the front row, directly behind the prosecution table. He settled into the wooden bench with the practiced ease of someone who owned every room he entered.

I forced myself to focus on Judge Morrison's voice. "—preliminary matters resolved, I'd like to set a trial date for six weeks from today. That gives both sides adequate time for discovery and witness preparation."

"Your Honor," Richardson said, "six weeks seems aggressive given the complexity—"

"The complexity, Mr. Richardson, is exactly why we need to move efficiently. This case will only get more complicated the longer we delay." Morrison made a note on his calendar. "Motion deadlines will be two weeks prior to trial. Any evidentiary disputes need to be resolved before we seat a jury."

I tried to focus on the scheduling details, but Thatcher's presence felt like a weight pressing against my back. Every few minutes, I caught myself glancing over my shoulder. He sat perfectly still, his attention seemingly focused on the proceedings, but something about his stillness felt calculated.

"Ms. Hayes?" Morrison's voice cut through my distraction. "Do you have any scheduling conflicts?"

"No, Your Honor. The government can meet those deadlines."

"Excellent. Now, regarding media access—"

The hearing continued for another twenty minutes, covering the mundane but necessary details that would shape the next several weeks. Jury pool size, courtroom security, press guidelines. Standard preliminary matters that felt anything but standard with Thatcher watching from the gallery.

When Morrison finally gaveled the session closed, I gathered my papers with deliberate care. Erin was already packing her briefcase, moving with the efficient speed of someone eager to leave.

"Ms. Hayes."

The voice came from directly behind me. Turning, I found Thatcher standing at the rail that separated the gallery from the well of the court. Up close, his eyes were pale blue, the kind that seemed to look through rather than at you.

"Judge Thatcher." I kept my voice level, professional. "I wasn't expecting to see you here."

"I try to attend when I can. This case has ... personal significance." His smile was perfectly practiced, the kind politicians and judges learned to deploy at will. "I hope you'll handle it with appropriate care."

Erin moved closer, positioning herself slightly between us. "Of course, Your Honor. We understand the sensitivity involved."

Thatcher's gaze shifted to her briefly before returning to me. "Ms. Mitchell, isn't it? I've heard good things about your work."

"Thank you."

"You'll need to guide your colleague through the complexities." His tone remained conversational, but something felt sharp underneath. "Federal court has its own rhythm. Different from state proceedings."

The heat rose in my chest. "I appreciate the concern, but—"

"I noticed you mentioned digital evidence and witness testimony in your filings." Thatcher continued, as if I hadn't spoken. "Have you considered the victim's background? Sometimes understanding the person helps clarify the circumstances."

"We've reviewed all relevant background information," I said carefully.

"Have you?" He tilted his head slightly. "Melissa was … complicated. Brilliant in many ways, but she had difficulty accepting boundaries. She believed rules were suggestions rather than requirements."

Erin stepped forward. "Judge Thatcher, perhaps this isn't the appropriate—"

"She was studying political science, you know. Always asking questions, always pushing." His expression shifted, something unreadable passing across his features. "I tried to teach her discretion, but young people today … they think everything should be transparent, every story should be told."

"She sounds passionate about her work," I offered neutrally.

"Passionate." He seemed to taste the word. "That's one way to describe it. Reckless might be another. She had notebooks full of … theories. About local politics, about people in positions of authority. Fantasy, mostly. The kind of conspiracies young people invent when they want to feel important."

The way he said it—dismissive but also watchful—made me pay closer attention.

"Did she share these theories with anyone?" Erin asked.

Thatcher's smile didn't reach his eyes. "Oh, she tried. But who listens to a college student playing detective? Still, it worried me. That kind of behavior can be … misunderstood. Can make enemies where none need exist."

"Are you suggesting someone might have—"

"What I'm suggesting," he interrupted smoothly, "is that my daughter didn't always exercise good judgment. And that young Mr. Costello took advantage of that. Love makes people vulnerable, Ms. Hayes. Especially when they're already prone to … flights of fancy."

I studied his face, trying to read what lay beneath the polished exterior. "You seem very certain about Costello's guilt."

"The evidence speaks for itself, doesn't it? They fought. He was possessive. She tried to leave." He shrugged, a gesture that seemed too casual. "Classic domestic violence escalation. I've seen it hundreds of times from the bench."

"Every case is unique," I said.

"Is it?" His gaze sharpened. "In my experience, prosecutors who look for complexity where none exists often find themselves ... disappointed. Sometimes the obvious answer is the correct one."

Erin's hand brushed my arm—a warning. "We appreciate your insights, Judge Thatcher."

"Do you?" He glanced between us. "I do hope so. It would be unfortunate if personal ... curiosities interfered with obtaining justice for my daughter. Melissa's dead because she trusted the wrong person. That's the only story that matters here."

The way he said "curiosities" felt deliberate, but I couldn't pin down why.

"We follow the evidence," I said. "Wherever it leads."

"How admirable." His tone suggested otherwise. "Though I wonder if you truly understand where evidence can lead. This city has a long memory, Ms. Hayes. Old stories have a way of resurfacing at inconvenient times." Pausing, he studied me. "You know, you remind me of someone. Another idealistic prosecutor from ... what, twenty years ago? Also thought every case had hidden depths. Tragic, really, how that turned out."

He shook his head as if dismissing an old memory. "But I'm sure you're nothing like that. Best to focus on the present, don't you think?"

Before I could respond, he checked his watch. "I should go. I have a meeting with the mayor—budget discussions. The mundane realities of civic service." He straightened his jacket. "Good luck with your case. I'm sure you'll do what's ... appropriate."

With that, he turned and walked toward the exit, his footsteps echoing off the empty walls. I watched him go, something cold settling in my stomach.

"Well," Erin said once the doors closed behind him, "that was interesting."

"Interesting?" I started packing my briefcase with more force than necessary. "He just spent ten minutes telling us not to investigate his daughter's death too thoroughly."

"That's not what I heard." But her expression was thoughtful.

"Though you're right—he did seem more concerned about her 'theories' than her actual murder."

"And the way he talked about her. Like she was an embarrassment."

Erin was quiet as we walked toward the elevator. "You know what struck me? He never once said he loved her. Never called her 'my baby' or talked about missing her. Just ... analyzed her like a case study."

"Yeah." I pressed the elevator button. "And that comment about old stories resurfacing—what was that about?"

"Could be nothing. Could be standard judicial ego—reminding us he's connected, he's important." The elevator arrived, and we stepped inside. "Or ..."

"Or he knows something about why I'm really interested in this case."

Erin studied me. "You think he knows about your mother?"

"I don't know what he knows. But that whole conversation felt like a chess match where I didn't know the rules."

The elevator descended in silence. Finally, Erin spoke. "You know what else was weird? Richardson didn't say a word after the hearing ended. Just packed up and watched."

"Like he was waiting to see what Thatcher would do."

"Or making sure Thatcher got his chance to talk to us alone." She shook her head. "This case is starting to feel like everyone knows something we don't."

As we exited the building into the morning sun, I replayed the conversation in my mind. Thatcher had been careful—nothing overtly threatening, nothing quotable. But the undercurrent was clear: stay in your lane, prove what we already know, don't dig deeper.

"So, what do we do?" Erin asked.

I looked at her. "We dig deeper."

"Even if Thatcher's warning was real?"

"Especially then." I pulled out my keys. "But we're going to be smart about it. If Melissa Thatcher was investigating something before she died, I want to know what it was."

Erin smiled grimly. "You know, when I woke up this morning, I thought this would be a straightforward domestic violence case."

"Nothing about this case is straightforward." I unlocked my car. "And I'm starting to think that's exactly how Judge Thatcher wants it—complicated enough to be convincing, but not so complicated that we look too close."

CHAPTER FIVE

"Richardson wants to talk plea," Erin said. We'd claimed a corner table at the café across from the federal building.

"Of course he does."

"Best case scenario? He knows his client is screwed and wants to see if we'll take manslaughter instead of murder one." Erin took a sip of her coffee and made a face. "Worst case? He's trying to figure out how much we actually know."

I took a sip from my own mug, the taste bitter against my tongue, but I needed the caffeine. I'd been up until two in the morning reviewing the case files, looking for something I might have missed. The conversation with Thatcher had left me unsettled, second-guessing every piece of evidence.

"What's your read on the defendant so far?" I asked.

"Privileged kid who's never faced real consequences. Clean record, but that doesn't mean much when daddy's money can make problems disappear." Erin pulled out her legal pad. "College senior at Georgetown, studying political science. Grades are decent but not stellar. Lives off a trust fund."

"Any red flags in his background?"

"Nothing obvious. A few noise complaints at his apartment, one underage drinking citation that got dismissed. Standard rich kid stuff." She flipped through her notes. "But here's what bothers me—

Richardson didn't just take this case for the money. He's connected, Alex. The kind of defense attorney who gets calls from senators when their kids get arrested."

I thought about that. Richardson's reputation preceded him—white-collar criminal defense, political corruption cases, the kind of lawyer who charged a thousand dollars an hour and was worth every penny. Taking on a college student's murder case seemed beneath his usual clientele.

"You think someone recommended him specifically?" I asked.

"I think someone wanted to make sure Blake Costello had the best possible representation." Erin's voice dropped. "And I think we need to be very careful about what we say in that room."

We finished our coffee and made our way back across the street. The federal building's security checkpoint was busier than usual, a line of lawyers and courthouse personnel waiting to clear metal detectors. By the time we reached the conference room on the fourth floor, it was exactly three o'clock.

Richardson was already waiting, his silver hair perfectly styled despite the humid October weather. He stood as we entered, extending a manicured hand.

"Ms. Hayes, Ms. Mitchell. Thank you for making time on such short notice."

"Mr. Richardson." I shook his hand briefly. "I understand your client is interested in discussing a resolution."

"Perhaps. First, I'd like you to meet Blake."

The young man sitting at the far end of the conference table looked exactly like what central casting would order for "privileged college student." Dark hair styled with expensive product, a navy blazer, and the kind of casual confidence that came from never doubting your place in the world.

Until you looked at his eyes. They were red-rimmed, darting around the room like he was looking for an exit that didn't exist.

"Blake Costello," Richardson said, "meet prosecutors Hayes and Mitchell."

Blake didn't stand. He barely looked up from the table. "Hi."

His voice was hoarse, like he'd been crying. Or screaming.

"Blake," Richardson continued smoothly, "as we discussed, this is an opportunity to share your perspective on what happened to Melissa."

The mention of the victim's name made Blake flinch. His hands, which had been resting on the table, curled into fists.

"I didn't kill her," he said, his voice stronger now. "I loved her."

Erin and I exchanged glances.

I leaned forward. "Tell us about your relationship with Melissa."

Blake's demeanor shifted, the vulnerability disappearing behind a wall of practiced arrogance. "We were together for eight months. She was... she was amazing. Smart, funny, beautiful. Way too good for most of the losers at school."

"But not too good for you?" Erin asked.

His jaw tightened. "I treated her right. Better than she'd ever been treated before."

"How so?"

"I protected her. From all the bullshit, all the drama. College girls, they get caught up in stupid stuff, you know? Gossip, social media, all that. Melissa was different, but sometimes..." He trailed off.

"Sometimes what?" I pressed.

"Sometimes she got ideas. About things that weren't her business."

The words hung in the air. Richardson's pen had stopped moving across his legal pad.

"What kind of things?" Erin asked.

Blake glanced at his lawyer, who gave an almost imperceptible shake of his head. "Just... family stuff. Her dad's work. She thought she could fix everything, make everything perfect." His voice cracked. "I told her to leave it alone."

"Leave what alone, specifically?"

"I don't know, okay?" The arrogance cracked, revealing something desperate underneath. "She wouldn't tell me details. Just kept saying her father wasn't who she thought he was, that she'd found something that would 'change everything.'" He made air quotes, his voice turning bitter. "Like she was some kind of investigative reporter instead of a college student."

I felt my pulse quicken. "Did she mention what she'd found?"

"No. But whatever it was, it scared her. The last few weeks, she was jumpy, paranoid. Kept saying someone was watching her, following her." Blake's hands were shaking now. "I told her she was being dramatic."

"And the night she died?"

Blake's face crumpled. Tears started flowing, and for a moment he looked exactly like what he was—a twenty-one-year-old kid in way over his head.

"I was at my friend David's place playing Call of Duty until around eight. We'd been online for hours—you can check the gaming logs if you want. Then I drove over to Melissa's apartment because we were supposed to talk, work things out. We'd been fighting a lot lately, and I …" He wiped his nose with his sleeve. "When I got there around eight-thirty, the door was unlocked. She was already dead."

"You didn't call the police," Erin observed.

"I panicked. I knew how it would look. Rich boy, dead girlfriend, everyone would assume …" He gestured helplessly. "So I left. Went home, tried to figure out what to do."

Richardson cleared his throat. "Blake called me the next morning, before the body was discovered. I advised him to contact the authorities immediately."

Which explained the timeline discrepancy in the police reports. Blake had known about the body twelve hours before anyone else.

"Blake," I said carefully, "when you found Melissa, did anything seem … off? Out of place?"

He considered the question. "Everything seemed off. She was lying in the living room, but there was no blood on the coffee table where she would have hit her head. And her laptop was missing."

"Missing how?"

"It was always on the kitchen counter, plugged in. She never moved it. But that night, it was gone."

Richardson's pen was moving again, but he was watching his client with an expression I couldn't read.

"Blake, did Melissa ever mention feeling threatened by anyone specifically?" I asked. "Someone who might have wanted to stop her from investigating whatever she'd found?"

"No, she just kept saying …" He stopped, his eyes widening. "Wait, she did say something weird. The day before she died. She said, 'Sometimes the people who are supposed to protect you are the ones you need to run from.'"

The room went quiet.

"Did she say who she meant by that?" Erin asked.

Blake shook his head. "I thought she was talking about her father. Like, being overprotective or whatever. But now …" He looked between us. "You think someone else killed her, don't you?"

I was about to respond when something occurred to me. "Blake, did she ever mention the name Katherine Hayes?"

The question came out before I could stop myself. Blake looked genuinely confused.

"No. Should she have?"

Richardson frowned. "I'm sorry, Ms. Hayes, but I'm not sure how that's relevant to—"

"It's not," Erin cut in smoothly. "My colleague was thinking of a different case." She shot me a warning look. "Blake, let's go back to the timeline. You said you were supposed to meet Melissa at eight o'clock …"

I tuned out the rest of the conversation. Blake's confusion had seemed genuine when I mentioned my mother's name. But his description of Melissa's final weeks—the paranoia, the fear, the sense that someone was watching her—sounded familiar.

After another twenty minutes of questions, Richardson called the meeting to an end. "I think that's enough for today. Blake, why don't you wait outside while I wrap up with the prosecutors?"

Blake nodded and shuffled toward the door, looking younger and more vulnerable than when we'd arrived.

"He's terrified," Richardson said once the door closed. "Whatever happened to that girl, it's destroyed him."

"Terrified of what?" I asked.

"Of whoever really killed her." Richardson's expression was grave. "That boy may be a lot of things, but he's not a murderer. And I think you both know it."

Richardson paused at the door. "One more thing. I've been practicing law in this city for thirty years. I've seen how certain cases ... resonate with old wounds. Be careful that history doesn't cloud your judgment, Ms. Hayes."

The comment was delivered so casually it almost sounded like general advice. Almost.

Erin and I left the building in silence. It wasn't until we reached the parking garage that she turned to me.

"Alex, what the hell was that?"

"What do you mean?"

"The Katherine Hayes question. Where did that come from?"

I leaned against my car, suddenly exhausted. "I don't know. Something about what Blake said—the way Melissa was acting before she died, the paranoia ..."

"It reminded you of your mother?"

"Maybe." I chose my words carefully. "Thatcher's comment yesterday about another prosecutor. I've been thinking about it."

Erin studied my face. "You think there's a pattern here? Between your mother and this case?"

"I think Judge Thatcher was very deliberate with his words yesterday. And I think Blake Costello is telling the truth about one thing—Melissa found something that got her killed."

"And you don't think Blake killed her."

"Do you?"

Erin was quiet for a long moment. "I don't know," she finally said. "But let's say he's not the killer. That doesn't mean we can prove it. And it also doesn't mean whoever did kill her won't try to pin it on him." She paused. "And Richardson's parting shot—about history and old wounds. That didn't feel random either."

"No," I agreed. "It wasn't."

CHAPTER SIX

I spread the forensic reports across my kitchen table, the overhead light casting harsh shadows over the crime scene photographs. The images were brutal—Melissa Thatcher sprawled on her living room floor, her blonde hair matted with blood, her college sweatshirt torn at the shoulder. Even in death, she looked young, vulnerable.

"The preliminary autopsy puts time of death between nine and midnight on October fifteenth," I said, flipping through the medical examiner's notes. "But Blake claims he found her at eight-thirty."

"Which would make him either the killer or the unluckiest boyfriend in D.C.," Erin said from behind me.

I turned to find her standing in my doorway, a bottle of wine in one hand and a stack of files in the other. Before I could greet her properly, my father appeared from the living room, holding a coffee mug and wearing the expression he reserved for people he didn't trust.

"So you're the one who got my daughter shot."

"Dad—" I started, but Erin didn't flinch.

"Mr. Hayes," Erin said smoothly, setting down the wine and extending her hand. "Erin Mitchell. And yes, I had a part to play in Alex's injuries. The other part, of course, being Alex's own insistence on playing the hero. But since she's still breathing and Andrews is behind bars, I'd say it worked out."

My father studied her for a long moment, then shook her hand with the grudging respect of someone recognizing a worthy opponent.

"She gets that from her mother," he said. "The hero complex."

"Dad, be nice."

"I am being nice." He turned back to Erin. "You drink coffee?"

"Only if it's stronger than battery acid."

A smile tugged at the corner of his mouth. "I think we'll get along fine."

Twenty minutes later, we were seated around the kitchen table with mugs of my father's industrial-strength coffee and the case files spread between us. Dad had retreated to the living room with a book, but I could feel him listening from the next room.

"Okay," Erin said, pulling out her legal pad. "Walk me through what we know."

I picked up the timeline the FBI had constructed. "October fifteenth. Melissa's last class ended at three-forty-five. She was seen at the campus coffee shop around four-thirty, alone. Her roommate says she got back to the apartment around six."

"What about phone records?"

"That's where it gets interesting." I pulled out the telecom report. "Her last outgoing call was to Blake at seven-fifteen. The call lasted three minutes. After that, nothing until her phone went dark around eight."

Erin frowned. "Went dark how?"

"Either turned off or destroyed. The cell tower data shows her phone disconnecting from the network at seven fifty-eight."

"But Blake says he didn't arrive until eight-thirty."

"Right. So either he's lying about when he got there, or someone else turned off her phone." I flipped to the next page. "Here's where it gets really weird. Blake claims they were texting back and forth between seven-thirty and eight, but there's no record of those messages on either phone."

"Deleted?"

"Maybe. But the phone company should still have routing data, and there's nothing." I pulled up the crime scene photos. "Look at this."

The images showed Melissa's apartment living room—overturned coffee table, scattered textbooks, a lamp knocked to the floor. But something about the placement of each object felt deliberate.

"Something's off about this," Erin said, leaning closer to study the photographs.

"I know what you mean. The positioning, the way everything's arranged—it doesn't feel natural. It's like someone staged it."

"And look at this." I pulled out the FBI's initial report. "No defensive wounds on her hands or arms. If someone attacked her, wouldn't she have tried to fight back?"

Erin was quiet for a moment, studying the photographs. "Unless she knew her attacker. Someone she trusted."

"Or someone who surprised her before she could react."

The sound of my father turning a page came from the living room. He was definitely listening in.

"What about the apartment itself?" Erin asked. "Any signs of forced entry?"

"None. The deadbolt was unlocked when Blake arrived, but that could mean anything. Maybe she was expecting someone."

"Or someone had a key."

I hadn't considered that possibility. "Blake had a key?"

"I don't know. We should ask." Erin made a note on her pad. "What about the missing laptop Blake mentioned?"

"Her roommate confirmed she always kept it on the kitchen counter, and it wasn't at the scene. It was a MacBook Pro, silver, with a Georgetown Law sticker on the back."

"Stolen during the attack?"

"Maybe. Or maybe whoever killed her took it because it contained something they didn't want found." I thought about Blake's description of Melissa's final weeks, her paranoia about being watched. "What if she documented whatever she'd discovered about her father?"

"So we're already assuming her father is somehow guilty?" Erin deadpanned.

I twisted my lips at the insinuation. I knew Erin was right. Maybe I was jumping to conclusions about the judge, but my gut was screaming at me to play hopscotch.

"I don't think we're at the stage where we can rule anybody out," I replied, slightly side-stepping her question.

"Alright. That's valid," Erin nodded. "So, the laptop's now conveniently missing." Erin leaned back in her chair. "This feels less like a domestic violence murder and more like—"

"A cover-up," I finished.

The sound of footsteps made us both look up. My father appeared in the doorway, coffee mug in hand.

"Mind if I take a look at those crime scene photos?" he asked.

I glanced at Erin, who shrugged. "Sure, Dad. But it's pretty gruesome."

He settled into the chair beside me and studied the photographs with the practiced eye of someone who'd seen his share of violent crime. After a few minutes, he tapped one of the images.

"This blood pattern here," he said, pointing to the spatter on the wall. "You're right about it being inconsistent with a fall. But look at the angle. Your killer was right-handed and about six inches taller than the victim."

"Blake fits that description," Erin said.

"This smearing on the coffee table edge? That's not from impact. Someone wiped blood on there after the fact." Dad picked up another photo. "And see how the furniture's arranged? The lamp's knocked over, but it fell away from the body, not toward it. Like someone staged the scene but didn't think about physics."

"So definitely not a crime of passion," I said.

"Nope. This was planned, executed, and then made to look like something else." He leaned back in his chair. "Twenty-five years on the force, I saw plenty of domestic violence murders. They're messy, emotional. This is clinical."

Erin was taking notes. "What about the missing laptop?"

"Smart move by the killer. Whatever was on there was important enough for the killer to take it with him." Dad's expression darkened. "The question is, what kind of person has the knowledge to stage a scene this well, and the connections to make evidence disappear?"

My Dad's implication was clear: Someone with power. Someone with resources.

"Speaking of powerful people," I said carefully, "we had an interesting encounter with Judge Thatcher at the courthouse."

Dad's attention sharpened. "What kind of encounter?"

I told him about Thatcher's comments, his warning about focusing on the case and not digging into things that didn't concern me. When I got to the part about him mentioning another prosecutor from twenty years ago, Dad's jaw tightened.

"He mentioned someone from twenty years ago? Made it sound like a warning?"

"Yeah. Said I reminded him of another 'idealistic prosecutor' and that it was tragic how that turned out."

"That son of a bitch." Dad stood abruptly, pacing to the window. "Alex, this isn't just about prosecuting a murder case anymore. If Thatcher knows something about—" He stopped himself. "If he's making veiled threats about the past ..."

"Then I need to find out what he knows," I finished.

"No." He turned back to us. "You need to be careful. Extremely careful. If someone killed this girl to cover up her father's crimes, what makes you think they won't kill again to keep those secrets buried?"

"Dad—"

"And you," he continued, looking directly at me, "are investigating a case involving a federal judge who's apparently been keeping tabs on prosecutors in this city for decades."

The room went quiet. Erin glanced between us before setting down her coffee mug. "Mr. Hayes, are you suggesting—"

"I'm suggesting that my daughter has a talent for finding trouble, and the people who want to silence her aren't going to play by the rules." His voice softened slightly. "I'm not trying to scare you, Alex. I'm trying to keep you alive."

After he went back to the living room, Erin and I worked in silence for several minutes, each lost in our own thoughts.

"Your dad's right, you know," Erin finally said. "If Thatcher is involved in whatever got his daughter killed, we're not just prosecuting a murder case. We're walking into the middle of something much bigger."

I picked up one of the photos—Melissa lying on her apartment floor, her eyes closed, her face peaceful despite the violence that had taken her life. She looked like she could have been sleeping.

"Maybe," I said. "But that girl deserves justice, regardless of who her father is or what he's done."

"Even if pursuing that justice gets us killed?"

I thought about my mother, about the chess pieces, about Thatcher's warning in the courthouse. About all the questions that had gone unanswered for too long.

"Especially then."

Erin gathered the files into a neat stack. "Okay. So what's our next move?"

"We need to talk to Melissa's roommate. Find out more about those final weeks, what was making her so paranoid." I stood and began clearing the table. "And we need to trace that missing laptop. If it contained evidence of whatever Melissa discovered, someone went to a lot of trouble to make sure we'd never see it."

"What about Blake's story?" Erin asked. "Do you believe him?"

I considered the question. "I think he's telling the truth about finding her dead. Whether he killed her beforehand and staged the body to find later, I'm not sure." I looked down at the photo. "But I also think he knows more than he's saying. The question is whether he's protecting himself or protecting someone else."

CHAPTER SEVEN

AFTER ERIN GATHERED the files and said her goodbyes, Dad walked her to the door with the practiced courtesy that had characterized his interactions with everyone I'd brought home over the years—law school friends, fellow prosecutors, the occasional boyfriend who'd been brave enough to meet my father. I could hear them talking quietly in the hallway, their voices carrying the tone of people who understood the weight of what we were undertaking, but I couldn't make out the specific words. When he came back to the kitchen, I was still staring at the crime scene photos, my mind trying to reconcile the clinical documentation of violence with the vibrant young woman whose life had been so brutally cut short.

The kitchen felt different now that it was just the two of us—more intimate, more familiar. This was where I'd done homework as a child, where we'd eaten countless dinners together after Mom died, where he'd taught me to see past the surface of things to the patterns underneath. The same skills that had made him a good police officer were now helping me navigate the complexities of federal prosecution.

"Erin seems solid," he said, settling back into his chair with the careful movements of someone whose body carried the accumulated wear of twenty-five years in law enforcement. His coffee mug bore the faded logo of the Houston Police Department, a gift from his retirement party that he still used every morning.

"She is. She's also the only person at the DOJ I trust right now." The admission came out heavier than I'd intended, carrying the weight of isolation that had been building for months as I'd pursued leads that others had dismissed or ignored.

"Smart. In a case like this, you can't trust too many people." He was quiet for a moment, studying me with the same intensity he'd used on the crime scene photos. "You look tired, kiddo."

The familiar endearment made me smile despite everything. He'd been calling me that since I was five years old and decided I wanted to be a police officer like him, following him around the house with a toy badge pinned to my shirt and asking endless questions about criminals and justice and how to tell the good guys from the bad guys.

I set down the photo I'd been holding—Melissa Thatcher smiling at a college party, unaware that her bright future would end in a dingy apartment with blood on the walls. "I am tired. And scared, if I'm being honest."

"Good."

"Good?" I looked at him in surprise, noting the way his weathered face had settled into the expression he'd worn when teaching me difficult lessons about the world's complexity.

"Fear keeps you alive. Your mother …" He paused, choosing his words carefully with the deliberation of someone who'd learned that careless phrases could carry more weight than intended. "She was fearless. It was one of the things I loved most about her, but it was also what got her killed. She never considered that someone might actually hurt her for asking the wrong questions."

I thought about that, trying to reconcile my memories of my mother —brilliant, determined, unshakeable in her convictions—with the idea that those same qualities might have been her downfall.

"I don't feel fearless," I said. "I feel like I'm in way over my head."

"That's called wisdom. And it means you'll be more careful than she was." Dad reached across the table and covered my hand with his, the callused skin speaking to years of physical work even after retirement. "Tell me about this investigation you've been doing. The one that's got you looking at old cases."

So I did. I told him about the chess pieces that had appeared at my office and home, each one a message I couldn't fully decode but understood was connected to something larger and more dangerous than any case I'd worked before. I described the connections I'd found between trafficking cases and certain judges, patterns that emerged only when you looked at years of data and had the patience to map relationships that others dismissed as coincidental.

I told him about the sleepless nights spent cross-referencing court records and financial documents, the constant feeling that I was being watched whenever I pursued certain leads, the way promising sources would suddenly become unavailable or evidence would disappear just when I thought I was getting close to something important. The mounting sense that I was walking through a maze designed by someone who understood the system better than I did and was always one step ahead.

"And now Thatcher shows up," I finished, my voice carrying the frustration of months of careful work that seemed to lead nowhere and everywhere at once. "Making veiled comments about prosecutors from twenty years ago. The timing, the way he said it—it felt deliberate."

Dad was quiet for a long time, processing everything I'd told him with the methodical approach he'd brought to every case he'd worked during his career. The kitchen clock ticked steadily, marking the passage of time while he weighed implications and possibilities against his own memories.

"You think he knows something about what happened twenty years ago?" he finally asked.

"I don't know. But I think he knows more than he's saying. And I think that's why his daughter was killed. She found out something about him, and it got her murdered." The words felt heavy as I spoke them, the weight of accusing a federal judge of being involved in his own child's death.

"Jesus, Alex." He rubbed his face with both hands, a gesture that spoke to the accumulated stress of watching his daughter pursue dangerous investigations. "Do you have any idea how dangerous this is? If you're right, if there's some conspiracy involving federal judges and human trafficking, you're not just risking your career. You're risking your life."

"I know. And that terrifies me." The admission came out quieter than I'd intended, carrying all the vulnerability I'd been trying to hide from colleagues and supervisors who needed to see me as competent and unshakeable. "But I can't just walk away from this. Not when I'm finally getting close to answers."

"What if those answers get you killed?" His voice cracked slightly, revealing the fear he'd been carrying since I'd started digging into old cases. "I've already lost ... I can't lose you too."

The raw pain in his voice made my chest tight, reminding me that my pursuit of justice wasn't just about abstract principles—it was about family, about the people who loved me and feared losing me to the same forces that had already caused so much damage. "Dad..."

"Your mother thought she was being careful too, you know. She thought she could handle whatever she'd gotten herself into." He looked at me with eyes that held twenty years of grief, regret, and unanswered questions. "The night she died, she was supposed to meet a source. Someone who claimed to have information about a trafficking ring operating out of the ports. She never came home."

I'd heard pieces of this story before, fragments shared during quiet moments when Dad's guard was down and the weight of carrying secrets became too much. But I'd never heard the details, never understood how close she'd come to breaking the case that ultimately broke her.

"What happened to the source?"

"Disappeared. Like they never existed." Dad's jaw tightened, the muscle jumping in the way it did when he was trying to control anger that had nowhere to go. "The case went cold within a week. No leads, no witnesses, no evidence. Like someone had swept it all away."

"Just like what's happening with Melissa's laptop."

"Exactly like that." He leaned forward, his expression intense with the urgency of someone trying to pass on hard-won wisdom. "I'm not going to try to stop you. I know you too well to think that would work. But promise me you'll be careful. Promise me you won't take unnecessary risks."

"I promise."

"And promise me you'll keep Erin close. Don't try to handle this alone." His voice carried the weight of experience, the understanding that isolation was often the first step toward becoming a victim rather than an investigator.

"I promise that too." I hesitated, then decided to voice something that had been weighing on me for months. "Dad, can I ask you something?"

"Of course."

"How do you do it? How do you live with not knowing what really happened to her?"

Dad went quiet, staring into his coffee mug as if the answers might be found in the dark liquid. When he spoke, his voice carried the exhaustion of someone who'd been carrying an impossible burden for two decades.

"Some days I don't do it very well. But seeing you fight for justice, even when it's dangerous ... it helps. It makes me feel like her death might actually mean something."

I squeezed his hand, feeling the strength in his fingers and understanding for the first time how much of his own healing had been tied to watching me pursue the career my mother had been building when she died.

"Thanks, Dad."

He smiled and then shook his head, as if trying to shake off the serious nature of our conversation and return to the normal rhythms of family life. "You're always so busy. I feel like I barely know what's going on anymore. How are things going with James?"

I felt heat rise in my cheeks, the familiar flush that came whenever anyone asked about my personal life in the context of my professional obsessions. "That's ... complicated."

Dad smirked. "Complicated how?"

"He's in D.C. working a case. We barely talk anymore." I picked at the edge of a photograph, using the physical action to avoid his eyes while I tried to articulate feelings I hadn't fully examined myself. "And when we do talk, I can't tell him about any of this. The chess pieces, the investigation, what I really think about this case—I have to lie to him about everything that matters."

"That must be lonely."

"It is." The admission hurt more than I'd expected, a hot pang in the center of my chest. "He thinks I'm obsessed with old cases. That I'm letting the past control my future."

Dad's expression darkened, his protective instincts flaring at the suggestion that someone was criticizing his daughter's choices. "He said that?"

"Sort of, but not in a mean way. I know he's just concerned for me. And maybe he's right. Maybe I am obsessed." The possibility had been haunting me for weeks, the growing suspicion that my pursuit of justice had become something unhealthy and consuming.

"There's a difference between obsession and justice, Alex. Your mother was murdered because she was trying to protect innocent people. If pursuing her killer makes you obsessed, then I'm proud of your obsession."

I felt tears prick at my eyes, unexpected emotion rising from the relief of having someone validate what felt like the organizing principle of my adult life. "Sometimes I wonder if I'm losing myself in all this. Like I don't know who I am anymore outside of this investigation."

"You know what I see when I look at you?" Dad's voice was gentle, carrying the unconditional love that had sustained me through law school, career changes, and the constant pressure of living up to my mother's legacy. "I see a woman who refuses to let evil go unpunished. I see someone who fights for people who can't fight for themselves. That's not obsession, kiddo. That's courage."

I shook my head. "It doesn't feel like courage. Feels more like I'm drowning."

"Good leaders doubt themselves. Good people question their motives. The fact that you're afraid, that you're questioning everything—that tells me you're approaching this the right way." He squeezed my hand with the gentle pressure of someone offering reassurance without dismissing legitimate concerns. "Your mother never doubted herself. Ever. And that confidence made her reckless."

We sat in comfortable silence for several minutes, the weight of shared grief and determination filling the space between us. The kitchen had grown darker as evening settled over the house, but neither of us moved to turn on the lights. There was something peaceful about sitting in the gathering dusk, connected by understanding and mutual support.

Finally, Dad stood to clear the mugs from the table, his movements careful and deliberate. The simple domestic action felt grounding after the intensity of our conversation, a return to the normal rhythms that had sustained our relationship through twenty years of loss and healing.

"Your mother would be proud of you, you know," he said quietly, his voice carrying across the kitchen as he rinsed dishes in the sink. "Proud that you're fighting for justice, even when it's dangerous."

"Think she'd approve of me going after a federal judge?"

A small smile crossed his face, the first genuine lightness I'd seen from him all evening. "Are you kidding? She'd probably want to help." Pausing at the sink, dish towel in hand, his expression grew more serious. "But she'd also want you to be smart about it. Don't let anger cloud your judgment. Don't let the need for answers make you reckless."

"What if I can't find the truth? What if whoever killed her is too powerful, too well-connected?"

"Then at least you'll know you tried. And maybe that's enough."

"Is it enough for you?"

Dad turned back to me, his expression serious but not despairing. "No. But it has to be, because the alternative is giving up entirely. And neither your mother nor you would ever do that."

"Dad?" I stood, suddenly needing to be closer to him, to feel the physical connection that had anchored me through every difficult moment of my life. "I'm scared I'm going to mess this up. That I'm going to get people hurt."

He pulled me into a hug, the kind that made me feel like I was ten years old again, safe in the knowledge that someone stronger and wiser was looking out for me. The embrace carried the accumulated comfort of thousands of similar moments—scraped knees soothed, nightmares banished, teenage heartbreaks mended through the simple power of unconditional love.

He pulled away and looked into my eyes, strong hands resting on my shoulders. "That fear you're feeling? That doubt? Hold onto those. They're what's going to keep you alive long enough to find the truth."

"I love you, Dad."

"I love you too, kiddo. More than you'll ever know."

After he'd gone to bed, I sat alone in the kitchen with the crime scene photos put away but their images still burned in my memory. Melissa Thatcher had been young, brilliant, full of potential—a pre-law student with dreams of exposing corruption, of making a difference in the world through the power of truth. Someone had stolen all of that from her, reducing a life of infinite possibility to evidence markers and forensic reports.

But as I turned off the lights and headed upstairs, I found myself holding onto my father's words. Fear and doubt weren't weaknesses—they were tools. And I was going to need every tool I could get if I was going to find justice for both Melissa and my mother, If I was going to honor their memories by ensuring that the people responsible for their deaths finally faced the consequences for their actions.

CHAPTER EIGHT

GRACIE'S STEAKHOUSE was exactly the kind of place that understood the unspoken rules of Houston legal circles—dimly lit booths perfect for confidential conversations, strong drinks served without judgment, and a staff that had perfected the art of selective hearing. The restaurant occupied a converted Victorian mansion in Montrose, its wood-paneled walls lined with photographs of prominent attorneys and judges from decades past, creating an atmosphere of old-school legal tradition.

I'd been coming here since my early days at the DA's office, back when a decent meal felt like a luxury I couldn't afford and every conversation with senior attorneys felt like a master class in how the legal system really worked. The hostess still remembered my name, and the bartender knew I preferred Cabernet to whatever trendy cocktail was popular that week.

Lisa Cooper was already waiting at our usual booth in the back corner, a glass of red wine in front of her and case files spread across the table like she was still at the office. The booth afforded privacy while maintaining a clear view of the restaurant's entrance—a habit both of us had developed after handling cases where paranoia had become a survival skill rather than a character flaw. Some things never changed, including Lisa's inability to completely disconnect from work even during social dinners.

"You look like hell," she said by way of greeting as I slid into the seat across from her, not bothering with pleasantries that wouldn't have fooled either of us.

"Thanks. You really know how to make a girl feel special."

"I'm serious, Alex. When's the last time you slept more than four hours?" Lisa signaled the waitress for another wine, her practiced gesture drawing immediate attention despite the busy restaurant. "And don't say last night, because I can see the caffeine jitters from here."

I accepted the glass of Cabernet when it arrived and took a generous sip, feeling the warmth spread through my chest and temporarily ease some of the tension I'd been carrying. "It's been a rough week."

"The Thatcher case?"

"Among other things." I glanced around the restaurant, scanning faces, noting exit routes, looking for anyone who seemed too interested in our conversation. "How much have you heard?"

"Enough to know you drew the short straw on a political landmine." Lisa closed her files and leaned back in the booth, her expression shifting from casual concern to professional analysis. "Judge's daughter, college boyfriend, domestic violence angle. Textbook case that should be a slam dunk, except nothing about it feels textbook."

"What do you mean?"

"Come on, Alex. We've both prosecuted enough DV murders to know the pattern. The escalation, the warning signs, the way evidence typically presents itself." She took a sip of her wine, her eyes never leaving my face. "This one's different, and not just because daddy wears robes. I've been asking around, doing some digging on your behalf."

"And?"

"And the number of people who suddenly discovered conflicts of interest when this case came up is ... interesting."

A familiar chill ran down my spine, the sensation I'd experienced when reviewing evidence that didn't fit expected patterns. "Define interesting."

Lisa pulled out a legal pad covered in her precise handwriting.

"Twelve senior AUSAs who would presumably be available for lead prosecutor. Seven recused themselves within forty-eight hours of the assignment being posted."

"That's not unusual for a high-profile case."

"No, but the reasons are." She ran her finger down the list, each name accompanied by detailed notes about their stated conflicts. "Bob Webb cited a prior professional relationship with Thatcher. Fair enough, except I checked—they've never worked a case together. Never even appeared in the same courtroom."

I took a sip of wine. "Maybe they know each other socially."

"Maybe. But then there's Patricia Valdez. Claims her husband's law firm has Thatcher as a client. So I called her husband's office. They've never heard of Judge Thatcher."

The chill spread through my chest now, icing over the wine's warmth. "What about the others?"

"Similar stories," Lisa said. "Vague conflicts that don't hold up under scrutiny. Professional relationships that don't exist, family connections that turned out to be fabricated, ethical concerns that evaporate when you dig deeper."

I set down my wine glass, my appetite gone despite the rich aromas drifting from the kitchen. "Lisa, what are you saying?"

"I'm saying these people weren't avoiding conflicts of interest. They were avoiding the case entirely." She leaned forward, lowering her voice to a conspiratorial tone. "And when senior prosecutors start running from a case this fast, it's usually because they know something you don't."

"Or they're scared of something."

"Or someone."

We sat in silence for a moment, the implications settling between us. Around us, the normal sounds of dinner chatter, laughter, and clinking glasses continued, muffled by the growing understanding that I'd walked into something far more dangerous than a straightforward murder prosecution.

"There's more," Lisa said.

"Of course there is."

"I had lunch with Leigh Morrison yesterday. You remember Leigh

—she worked white-collar crime before moving over to the Eastern District."

I nodded. Leigh was solid, experienced, the kind of prosecutor who didn't spook easily and had built her reputation on successfully prosecuting complex financial crimes that other attorneys avoided.

Lisa's expression grew more serious. "She told me something interesting about Judge Thatcher. Apparently, about two years ago, she had a case involving offshore banking and money laundering. Complex financial crimes, shell corporations, the works. The case was assigned to Thatcher's court."

"And?"

"And Leigh said Thatcher seemed unusually interested in the details. Kept asking questions during pretrial hearings that went beyond normal judicial curiosity. Questions about specific bank accounts, routing numbers, corporate structures."

"That could be normal due diligence."

"Could be. Except Leigh also said that every time her team got close to a breakthrough, something would go wrong. Key witnesses would recant their statements. Financial records would disappear. Search warrants would get challenged and overturned on technicalities."

My stomach was knotting itself into increasingly complex configurations as the pattern Lisa was describing became clear. "What happened to the case?"

"Dismissed. Lack of evidence. The defendants walked free. Leigh said it felt like someone had been systematically dismantling her case from the inside."

"Jesus."

"Gets better. About six months after the case was dismissed, Leigh heard through the grapevine that several of the defendants had been quietly arrested on federal charges in other jurisdictions. Different prosecutors, different courts."

"They rebuilt the cases somewhere else."

"Exactly. Away from Thatcher's influence." Lisa finished her wine and signaled for another, her movements carrying tension. "Alex, I think your judge has been protecting people. And I think the people who would normally prosecute those kinds of cases know it."

The pieces were starting to form a picture I didn't want to see, a pattern of corruption that extended far beyond a single murder case. "So when Thatcher's daughter turns up murdered ..."

"Everyone who knows his reputation suddenly finds a reason to be elsewhere. Nobody wants to be the prosecutor against a dirty judge."

"Except me," I said, leaning back. "Because I didn't know."

"Because you didn't know. And because ..." Lisa hesitated, clearly weighing whether to share something that might be difficult to hear.

"Because what?"

Lisa shot me a look. "Because you have a reputation for not backing down when things get complicated. Word is you're the prosecutor they call when they need someone who won't be intimidated."

I wasn't sure if that was a compliment or a death sentence. "Great. I'm the sacrificial lamb, then."

"Or you're the only one with the guts to do the job." Lisa reached across the table and squeezed my hand, her gesture carrying both support and concern. "Look, I know this isn't what you signed up for. But if Thatcher is dirty, if he's been using his position to protect criminals, then his daughter's murder might be connected."

"You think she found out about his activities."

"I think it's possible. And I think if you can prove it, you might be able to clean up more than just one murder case."

The waitress appeared at our table, clearly expecting to take our food order. We both declined, and she retreated with the practiced discretion of someone who'd seen plenty of serious conversations over the years and understood when not to interrupt.

"Lisa, there's something else I haven't told you." I looked around the restaurant again, then leaned closer, preparing to share information that could put both of us in danger. "I think this case might be connected to my mother's murder."

Her eyebrows rose, genuine surprise replacing professional concern. "What makes you think that?"

I told her about the chess pieces, about the conversation with Thatcher at the courthouse, about his comment. Lisa listened without interrupting, her expression growing more concerned with each detail.

"Alex, none of that is a coincidence."

"I know."

"If Thatcher knows something about Katherine's death, if he's been sitting on that information for twenty years ..." She shook her head, the magnitude of the situation clearly overwhelming even her experienced perspective. "You realize what this means, don't you?"

"That I'm probably walking into a trap."

"That you might finally get answers. But yes, also that you're walking into a trap." Lisa gathered her files and stuffed them into her briefcase with quick, efficient movements. "What are you going to do?"

"My job," I said. "Prosecute Melissa Thatcher's murder and see where the evidence leads."

"Even if it leads somewhere dangerous?"

I thought about my conversation with Dad the night before, about fear being a tool rather than a weakness, about the importance of pursuing justice even when the personal cost was high.

I nodded. "Especially then."

Lisa stood and dropped money on the table for our drinks. "Okay. But promise me something."

"What?"

"Promise me you won't do this alone. Trust your instincts, and for God's sake, watch your back. If Thatcher really is what we think he is, he's not going to just let you destroy him."

As we walked toward the parking lot through the humid Houston evening, a weight settled on my shoulders. The case I'd thought was a straightforward domestic violence murder was turning into something much more complex and dangerous. People feared Judge Thatcher, enough to abandon their professional responsibilities rather than cross him.

The question was, what exactly were they afraid of?

And more importantly, was I brave—or foolish—enough to find out?

"Alex," Lisa called as we reached our cars, her voice carrying across the parking lot with obvious reluctance. "Leigh Morrison said something else about that financial crimes case. That she always suspected someone inside the system was feeding information to the defense. Someone with access to prosecution strategy, witness lists, evidence."

"Someone in the prosecutor's office?"

"Or someone with enough influence to get that information. Someone judges and prosecutors would trust." Lisa's expression was grim as she prepared to voice the suspicion that had clearly been troubling her. "Someone like another federal judge."

If Thatcher had been using his position to obstruct justice, to protect criminals involved in human trafficking, then his daughter's death took on an entirely different significance.

Melissa Thatcher hadn't just been a pre-law student with dreams of following in her father's footsteps. She'd been smart, idealistic, the kind of person who would have been horrified to discover her father's corruption. The kind of person who might have tried to do something about it.

And now she was dead.

Just like Katherine Hayes.

CHAPTER NINE

The drive home from Gracie's took longer than usual. The Houston traffic crawled along I-10, giving me too much time to think about federal judges who protected criminals and prosecutors who disappeared when cases got too close to the truth.

By the time I pulled into my driveway, it was nearly ten o'clock. The floodlight illuminated the front steps as I pulled up, and I noticed a small manila envelope propped against my front door.

My blood went cold.

I sat in my car for a full minute, engine running, studying the envelope from a distance. From what I could see, it was unremarkable. Standard office size, no return address, my name written in block letters across the front.

I grabbed my pepper spray from my purse and approached the door carefully, scanning the street for any sign of movement. The neighborhood was quiet, porch lights glowing from the houses on either side, but no one in sight. Whoever had left this was long gone.

The envelope was light, almost empty feeling. I carried it inside, locking the deadbolt behind me and checked all the windows before settling at the kitchen table to examine it properly.

My hands trembled as I tore open the sealed flap. Inside was a single piece of paper and something else—something small and hard that clinked against the table when I turned the envelope upside down.

A chess piece. A white bishop.

The paper was simple, ordinary computer paper with two words printed in the same block letters as my name on the envelope:

One down.

I stared at the message, my pulse hammering in my ears. One down. One what down? One judge? One case? One person who'd gotten too close to the truth?

I picked up the chess piece, feeling its smooth porcelain surface between my fingers. In chess, bishops moved diagonally, could travel across the entire board in a single move if the path was clear. They were powerful pieces, capable of controlling large sections of the game from a distance.

But they could also be captured, removed from the board entirely.

I sat at my kitchen table until nearly midnight, turning the bishop over in my palm, trying to decode the message. Was this a threat? A warning? Some kind of sick game being played by whoever had killed my mother?

One thing was certain. Whoever had sent this knew where I lived. They'd been close enough to my front door to leave an envelope, confident enough to approach my house in broad daylight or under cover of darkness. The thought made my skin crawl.

I considered calling the police, filing a report, turning the chess piece over to someone who might be able to trace its origin. But what would I tell them? That I'd received an anonymous chess piece? That I suspected it was connected to a case involving a federal judge who might be corrupt?

They'd think I was paranoid. Or worse, they'd think I was manufacturing evidence to support a conspiracy theory.

This was something I needed to handle carefully. Something I needed to think through before making any moves that couldn't be undone.

I locked the chess piece and note in my home safe. Tomorrow, I'd show them to Erin. She'd know what to do.

The next morning arrived gray and drizzly, the kind of Houston weather that made everything feel oppressive and close. I'd slept poorly, waking every few hours to check the locks on the doors and windows, jumping at every sound from the street outside.

Erin was already at her desk when I arrived at the federal building, a cup of coffee in one hand and case files spread across her workspace. She looked up as I approached, and her expression immediately shifted to concern.

"You look terrible," she said. "Again."

"Thanks. You're really good for my self-esteem."

"I'm serious, Alex. Did you sleep at all last night?"

I closed her office door and took the chair across from her desk. "We need to talk."

"About the case?"

"About this." I pulled the manila envelope from my briefcase and placed it in front of her. "I found it on my doorstep when I got home from drinks with Lisa."

Erin's eyebrows rose as she carefully extracted the chess piece and note. She studied both items for a long moment, turning the bishop over in her hands just as I had the night before.

"Alex, this is …"

"I know."

"When did you find this?"

"Last night. Around ten."

"And you didn't call the police? You didn't call me?"

I squirmed in my chair. "I wanted to think about it first. Figure out what it means before we involve anyone else."

"What it means?" Erin's voice rose. "Alex, someone left a threatening message at your house. Someone who knows where you live, knows what case you're working on, knows enough about your history to reference your previous chess piece incidents."

"It's not necessarily a threat."

She held the sparse note between her fingers, shaking the page until it rustled. "'One down' isn't a threat? What else could it possibly mean?"

I had been asking myself the same question all night. "Maybe it means one piece of the puzzle has been solved. Maybe it's acknowledgment that I'm getting closer to the truth. Maybe it's someone supporting my quest for the truth."

"Or maybe it means one person has been eliminated," Erin said, "and you're next."

Her words gave a voice to the fear I'd been trying to suppress.

"Erin, I think whoever sent this is connected to Judge Thatcher. The timing is too perfect—his daughter dies, I get assigned the case, I start asking questions about his background, and suddenly I'm getting anonymous chess pieces."

"Which is exactly why you need to report this. Turn it over to the FBI, let them investigate."

"And tell them what? That I suspect a federal judge of corruption based on office gossip and anonymous chess pieces? They'll think I'm crazy."

"They'll think you're being threatened by someone connected to an active murder investigation. Which you are."

I stood and began pacing in front of her desk. "Erin, don't you see? This proves we're on the right track. Someone is scared enough to try intimidating me, which means there's something real to find."

"Or someone is dangerous enough to kill a federal judge's daughter and confident enough to threaten a federal prosecutor." She leaned forward, her expression intense. "Alex, this isn't a game. Whoever sent this has already killed at least once. Maybe more than once, if your suspicions about your mother are correct."

"Which is exactly why I can't back down now."

"And it's exactly why you need protection. Official protection."

We stared at each other across her desk, the chess piece sitting between us like a small white monument to everything we didn't know and couldn't prove.

"What if reporting this compromises the investigation?" I asked finally. "What if whoever sent it has connections inside law enforcement? What if turning this over to the FBI just gives them advance warning that we're getting close?"

Erin was quiet for a moment, considering the possibility. "You really think the corruption goes that deep?"

"I think my mother was investigating human trafficking when she was killed twenty years ago. I think she got too close to something big, something involving powerful people, and it cost her life." I sat back down, leaning forward. "And I think Judge Thatcher knows exactly what happened to her."

"Based on what he said at the courthouse."

"Based on what he said, and the fact that his daughter is now dead under suspicious circumstances, and the fact that I'm receiving a chess piece when Leland's files showed a chess board with his name written on it." I picked up the white bishop. "This isn't random, Erin. This is all connected."

She rubbed her temples like she was fighting a headache. "Okay. Let's say you're right. Let's say there's some massive conspiracy involving federal judges and human trafficking and your mother's murder. What exactly do you propose we do about it?"

"We solve Melissa Thatcher's murder. We follow the evidence, even if it leads to her father. And we use this"—I held up the chess piece —"as proof that we're getting close to something someone desperately wants to keep buried."

"Alex …"

"I'm not backing down, Erin. Not when I'm finally getting answers about my mother. Not when some anonymous coward thinks they can scare me away with chess pieces and cryptic notes."

Erin stared at me for a long moment, then sighed. "You're not going to report this, are you?"

I shook my head. "Not yet. Not until we have more evidence."

"And you're not going to drop the case."

"Absolutely not."

"And you're not going to be careful or take precautions or do anything remotely sensible to protect yourself."

"I didn't say that."

"You didn't have to." Erin glared at me from across the desk. "I know you, Alex. You get that look in your eyes when you're about to do something incredibly brave and massively stupid." She leaned back in her chair. "Fine. But I have conditions."

I squinted back at her. "What kind of conditions?"

"First, you don't investigate anything alone. If you're going to poke the bear, I'm going with you. Second, we keep this between us for now, but if anything else happens—any more chess pieces, threats, anything—we report it immediately."

"And third?"

"Third, you start carrying a gun. All the time. Because if someone is willing to kill a federal judge's daughter, they won't hesitate to kill a federal prosecutor who's asking too many questions."

I nodded, accepting her terms. They were reasonable, and honestly, having Erin watch my back made me feel marginally safer.

"There's something else," I said. "Lisa told me last night that Leigh Morrison thinks someone inside the system was feeding information to defense teams in cases involving Thatcher. Someone with access to prosecution strategy and evidence."

"Someone like who?"

"Someone judges and prosecutors would trust implicitly. Someone with enough influence to make evidence disappear and witnesses recant their statements." I met her eyes. "Someone like another federal judge."

Erin's expression darkened. "You think there's more than one dirty judge involved."

"I think we're looking at something much bigger than one corrupt federal judge protecting a few criminals. I think we're looking at a network."

"A network that's been operating for at least twenty years."

"At least."

She picked up the white bishop again, examining it in the morning light streaming through her office window. "You know what this means, don't you?"

"What?"

"It means we're not just prosecuting a murder case. We're walking into the middle of a war zone."

CHAPTER TEN

THE THATCHER FAMILY home sat in River Oaks, one of Houston's most exclusive neighborhoods, where the houses were set back from tree-lined streets behind wrought-iron gates and the price tags started at seven figures. Even in the gray morning light that filtered through the canopy of ancient oak trees, the Georgian colonial was impressive—red brick weathered to the perfect shade of distinction, white columns that spoke to old Southern money, and a perfectly manicured lawn that probably cost more to maintain than most people made in a year.

The neighborhood itself whispered wealth in the way that only true money could—understated elegance rather than flashy displays, the kind of refined taste that came from generations of privilege rather than recent fortune. Security cameras tucked discreetly among the landscaping, private patrol cars making their rounds, and the subtle signs that reminded visitors they were entering a world where different rules applied.

"Subtle," Erin muttered as we pulled into the circular driveway that curved past a fountain depicting some classical figure I couldn't identify.

"Federal judges do pretty well for themselves," I replied.

"Not this well. Not on a government salary." She gestured toward the three-car garage that probably housed vehicles worth more than our annual salaries combined.

That point had been nagging at me since I'd first started researching Judge Thatcher's background. The house screamed old money, the kind of wealth that came from family connections, trust funds, and investments carefully managed over decades—not the steady but modest paycheck of public service. Another piece of the puzzle that didn't quite fit the image of a dedicated federal judge who'd risen through the ranks on merit alone.

A housekeeper answered the door—a middle-aged Hispanic woman wearing a crisp uniform who looked like she'd been crying recently, her eyes red-rimmed despite careful makeup.

"We're here to see Judge or Mrs. Thatcher," I said, showing my credentials. "I'm Alex Hayes from the U.S. Attorney's office."

"They are not home," she said in accented English. "The Judge is at court, and Mrs. Thatcher …" She trailed off, clearly uncomfortable.

"We can come back," Erin offered.

"No, wait." A young voice came from behind the housekeeper. A teenage girl appeared in the foyer—fifteen at most, with pale eyes that looked too old for her face. "Maria, it's okay. These are the prosecutors Dad mentioned might come by."

The housekeeper looked uncertain. "Miss Becca, your father said—"

"He said to cooperate fully with the investigation." The girl's voice was steady despite obvious grief. "I'm sure he meant that."

I exchanged a glance with Erin. We'd come hoping to speak with the parents, but finding Becca alone presented both an opportunity and an ethical minefield.

"Becca," I said carefully, "we actually came to speak with your parents. We should probably come back when—"

" Mom hasn't left her room in three days," Becca interrupted. "And Dad's always at the courthouse or his office. If you want to know about my sister, I'm the only one here who can tell you anything useful."

"We really should wait for a parent or guardian," Erin said, following proper protocol.

Becca's composure cracked slightly. "Please. Everyone keeps telling me I'm too young to understand, too young to help. But I knew her better than anyone. I have things that might help you find who really killed her."

That stopped us both. I weighed the options quickly. Technically, we weren't interrogating her as a suspect or even a witness to the crime itself. We were gathering background information about the victim. Still, speaking to a minor without parental consent was risky.

"How about this?" I suggested. "We can sit and talk informally. If at any point you feel uncomfortable or want to wait for your parents, we stop immediately. And I'll leave my card so your father knows we were here. Would that be okay?"

Becca nodded eagerly. "Yes. Please. I just ... I need to do something to help."

Leading us through a marble foyer that echoed our footsteps, we entered a sitting room that belonged in an architectural magazine—all carefully arranged antiques, oil paintings in gilded frames, and furniture that had been selected by someone with impeccable taste and unlimited resources.

Fresh flowers filled crystal vases on carefully polished surfaces, and the faint scent of lemon oil spoke of meticulous housekeeping. Everything was perfect, from the positioning of throw pillows to the arrangement of coffee table books about art and architecture. It was the kind of room designed to impress visitors with its understated elegance and quiet display of wealth.

"I'm Becca," she said, settling into an antique chair with practiced grace.

"Becca, I'm Alex Hayes, and this is Erin Mitchell." I kept my voice gentle, drawing on years of experience with young witnesses processing trauma they shouldn't have had to face.

She nodded solemnly and gestured for us to sit on a cream-colored sofa that looked like it had never been used for anything as mundane as watching television or casual conversation.

Settling onto the sofa, I chose my words carefully. "Just remember, you can stop at any time if you want to wait for them. I know this is difficult, but anything you can tell us about Melissa might help us find out what happened to her."

Becca's composure cracked slightly, revealing the fifteen-year-old girl beneath the carefully maintained facade. "Everyone keeps saying

Blake killed her. The news, people at school, even some of Mom and Dad's friends. But I don't think he did."

Erin leaned forward, her voice carrying the same gentle tone I'd used. "Why not?"

"Because he loved her. Like, really loved her. The crazy, obsessive kind that's probably not healthy but isn't violent either." She tucked her legs under her on the chair with the unconscious grace of someone still comfortable moving like a child despite the adult circumstances she was facing. "He was always texting her, calling her, buying her things. Expensive things—jewelry, clothes, books for her classes. Melissa thought it was sweet at first, but lately …"

"Lately, what?" I asked.

"Lately she said it was getting weird. Like he was scared of losing her." Becca's voice grew more confident as she warmed to the subject, clearly relieved to have someone who wanted to hear what she'd observed. "She said he'd started asking strange questions about her friends, about her professors, about what she was working on for school."

I made a note, sensing we were approaching something important. "Did she say what she thought he was afraid of?"

"Not really. Just that he kept asking her not to go places without him, not to talk to certain people. He didn't want her working on some project for school." Becca's brow furrowed as she tried to remember details that hadn't seemed significant at the time but now carried new weight.

"What kind of project?" I asked.

Becca shrugged, a gesture that seemed too casual for the serious conversation we were having. "I don't know exactly. Something for her pre-law thesis. She was supposed to research judicial ethics or something like that. She picked local judges as her topic."

Exchanging a glance with Erin, I felt the familiar tingle that came when pieces of a case started connecting in unexpected ways.

"Why did she choose local judges?"

"She thought it would be easy because of Dad. Like, she could interview him and maybe some of his colleagues, get insider information that other students couldn't access." Becca's voice dropped, taking on the conspiratorial tone of someone sharing information they weren't entirely sure they should be revealing. "But then she started acting weird about it."

"Weird how?"

"Secretive. She'd close her laptop whenever I came into her room, which she'd never done before. Started asking strange questions about Dad's work, about people he knew, about cases from years ago. And she was always writing in that journal of hers, more than usual."

"What do you know about her journal?" I asked, keeping my voice casual despite the quickening of my pulse.

"She's kept one since middle school. Writes in it every night before bed, like a ritual. Used to read me funny parts sometimes—stories about college parties or stupid things her professors said. But not lately." Becca's eyes filled with tears, the first real break in her composure since we'd arrived. "Not for the last few months."

I felt my pulse quicken, recognizing the potential significance of contemporaneous documentation by someone who might have stumbled onto something dangerous. "Becca, do you know where that journal is now?"

"The police asked about it when they searched her apartment. FBI agents, actually. But they didn't find it." She wiped her eyes with the back of her hand, a gesture that reminded me how young she really was despite her attempts at adult sophistication. "I think that's because Melissa hid it. She was paranoid about people reading her private thoughts, especially after she started working on that project."

"Do you have any idea where she might have hidden it?"

Becca went quiet, seeming to wrestle with something internal—perhaps loyalty to her sister's privacy balanced against the desire to help find her killer.

Finally, she stood up with the quick decisiveness of someone who'd made up her mind. "Wait here."

She disappeared upstairs, leaving Erin and me alone in the pristine sitting room. I could hear footsteps overhead, the sound of drawers opening and closing, furniture being moved. The house felt different without her presence—larger, more formal, somehow less welcoming despite its obvious luxury.

"Pre-law thesis on local judges," Erin said quietly, her voice carrying the same sense of dawning understanding I was feeling. "Jesus, Alex."

"I know."

"She was researching judicial ethics and stumbled onto something about her own father."

Becca's footsteps came back down the stairs, quicker now, carrying a sense of urgency. She returned carrying a leather-bound book, the kind of journal you'd buy at an expensive stationery store—rich brown leather with gold-edged pages and a ribbon bookmark.

"I found it yesterday when I was going through her things. She hid it under the false bottom of her jewelry box." Becca held the journal against her chest like it was precious, her knuckles white with the intensity of her grip. "I started reading it, but... some of it's pretty private. And some of it's scary."

"Scary how?"

"She wrote about being followed. About phone calls where no one would speak when she answered. About finding her apartment searched when she came home from class, like someone had been looking through her things." Becca's voice was barely above a whisper, as if speaking too loudly might make the dangers more real. "She was terrified, Ms. Hayes. Especially the last week."

I stood and approached her carefully, recognizing the delicate balance between gaining her trust and not pressuring a grieving teenager. "Becca, this journal could be very important evidence. It might help us find out who really hurt your sister."

She looked up at me with those pale eyes. "You don't think Blake killed her?"

"I think your sister was investigating something dangerous, and that investigation might have put her in harm's way."

Becca looked down at the journal, then back at me, her pale eyes searching my face for something—honesty, competence, the promise that her sister's death would mean something. "Will this help you catch whoever did it?"

"It might."

She held out the journal with trembling hands, the gesture carrying the weight of trust and hope and desperate faith that adults could fix what had been broken. "Then you should have it. Melissa would want you to have it."

I took the journal gently, feeling the weight of it in my hands—not just the physical weight of leather and paper, but the weight of a young woman's private thoughts and fears, her final attempts to document something that had ultimately cost her life. The leather was soft, well-worn from months of daily use. Melissa's initials were embossed in gold on the cover: M.E.T.

"Becca, one more question." She nodded for me to continue. "Did your sister ever mention feeling threatened by anyone specifically? Anyone who might have wanted her to stop her research?"

"Not exactly." The girl bit her lip, a gesture that made her look even younger. "But she did say something weird a few days before she died."

"What did she say?"

"That sometimes the people who are supposed to protect you are the ones you need to run from." Becca's pale eyes met mine with an intensity that seemed too old for her face. "I asked her what she meant, but she just said I was too young to understand."

The same words Blake had mentioned during our interview. They suggested Melissa had discovered something that challenged everything she believed about justice and protection.

"Becca, has your father said anything about Melissa's research? About her school project?"

"He doesn't know about it. At least, I don't think he does. Melissa made me promise not to tell him." She paused, her expression troubled. "She said it would ruin everything if he found out."

We left the Thatcher residence twenty minutes later, the journal secure in my bag and a dozen new questions swirling in my head. Becca had walked us to the door, looking younger and more fragile than when we'd arrived, but also somehow relieved, as if sharing her sister's secrets had lifted some of the burden she'd been carrying alone.

"Ms. Hayes?" she'd called as we reached our car. "Will you find out who really killed my sister?"

"I'm going to try, Becca. I promise."

As promised, I left my business card with the housekeeper, along with a note for Judge Thatcher explaining that we'd stopped by and spoken briefly with Becca about background information regarding Melissa. It was a calculated risk, but one that would cover us procedurally while hopefully not alerting him to exactly what his younger daughter had shared.

Now, driving back toward downtown Houston through neighborhoods that grew progressively less affluent as we moved away from River Oaks, Erin and I sat in silence for several blocks before she finally spoke.

"That girl just handed us potential evidence that her father is involved in something that might have gotten his daughter killed."

"Yes, she did."

"And she has no idea what she's done."

"She knows her sister is dead and Blake Costello didn't kill her. That's enough for now."

Erin stared out the passenger window at the passing neighborhoods—middle-class homes with smaller yards and older cars, the kind of places where federal prosecutors lived rather than federal judges with mysterious sources of wealth.

"What do you think we're going to find in that journal?" she asked.

"Hopefully, the truth," I replied. "Or at least part of it."

"And what if the truth shows Judge Thatcher was involved in his daughter's murder?"

I thought about Becca's pale eyes, about the trust she'd placed in us by handing over her sister's most private thoughts. About Melissa, lying dead on her apartment floor while her killer walked free, and about a fifteen-year-old girl who deserved to know that her sister's death had meaning.

I gripped the steering wheel tighter. "Then we're going to prove it. No matter how powerful he is, no matter how many people are scared of him. If Henry Thatcher was involved in his daughter's death, I'm going to make sure he faces justice."

"Even if it puts us in danger?"

I remembered the white bishop sitting in my office safe, the cryptic message that had been left on my doorstep. Whoever was behind this was already escalating, already making threats that suggested they viewed us as obstacles to be removed rather than prosecutors to be respected.

"The danger's already here, Erin. We might as well find out why."

CHAPTER ELEVEN

BACK AT THE OFFICE, I closed my door and placed Melissa's journal on my desk like it was made of glass. The leather cover felt warm under my hands, like it still held some trace of its owner's life.

I took a deep breath and opened it to the first page.

A small slip of paper fell out, fluttering to the floor. I picked it up—a business card for Sullivan & Associates, CPAs, with a downtown Houston address. The name "Nicole Sullivan, CPA" was printed in conservative blue lettering.

I flipped the card over. In Melissa's handwriting: "Call about Dad's foundation documents."

Foundation documents. Judge Thatcher ran a foundation? That could explain the wealth, the River Oaks house that seemed beyond a federal judge's salary.

I picked up my phone and dialed the number on the card.

"Sullivan & Associates," a woman answered. "This is Nicole Sullivan."

"Ms. Sullivan, this is Alex Hayes with the U.S. Attorney's Office. I'm calling about Melissa Thatcher."

A pause. "Oh my God. That poor girl. I heard about what happened on the news."

"I understand she contacted you recently?"

"Yes, about three weeks ago. She said she was working on a research project and needed some financial documents. Corporate filings, governing documents, that sort of thing."

"What specific corporate and government documents?"

"Well, she was asking about the Thatcher Family Foundation—tax returns, board meeting minutes, financial statements going back several years. I told her she'd need authorization from the foundation's board to access most of that information."

I grabbed a pen and started taking notes. "Did she say why she needed these documents?"

"She mentioned it was for a college project about nonprofit governance. Something about how family foundations operate in Texas." Nicole's voice dropped. "But between you and me, she seemed more nervous than you'd expect for a school assignment."

"Nervous how?"

"She kept looking over her shoulder, asking if our conversation was confidential. And she wanted to meet in person rather than handle everything by phone. We met at a coffee shop instead of my office. Her request. Which also felt odd."

"Did you provide her with any documents?"

"Just the basic public filings—the stuff that's available through the Secretary of State's office anyway. But she seemed particularly interested in the foundation's board composition and funding sources."

A chill ran through me. "Ms. Sullivan, in your professional opinion, was there anything unusual about her requests?"

"Hard to say," she replied. "But most college students doing research projects don't typically ask about offshore banking relationships and wire transfer records. Especially not when the founder of the foundation is their own father."

"Thanks for your time," was all I could manage to say.

After hanging up, I sat staring at the business card for several minutes. Melissa hadn't just been researching judicial corruption in general—she'd been specifically investigating her father's foundation. And based on Nicole Sullivan's description, she'd been asking very sophisticated questions about financial irregularities.

I opened the journal to the first entry, dated eight months earlier.

August 15th

Blake took me to dinner at that expensive place downtown. He's sweet, but sometimes I think he tries too hard. Ordered a bottle of wine that probably cost more than my textbooks. I keep telling him he doesn't need to impress me, but he says his parents expect him to "maintain appearances." Whatever that means.

Starting senior year tomorrow. Can't believe this is it—last year before law school. Dad's so proud I got into Georgetown. Says I'm going to be a better lawyer than he is a judge. We'll see.

The early entries were exactly what you'd expect from a college senior—complaints about professors, excitement about law school, mundane details about classes and social events. But as I read chronologically through the months, I noticed changes in tone.

October 3rd

Blake was weird at lunch today. Got angry when I mentioned my research project for PoliSci. Says I should pick a different topic, something that won't "cause problems." I asked him what he meant, and he just said some stones are better left unturned. Since when does Blake care about my academic work?

October 10th

Another fight with Blake. He saw me at the library with research materials about judicial ethics and freaked out. Said I don't understand how complicated these things can be, that I could hurt people by digging into stuff I don't understand. He grabbed my arm hard enough to leave marks. I've never seen him like that.

I stopped moving my pen across the notepad. Blake had been trying to discourage Melissa's research from the beginning. And he'd gotten physical about it.

October 18th

Blake keeps calling and texting, wants to know where I am every minute. Says he's worried about me, but it feels more like he's keeping tabs. When I told him I was meeting with an accountant for my research, he got that look again. The angry one that scares me.

I'm starting to think this relationship isn't healthy. But every time I try to talk to him about it, he gets emotional and says he loves me too much to lose me. Then he'll do something sweet, and I feel guilty for doubting him.

The pattern was becoming clear—escalating control, emotional manipulation, physical aggression. Classic signs of an abusive relationship. But there was something else, something different from the typical domestic violence cases I'd prosecuted.

October 25th

Blake hit me today. Actually hit me, not just grabbed my arm. We were arguing about my research again, and I told him he didn't get to control what I studied. He slapped me across the face and then immediately started crying, saying he was sorry, that he was just scared for me.

I should break up with him. I know I should. But he says if I leave him, he'll have to tell people things that will hurt my family. What does that even mean? What could he possibly know about my family?

My blood ran cold. What kind of information would a college student have that could hurt a federal judge's reputation? And why was he using it to threaten her to stay with him?

November 2nd

Something's really wrong. I found my room searched yesterday—clothes moved, papers shuffled through. When I asked my roommate about it, she said she'd been in class all afternoon. Someone else was in here.

Blake swears it wasn't him, but who else would do something like that? I'm starting to hide my research materials in different places. I don't feel safe in my own apartment.

November 8th

Called the accountant about Dad's foundation documents. Some of the financial flows don't make sense. Large donations from corporations I've never heard of, money moving through multiple accounts before landing in the foundation's coffers. When I asked Dad about it over dinner, he got quiet and said foundation business was complicated.

Blake was there for dinner. He kept watching me, like he was waiting for me to say something I shouldn't. After Dad went to his study, Blake cornered me in the kitchen and said I needed to drop the research project. Said there were things about my family I didn't understand, things that could hurt a lot of people if they came out.

I'm scared. Not just of Blake anymore, but of what I might be uncovering.

I had to stop reading and pour myself a glass of water. The picture emerging from Melissa's journal was far more complex than a simple domestic violence case. Blake wasn't just an abusive boyfriend—he was actively trying to stop her from investigating her father's foundation. Because if she didn't, he'd have to reveal damaging information about the Thatcher family.

But that didn't change the fact that he'd been hitting her. That the violence had been escalating. That she'd been afraid of him.

November 12th

Blake cornered me after class today. Said his family has connections, that they know things about Dad's business dealings that could destroy his career. He says if I keep pushing with my research, if I don't drop the project and stop asking questions, those connections might decide to share what they know as a way to control the narrative.

Is he threatening to expose Dad? What could my father have done that would give Blake's family leverage over him?

I don't know what to do. I can't tell Dad about Blake's threats—what if Blake's telling the truth about having damaging information? But I can't keep living like this, scared of my own boyfriend, jumping at shadows.

The final entries were the most disturbing:

November 18th

Blake grabbed me by the throat today. Actually squeezed until I couldn't breathe. Said this was his last warning about the research project. That some people don't give second chances.

When he let go, I asked him who he was talking about. Who were these "people" he kept mentioning? He just said I should be grateful that he cares enough to protect me from them.

I think Blake's family is involved in something with Dad's foundation. Something bad enough that they're willing to hurt me to keep it quiet.

November 20th

Someone's been following me. I see the same car parked outside the library, the same man in the coffee shop where I study. When I told Blake about it, he said I was being paranoid. But then he asked if I'd told anyone about my research, if I'd shared any documents with my professors or classmates.

I lied and said no. But I've been copying everything and hiding it in different places. If something happens to me, at least there will be a record.

The final entry was dated just three days before her death:

November 22nd

I know too much. I know about the money laundering through Dad's foundation. I know about the shell companies and the offshore accounts. And I know Blake's family is somehow connected to all of it.

Blake keeps saying he's trying to protect me, but I think he's really trying to protect them. Tonight he said something that terrified me: "Sometimes people who ask too many questions just disappear."

I don't think he meant it as a threat. I think he meant it as a warning. Which is somehow worse.

If anything happens to me, look at the foundation. Look at the money. And look at who's really pulling the strings.

I closed the journal and sat back in my chair, my hands trembling. Melissa had discovered something significant about her father's foundation. Blake had already known about it and had been trying to stop her investigation through increasingly violent means.

But the journal also revealed something else: Blake might not have been acting alone. He'd mentioned his family's connections, people who "don't give second chances," threats that seemed to come from someone with real power.

Had Blake killed Melissa to silence her? Or had he been trying to protect her from someone else, using the wrong methods but acting out of genuine fear?

I picked up my phone to call Erin, then hesitated. The journal painted Blake as an abusive boyfriend who'd been escalating toward violence. It supported the prosecution's theory of the case. But it also suggested a much larger conspiracy involving Melissa's father and Blake's family.

One thing was certain: Melissa Thatcher had died because she'd uncovered a powerful secret. The question was whether Blake Costello was one of those people who'd wanted it kept in the shadows, or if he was just another victim caught in the crossfire.

Either way, the journal had given me a roadmap. We needed to investigate the Thatcher Family Foundation. We needed to find out what Melissa had discovered about the money laundering and shell companies.

And we needed to figure out who Blake's family really was, and what connections they had to Judge Thatcher's world.

This case was about much more than a college student killed by her abusive boyfriend. This was about corruption that reached the highest levels of the federal judiciary.

And if the chess piece on my doorstep was any indication, someone was willing to kill to keep those secrets buried.

CHAPTER TWELVE

"So Blake was hitting her," Erin said as we drove through downtown Houston toward Melissa's apartment complex. "Her journal entries make that crystal clear."

"It does," I replied, tapping my thumb against my knee. "But they also make something else clear—he was trying to get her to stop investigating her father's foundation. The violence escalated whenever she pushed forward with her research."

Erin navigated around a slow-moving delivery truck. "Which supports our theory that this was about silencing her, not typical domestic violence."

"Exactly. Look at the timeline." I flipped through my notes from the journal. "Blake starts getting aggressive in early October, right after she mentions her research project. By November, he's making threats about his family's connections and people who 'disappear' when they ask too many questions."

"His family's connections," Erin repeated. "What do we know about the Costellos?"

"Not enough. But Melissa seemed to think they were involved with whatever money laundering scheme she'd uncovered through her father's foundation."

We pulled into the parking lot of Melissa's apartment complex—a modern development near campus that catered to students whose parents could afford the premium for safety and convenience. The kind of place with security cameras, electronic key fobs, and monthly rent that exceeded most people's mortgage payments.

"Here's what bothers me," I said as we walked toward the building. "If Blake was part of some family conspiracy to protect Judge Thatcher's foundation, why would he date the judge's daughter in the first place? Why put himself in a position where she might discover the connection?"

"Maybe the relationship started before the foundation became an issue. Or maybe dating her was part of the plan—keep your enemies close sort of thing."

The building manager met us at the entrance, a nervous-looking man in his fifties who kept checking his watch like he had somewhere more important to be.

"The FBI finished with the scene yesterday," he said, leading us to the elevator. "The family's hired a cleaning company to come in next week. Tragic situation, just tragic."

Melissa's apartment was on the third floor, an end unit with windows facing the courtyard. Crime scene tape still stretched across the door, but the manager had keys and the authority to let us in.

"We'll need about an hour," I told him.

"Take your time. I'll be in the office if you need anything."

The apartment felt different from the crime scene photos—smaller somehow, more intimate. Without Melissa's body on the floor, it looked like what it was: a college student's living space, complete with textbooks stacked on the coffee table and laundry basket by the bedroom door.

"No forced entry," Erin observed, examining the front door. "Lock's intact, no scratches or tool marks. Just like the photos showed."

I walked into the living room, trying to visualize the scene as Blake had described it. According to his statement, he'd found the door unlocked upon his arrival at eight-thirty. Melissa was already dead, lying near the overturned coffee table. He'd assumed she must have fallen and hit her head.

But seeing the space in person confirmed what we'd suspected, and my father had concluded from analyzing the crime scene photos.

"The staging is even more obvious here," I said, looking at the righted coffee table. They must have turned it back over after processing. "Dad was right about the blood patterns. This wasn't an accidental fall."

Erin nodded, studying the wall where the dried blood spatter had been marked by forensics. "Seeing it in person, the cleanup area on the floor is really obvious too."

We spent the next forty minutes going through the apartment room by room. Melissa's bedroom had been thoroughly searched by the FBI, but it was easy to see signs of an earlier search—like Melissa had written about in her journal. Dresser drawers that didn't quite close, books on shelves that weren't quite aligned. Subtle signs that someone had been looking for something.

"Her laptop's definitely gone," Erin said from the kitchen. She pointed at a white block against the wall. "The charger is still plugged into the wall."

I was examining the living room windows when I heard footsteps in the hallway. Heavy, deliberate steps that didn't belong to the building manager.

"Ms. Hayes?" A man's voice, authoritative and slightly annoyed.

I turned to see a tall, broad-shouldered man in a dark suit standing in the doorway. He had the look of federal law enforcement—conservative haircut, serious expression. A quiet confidence that came from years of telling people what to do.

"I'm Special Agent Rick Morrison, FBI. I understand you're the prosecutor on the Thatcher case."

"That's right," I replied. "And you are?"

"Lead investigator. I'm curious about what brings you back to a crime scene we've already processed."

His tone was polite but pointed, professional courtesy that barely concealed irritation. I'd dealt with FBI agents like Morrison before—territorial, protective of their cases, suspicious of prosecutors who wanted to do more than just review reports.

"I like to see crime scenes for myself. Get a feel for what happened."

"And what's your feeling, counselor?"

"That your team did thorough work documenting the evidence." I kept my voice neutral, professional. "Though I do have some questions about the scene reconstruction."

Morrison's eyebrows rose slightly. "Questions?"

"The blood spatter patterns don't support Blake's assumption that Ms. Thatcher died from striking her head during a fall. We analyzed the photos extensively, and the angles are wrong. There's also evidence of selective cleanup in the area where the heaviest blood concentration should have been."

"Are you suggesting our forensics team missed something?"

"I'm suggesting the scene might have been staged to look like an accident."

Morrison walked further into the apartment, his eyes scanning the living room with the practiced gaze of someone who'd processed hundreds of crime scenes.

"Ms. Hayes," he said. "With all due respect, our forensics experts have decades of experience in blood pattern analysis. They've concluded that the evidence is consistent with blunt force trauma resulting from a fall."

"Even with the cleanup patterns we identified from the crime scene photos?"

"What cleanup patterns?"

I gestured toward the area of floor we'd noted in our earlier analysis. "The absence of blood transfer in the area where Melissa's body was found, combined with the spatter pattern on the wall, suggests someone cleaned up evidence of the actual murder scene. We noticed it when reviewing the photographs, but seeing it in person confirms it."

Morrison studied the area for a moment, then looked back at me with an expression that was equal parts patronizing and concerned.

"Counselor, I appreciate your thoroughness, but sometimes the simplest explanation is the correct one. We have a young woman with a history of domestic violence, a boyfriend with anger issues and no solid alibi, and a crime scene consistent with a fatal assault during an argument."

"What about the missing laptop?"

"What about it? Laptops get stolen during break-ins all the time."

"There was no break-in. No signs of forced entry, and nothing else taken."

Morrison's patience was clearly wearing thin. "Look, Ms. Hayes, I understand this is a high-profile case. Judge's daughter, media attention, political pressure. But sometimes prosecutors get so focused on finding a conspiracy that they miss the obvious answer staring them in the face."

The comment hit close to home. How many times had people suggested I was seeing patterns that didn't exist, connections that were purely coincidental?

"Agent Morrison, I'm not looking for a conspiracy. I'm looking for the truth."

"The truth is that Blake Costello killed his girlfriend during a violent argument. Everything else is just details."

Erin stepped closer, her voice carefully controlled. "What about Melissa's research into her father's foundation? Her journal entries about being followed and threatened?"

Morrison's expression didn't change, but I caught a flicker of something in his eyes. Surprise? Concern?

"What journal?" he asked

"The journal her sister gave us yesterday," I said, folding my arms. "Melissa's personal diary documenting the weeks leading up to her death."

Morrison sized me up, folding his own muscular arms in front of his torso. "We didn't find any journal during our search of the apartment or her belongings."

"Because she hid it," I told him. "Her sister found it yesterday in the false bottom of a jewelry box."

Morrison was quiet for a beat. When he spoke again, his tone had shifted from patronizing to genuine concern.

"Ms. Hayes, are you telling me there's evidence in this case that my team wasn't aware of?"

"Yes, I am." I cast a glance at Erin, and she nodded for me to reveal what we knew so far. "Melissa Thatcher was investigating financial irregularities in her father's foundation. She believed she'd uncovered money laundering and shell company operations, and that she was receiving threats to stop her research."

"Threats from who?"

"According to her journal, from Blake and his family's 'connections.' People who, in her words, make problems disappear."

Morrison pulled out a small notebook and started writing. The patronizing federal agent was gone, replaced by a cop who realized his case might be more complicated than he'd thought.

"I'm going to need to see that journal," he said without looking up.

"Of course," I replied. "But Agent Morrison, I have to ask—did your investigation look into Judge Thatcher's foundation at all?"

He returned my stare. "Why would we? The judge wasn't a suspect."

"His daughter died three days after documenting financial irregularities involving his foundation. According to her journal, she believed her discoveries had attracted dangerous attention from powerful individuals."

Morrison closed his notebook and looked around the apartment one more time, as if seeing it with fresh eyes. "Ms. Hayes, are you suggesting that a federal judge had his own daughter killed?"

"I'm suggesting that Melissa Thatcher discovered something that got her murdered, and that something involved her father's foundation. Whether Judge Thatcher knew about it or was involved in it, I don't know. But I think Blake Costello was either part of the coverup or trying to protect her from people who were."

"And you base this on journal entries?"

"I base it on the fact that nothing about this crime scene makes sense if Blake simply lost his temper and killed her during an argument. But it makes perfect sense if someone staged the scene to look like domestic violence while covering up evidence of a more calculated murder."

Morrison was quiet for several minutes, studying the blood patterns on the wall with new attention. Finally, he turned back to us.

"I'm going to be honest with you. When this case was assigned to me, I was told to keep it simple. Domestic violence, open and shut, don't complicate things unnecessarily."

"Told by whom?"

"People above my pay grade." He met my eyes directly. "People who don't like it when federal judges' families get dragged through high-profile investigations."

The implication was clear: Morrison had been pressured to avoid digging too deep into the Thatcher family's affairs. The FBI had been told to treat this as a simple domestic violence case and not ask inconvenient questions about judicial corruption.

"Agent Morrison, are you saying your investigation was compromised?"

"I'm saying my investigation followed the evidence as it was presented to me. But if there's additional evidence—like a journal documenting threats and financial crimes—then maybe we need to take another look at where that evidence leads."

As we left the apartment complex, Erin and I walked in silence to the car. The conversation with Morrison had revealed something disturbing: the FBI's investigation had been guided from above, steered away from any examination of Judge Thatcher's possible involvement.

"Someone doesn't want us looking too closely at the foundation," Erin said as we drove away.

"Someone with enough influence to direct an FBI investigation," I replied.

"The question is whether Morrison is going to help us or continue following orders to keep things simple."

I thought about the change in Morrison's demeanor when he realized there was evidence his team hadn't seen. He'd gone from dismissive to concerned, from federal agent protecting his turf to cop seeking the truth.

"I think Morrison's a good agent who was told to avoid complications," I said. "Now that he knows there are complications, whether he likes it or not, I think he'll follow the evidence."

"And if the evidence leads to Judge Thatcher?"

I tapped my thumb against the table. "Then we'll find out just how much influence the judge really has. And whether the people protecting him are willing to kill again to keep their secrets safe."

CHAPTER
THIRTEEN

My phone buzzed just as I was settling in with takeout Thai food and Melissa's journal spread across my kitchen table. The familiar containers of pad thai and green curry cooled beside stacks of legal documents and photographs.

James's name lit up the screen, and despite everything weighing on my mind—the chess piece locked in my office safe, the growing certainty that Judge Thatcher was somehow involved in his daughter's death, the isolation that came from pursuing a case everyone else seemed afraid to touch—I felt a flutter of anticipation.

I leaned back in my seat and answered. "Hey, stranger."

"Alex." His voice carried that familiar warmth that could still make my stomach flip after all these months. His deep, measured tone had first attracted me to him. "How's Houston treating you?"

"Hot, humid, and full of surprises. The usual." I closed the journal, grateful for the connection to someone who existed outside the increasingly claustrophobic world of my investigation. "How's D.C.?"

"Gray, cold, and bureaucratic. Also the usual." A pause, and I could hear the exhaustion in his voice that came from too many late nights and too much pressure. "I miss you."

The simple words hit harder than they should have, carrying the weight of months of snatched phone calls and canceled plans, of a relationship trying to survive the demands of two careers that consumed everything in their path. "I miss you too."

"This case is consuming my life. Eighteen-hour days, sleeping at the office, living on coffee and whatever passes for food in federal vending machines." His laugh was humorless, the sound of someone who'd forgotten what work-life balance meant. "I can't remember the last time I had a real meal or slept in my own bed."

"Sounds familiar." I twisted the phone cord around my finger, a nervous habit from childhood that I'd never outgrown. "What kind of case?"

"The kind I can't talk about over the phone. But it's big, Alex. Career-defining big. The kind that either makes you or destroys you, with no middle ground."

I understood that feeling intimately, having spent my own career walking the line between breakthrough victories and spectacular failures. Federal prosecution was an unforgiving field where one mistake could end everything you'd worked for, but one major success could open doors that remained closed to others for decades.

"When will you be back?" I asked.

"That's the thing. It could be weeks. Maybe longer." His voice dropped, taking on the intimate tone that reminded me of lazy Sunday mornings and quiet conversations about building a future together. "I hate this distance. Hate that we barely talk anymore."

"We're talking now."

"You know what I mean. Real conversation. Being in the same room. Touching you." The longing in his voice was unmistakable, and I felt an answering ache in my chest.

Heat crept up my neck as I remembered the last time we'd been together, the way his hands felt against my skin, the safety of falling asleep next to someone who understood the pressure that came with our chosen profession. "James …"

"Sorry. I know this isn't fair. You have your own cases, your own life. I just …" James sighed, the sound carrying months of frustration and missed connections. "I keep thinking about that weekend in Austin. How easy everything felt."

Our weekend in Austin had happened three months ago, before

this case, before the chess piece, before everything got complicated. We'd driven over for a long weekend, stayed at a boutique hotel on South Congress, pretended we were normal people with normal jobs who could plan a future together without considering the demands of federal law enforcement and the unpredictable nature of high-stakes prosecutions.

I allowed myself a smile at the memory. "That was a good weekend."

"The best." Another pause, and I could picture him in his D.C. office, probably surrounded by the same kind of case files and evidence photos that covered my own workspace. "Alex, are you okay? You sound different."

My chest tightened. James always could read me, even over the phone, picking up on subtle changes in tone and inflection that spoke to emotional states I thought I was hiding. It was one of the qualities that made him an excellent prosecutor and a dangerously perceptive boyfriend.

"Just tired. This case is …" I searched for words that wouldn't be outright lies while still protecting him from information that could put both of us in danger. "It's more complicated than I expected."

"The judge's daughter's murder? I saw something about it on the news."

"Yeah, that one."

"Domestic violence?"

"That's the theory." Staring at the closed journal, I thought about all the evidence inside contradicting that simple explanation.

"But you don't buy it."

I could hear the shift in his voice, the subtle change that indicated he was moving from personal concern to professional analysis. "There are inconsistencies. Things that don't add up."

"There always are in cases like this," he said. "Doesn't mean there's a conspiracy."

The words stung, echoing the dismissive comments I'd heard from colleagues and supervisors who thought my investigative instincts were shaped more by paranoia than evidence.

"I didn't say anything about a conspiracy."

"You didn't have to. I know that tone." His voice softened, taking on the patient quality he used when he was trying to guide me away from what he saw as dangerous territory. "Alex, I worry about you sometimes. This need to find the deeper story, the hidden connection. Not everything is related to your mother's case."

"I never said it was."

"You didn't have to."

We sat in silence for a moment, the distance between Houston and D.C. feeling larger than the actual miles that separated us. I could hear the hum of his office in the background—phones ringing, the distant murmur of conversations, the normal sounds of a federal building that never really slept.

"I'm not imagining things, James."

"I didn't say you were. I just ... I know how you get when a case grabs you. You disappear into it. You stop sleeping, stop eating, stop returning phone calls." His voice carried the weariness of someone who'd watched this pattern repeat itself too many times.

"I returned your call last week."

"After three days."

Had it been three days? I'd lost track of time since finding the chess piece, since reading Melissa's journal, since discovering that multiple prosecutors had lied about conflicts to avoid this case. The investigation had consumed my days and invaded my dreams, blurring the boundaries between personal obsession and professional responsibility.

"This is important to me," I said.

"They're all important to you. Every case, every victim, every injustice. It's one of the things I love about you, but it's also ..." He trailed off, clearly searching for words that would express his concern without triggering my defensive instincts.

Yet, my guard crawled its way over my body and through to my heart. "Also what?"

"Also exhausting. Loving someone who's always fighting other people's battles."

His words cut deeper than intended. My commitment to justice often came at the cost of personal relationships. That's why, before him, I had none.

"That's my job, James." Emotion crept its way up my throat. "That's what prosecutors do."

"No, that's what you do," he said, not bothering to hide his frustration. "Most prosecutors try cases and go home. You turn every case into a personal crusade."

"And that's a problem?"

"It is when it keeps you from living your own life, yes. When it keeps you from being present in this relationship." His voice carried genuine pain, like he was competing with ghosts and abstract principles for his girlfriend's attention.

Standing, my chair scraped against the floor, and I started pacing around my kitchen, my bare feet silent against the cold tile floor. "So what are you saying? That I should care less? Do my job halfway?"

"I'm saying maybe you could try trusting the system sometimes instead of assuming everyone else got it wrong."

"The system that failed my mother."

"Alex ..." His voice carried a warning I'd heard before, the gentle but firm tone that indicated I was approaching territory he thought was unhealthy for me to revisit.

"Don't. Don't tell me to let it go. Don't tell me I'm obsessed."

"I wasn't going to say obsessed." He paused for a moment, his voice growing quieter. "I was going to say haunted. There's a difference."

Haunted, turning the word over in my mind.

Maybe he was right. Maybe I was haunted by my mother's unsolved murder, by the questions that had shaped my career and my understanding of justice. But being haunted didn't make me wrong about what I was seeing in this case.

"Look," James continued, "I have to get back to work. This call is already longer than I should have taken."

"Right. Your career-defining case." The words came out sharper than I'd intended, carrying the resentment that had been building as our relationship took a backseat to professional demands.

"Don't do that," he said. "Don't make this about work."

"Isn't it? You just told me I'm haunted and exhausting. Doesn't sound like someone eager to rush back to Houston."

"Alex, that's not what I meant."

"Then what did you mean?"

I could picture him in his office, probably running his hands through his hair the way he did when he was frustrated. When he spoke again, his voice was careful, measured. "I meant that I love you. And I'm worried about you. And I wish you'd talk to me about what's really going on instead of pretending everything's fine when it clearly isn't."

I sank back into my chair, suddenly exhausted by the weight of maintaining facades and protecting secrets that felt too dangerous to share. "Everything's not fine."

"Tell me."

I looked at the journal, thought about the chess piece locked in my safe, at all the secrets I was carrying—evidence of judicial corruption, connections to my mother's murder, theories that could destroy careers or get people killed.

"I can't. Not over the phone."

"Then I'll come to Houston this weekend."

"You just said your case could consume weeks."

"Some things are more important than cases."

The offer tempted me more than it should have. Having James here, having someone to share the burden, someone who understood the weight of federal prosecution and the isolation that came with pursuing dangerous truths. But I also knew that bringing him into this would mean explaining about the chess piece, about my investigation into my mother's death, about all the theories he thought were conspiracy thinking.

"James, you don't need to—"

"I want to. Let me help with whatever's going on."

"You can't help with this."

"Why not?"

"Because you think I'm haunted. Because you think I see patterns that don't exist. Because if I tell you about the chess piece and the journal and the foundation investigation, you'll tell me I'm turning another case into a personal crusade, just like everyone else in my life.

"Because it's my case," I said. "My responsibility."

"And as your what, boyfriend? Partner? I don't even know what we're calling this anymore, but clearly I'm not allowed to help."

We'd been dancing around definitions for months, both too busy with our careers to have the conversation about what we wanted this to be, what kind of future we were building together, whether our relationship could survive the demands of two consuming professions.

"James ..."

"You know what? Forget it. Handle your case however you want. I'll be here in D.C., trying not to worry about you getting yourself killed chasing ghosts."

"They're not ghosts."

"Prove it."

The line went dead, leaving me staring at my phone in the sudden silence of my kitchen. The takeout containers were cold, steam no longer rising. The journal lay closed beside my legal pad, and I was alone again with secrets that felt too heavy to carry but too dangerous to share.

CHAPTER FOURTEEN

ERIN APPEARED in my office doorway the next morning with coffee and the satisfied expression of someone who'd just cracked a case wide open.

"Blake Costello lied to us."

I looked up from the foundation documents I'd been reviewing since six AM. "About what?"

"His alibi." Her eyes were wide, grin even wider. "Remember how he claimed he was gaming with his friend David until eight the night Melissa died?"

"Yeah. Said we could check the gaming logs."

Erin settled into the chair across from my desk and pulled out her notebook. "And I did. Called David Chen yesterday afternoon, very casual, just verifying details for our case file."

I set down my documents, closing them on my desk. "And?"

"And David got nervous the second I mentioned Blake's name. Started stumbling over his words, contradicting himself." She flipped through her notes. "First he says yeah, they were gaming all evening. Then when I ask about specific times, he says well, maybe Blake stepped away for a while. Then I pressed him on how long 'a while' was. He admits Blake was offline for at least an hour."

"How long exactly?"

"According to David, Blake logged off around seven-fifteen and didn't come back online until after nine PM. That's not 'stepping away for a while'—that's gone for nearly two hours."

"Two hours is enough time to drive to Melissa's apartment, kill her, stage the scene, and get back home."

"Exactly." Erin's eyes were bright with the thrill of a breakthrough. "But here's the best part—David says Blake called him around nine-thirty that night, all panicked, asking him to say they'd been gaming together the whole time if anyone asked."

I leaned back in my chair. Blake's alibi was falling apart, just like it should if he'd murdered his girlfriend. But something about the timing nagged at me.

"What made David decide to tell you the truth?" I asked.

"I think he's been feeling guilty about lying. He kept saying he didn't want to get Blake in trouble, but he also didn't want to lie to the FBI." Erin flipped to another page. "He's a good kid, Alex. Engineering major, no criminal record, probably never been questioned by law enforcement before in his life."

"And Blake asked him to lie that same night."

"Right after it happened. Which shows consciousness of guilt, premeditation to cover his tracks."

Everything Erin said made perfect sense. Blake had lied about his whereabouts during the time of the murder. He'd immediately tried to establish a false alibi. His friend's recantation was exactly the kind of break we needed to strengthen our case.

So why did I feel uneasy about it?

"Let's think about the timeline here," I said, leaning forward and propping my elbows on the desk. "Blake logs off at seven-fifteen, which matches exactly when Melissa's last phone call to him ended. Her phone goes dark at seven fifty-eight. He's back online by nine PM, which gives him time to establish his presence before calling David to coordinate their story."

"Right." Erin nodded her head once. "It's almost too perfect."

"That's what bothers me."

Erin's enthusiasm dimmed. "What do you mean?"

I stood and walked to the window overlooking downtown Houston. "Blake's not that smart. We've interviewed him—he's emotional, impulsive, the kind of guy who acts first and thinks later. But this timeline suggests careful planning."

Erin hitched her shoulders. "Maybe he's smarter than we gave him credit for."

"Or maybe someone else planned it and Blake followed their instructions."

"Alex …" Erin's voice carried a warning tone I was becoming familiar with. "Sometimes a lying boyfriend is just that: a lying boyfriend. Sometimes the obvious answer *is* the correct one."

"But what if it's not?" I turned back to face her. "What if someone had ordered Blake to be at that apartment, but not to kill Melissa?"

"What else would they have sent him there to do?"

"Stop her from going to that meeting with her source. Convince her to drop the research. Keep her away from whatever she'd discovered about the foundation."

Erin was quiet for a moment, considering. "You think someone else killed her while Blake was there?"

"I think Blake knows more than he's telling us about what happened that night. And I think David's sudden honesty might not be as spontaneous as it seems."

"You think someone told David to recant his statement?" Erin asked.

"I think someone wants us to focus on Blake's lying about the gaming instead of digging deeper into why Melissa was killed."

Erin closed her notebook and studied my face. "David approached me, Alex. I didn't even ask him about discrepancies in the timeline—he volunteered the information about Blake being offline."

"Which makes it even more convenient."

"Or it's evidence. Real evidence that our suspect lied about his whereabouts during the murder."

I sat back down, trying to organize my thoughts. "Let me ask you something. If you were going to kill your girlfriend, would you do it during a two-hour window when you'd already established your presence online with a friend? Wouldn't you create a more solid alibi?"

"Maybe he panicked," Erin said. "Maybe the fight escalated faster than he expected."

"Then why the careful staging of the crime scene? Why the cleanup? Why take her laptop?" I picked up one of the foundation documents. "Erin, everything about this case points to someone with resources, someone with experience covering up crimes. That doesn't sound like Blake Costello."

"It sounds like you're determined to find a conspiracy."

The accusation stung because it echoed what James had said the night before. "I'm determined to find the truth."

Erin leaned forward, her eyes pleading. "What if the truth is that Blake killed his girlfriend during a domestic dispute and then tried to cover it up? What if that's all this is?"

"Then why are multiple federal prosecutors scared to touch this case?" I didn't stop the rising pitch of my voice. "Why did FBI Agent Morrison get told to keep the investigation simple? Why am I receiving anonymous chess pieces warning me off the case?"

Erin's expression tightened. "Alex, we talked about this. You were supposed to keep me in the loop if anything else happened."

"Nothing else has happened. I'm talking about the same chess piece I showed you."

"Right, the one you refused to report to anyone."

"Because reporting it wouldn't help us solve Melissa's murder."

"Reporting it might help keep you alive."

We stared at each other across my desk, unblinking, the foundation documents scattered between us like evidence of all the secrets we were keeping from each other.

"Erin, someone killed Melissa Thatcher because she discovered financial crimes involving her father's foundation. Someone with enough power to influence FBI investigations and scare off federal prosecutors. And now, that same someone is sending me chess pieces, which means we're getting close to something they want to keep buried."

"Or someone's playing games with you because they know you'll see patterns everywhere."

"The patterns are real."

"Are they? Or are you so focused on finding connections to your mother's case that you're missing the obvious explanation right in front of you?"

I opened my mouth to speak but breath was all that came out. Was Erin right? Was I so determined to find a larger conspiracy that I was dismissing clear evidence of Blake's guilt?

David Chen's sudden honesty was just entirely too convenient. It led exactly where someone wanted us to go.

"Let's say you're right," I said finally. "Let's say Blake killed Melissa and David is telling the truth about the gaming alibi. What do we do with that?"

Erin splayed her palms open, as if the answer to that were obvious. "We build a case. We present the evidence to a jury. We get a conviction."

"And if I'm right? If Blake's being set up to take the fall while the real killers walk free?"

"Then we'll figure that out when we have actual evidence to support it."

"But if Blake's innocent?"

"Then we'll make sure he's exonerated."

Without another word, Erin gathered her things and stood to leave. At the door, she paused and looked back at me.

"I'm on your side, Alex. I want to find the truth as much as you do. But right now, the truth looks like Blake Costello lied about his alibi and killed his girlfriend. Everything else is speculation."

She left, and I sat alone with the foundation documents and the uncomfortable possibility that she was right. Maybe Blake was guilty. Maybe David's recantation was genuine. Maybe the chess piece was unrelated to the case.

But if that was true, why did every piece of evidence feel like it was being handed to us at exactly the right moment?

And why did I have the growing sense that we were walking into a trap?

CHAPTER FIFTEEN

Lisa had claimed a corner booth at our usual place, but this time her files were organized in neat stacks instead of scattered across the table. The documents were arranged with military precision, each folder labeled and positioned at precise angles. When she saw me approaching, she gestured to the empty seat across from her with the kind of expression that meant she'd found something significant.

"You're not going to like what I've dug up," she said without preamble.

I slid into the booth, the worn vinyl creaking under my weight. The restaurant carried its usual aroma mix of bacon grease and industrial coffee, scents that had become associated with difficult conversations and uncomfortable truths. I signaled the waitress for coffee, needing the caffeine to process whatever Lisa was about to dump on me.

"Try me," I said.

Lisa opened the first file folder with deliberate care, her movements betraying the nervous energy she was trying to control. "I've been researching Judge Thatcher's case history, going back five years. Specifically looking at any rulings involving financial crimes, money laundering, or trafficking cases."

The waitress appeared with a steaming mug and placed it on the table. I wrapped my fingers around it, the ceramic hot against my palms and steam wafting into my nose. "And?"

"Three cases stand out. All involving complex financial structures, shell corporations, offshore banking. And in all three, Thatcher ruled in favor of the defense in ways that seem …" She paused, searching for the right word while her fingers drummed against the table's surface. "Unusual."

I leaned forward, the booth's already cramped space caving in. The restaurant's background noise–clinking silverware, muted conversations, the occasional laugh–faded as I focused on Lisa's words. "Unusual how?"

"Take this one." She pulled out a case file, the contents thick with legal documents and financial records. "United States v. Meridian Holdings. Money laundering operation using a network of shell companies to move funds from human trafficking. The government had solid evidence—financial records, wire transfers, witness testimony."

I could see the prosecution's case outlined in her notes, the careful building of evidence that should have resulted in convictions. Financial crimes always left paper trails, and good prosecutors knew how to follow them.

"What happened?" I asked.

"Thatcher suppressed key financial evidence on a technicality. Said the search warrant was overly broad. Then he excluded testimony from a cooperating witness because of alleged prosecutorial misconduct that was pretty minimal." Lisa flipped through the pages, her frustration evident in the sharp way she handled the documents. Each page turn was accompanied by a small sigh, the sound of someone who'd spent hours reviewing material that should have resulted in justice. "The case fell apart. All defendants walked."

The goosebumps that rose on my arms had nothing to do with the restaurant's air conditioning.

"What about the other two cases?" I asked.

"Similar patterns," Lisa said. "Evidentiary rulings that gutted the prosecution's case, procedural decisions that favored wealthy defendants with expensive lawyers." She opened another folder, this one containing copies of court transcripts and judicial opinions. The text was dense, filled with legal citations and technical arguments that obscured the human cost of these decisions. "But here's what's really interesting—some of the shell companies that benefited from Thatcher's rulings show up in cases from other jurisdictions."

I set down my coffee cup, the ceramic making a sharp sound against the table. "What kind of cases?"

"Cases you worked on. Remember Lydia Kane and the Scorpion trafficking ring?"

The names made me flinch, muscle memory from wounds that hadn't quite healed. Lydia had been a key witness who'd turned out to be the real mastermind behind a massive trafficking operation. Scorpion had been her enforcer, the one who'd nearly killed me in that warehouse. Their ties to my mother were still something that I didn't have a clear picture on. My hand instinctively moved to my ribs, where my shirt hid the scar from his knife.

"I remember."

"Well, two of the shell companies Thatcher protected in the Meridian Holdings case were also moving money for organizations connected to their trafficking ring. Different names, different corporate structures, but the same bank routing numbers, same offshore accounts." Lisa spread out a series of financial documents, the numbers and account details creating a web of connections across multiple pages. "The paper trail links back to the same source."

I stared at the documents spread across the table, my vision blurring as the implications sank in. The numbers and company names swam before my eyes, but the pattern Lisa had uncovered was clear enough. Financial connections that should have been severed when we'd taken down the trafficking ring but had apparently survived through Thatcher's intervention.

"You're saying Thatcher was protecting part of the same network I helped take down?"

"I'm saying there are connections. Financial links between cases Thatcher dismissed and the trafficking operation you exposed. Could be coincidence." But her tone suggested she didn't believe that.

"You don't believe in coincidence any more than I do."

Lisa closed the folders and leaned back in the booth, the vinyl squeaking in protest. Her shoulders sagged with the weight of what she'd discovered, and for the first time since I'd known her, she looked genuinely worried about the implications of her research.

"No, I don't. But Alex, what I believe and what I can prove in court are two different things. And going after a federal judge based on patterns and connections ..." She shook her head, the movement sharp and definitive. "That's career suicide."

"Not if you're right."

"Especially if *you're* right. Federal judges have friends. They have influence. They can make careers disappear with a few phone calls." Lisa's tone spoke to the ambitious prosecutors destroyed for taking on targets too powerful for their own good. "The legal community is smaller than you think, and memories last a long time."

I thought about Agent Morrison's admission that he'd been told to keep the investigation simple. About the multiple prosecutors who'd fabricated conflicts to avoid this case. About the chess piece that had appeared on my doorstep, a reminder that someone was watching my every move.

"People are already trying to make my career disappear," I said.

"Then don't give them more ammunition." Lisa reached across the table, her fingers briefly touching mine before withdrawing. "Look, I know you think this case is connected to your mother's death. And maybe it is. But you need to be smart about how you approach it."

I scoffed. "Smart like backing down when things get complicated?"

"Smart like staying alive long enough to actually get justice."

I picked up one of the case files, scanning Thatcher's ruling in the Meridian Holdings case. His legal reasoning was technically sound, his arguments properly cited and logically constructed. Any law student could follow his rationale. But the cumulative effect of his decisions had been to protect a money laundering operation that should have been dismantled. The precision of his destruction of the prosecution's case suggested knowledge that went beyond legal expertise.

"Lisa, this isn't the first federal judge I've taken down."

Her eyebrows rose, surprise flickering across her features. "Leland?"

I nodded, remembering the months of investigation that had preceded that case. "He took bribes, fixed cases, worked with the same trafficking network these shell companies were funding." I met her eyes, seeing my own determination reflected in her worried expression. "He's in federal prison right now because I didn't back down when people told me going after a judge was career suicide."

"That was different."

"How?"

"You had evidence. Concrete proof of bribery, recorded conversations, financial records showing direct payments." Lisa gestured to the files between us, her hand sweeping over the documents with evident frustration. "This is circumstantial. Patterns and connections that could be explained away by any competent defense attorney."

"Leland seemed untouchable too," I said. "Right up until he wasn't."

"Yet how many people tried to kill you during that investigation?"

I was quiet for a moment, remembering the airport holding cell where I'd been held without charges. The gunshot that had shattered glass and ended a life inches from where I'd been standing. The feeling of watching a man murdered execution style in front of me, unsure whether I was next on the list. The taste of fear that had lingered for weeks after the case was closed.

I folded my arms. "That's not the point."

"That's exactly the point. Alex, you almost died going after that trafficking ring. And now you're talking about investigating another federal judge who might be connected to the same network." Lisa's voice dropped to barely above a whisper, as if speaking the words too loudly might summon the danger she was describing. "What makes you think they won't try to finish what they started?"

"What makes you think they won't try anyway, whether I investigate Thatcher or not?"

"Because if you back down, if you prosecute Blake Costello and close the case, maybe they'll decide you're not a threat."

"And if they decide I know too much anyway?"

Lisa didn't have an answer for that. She stared into her coffee cup, the liquid long since gone cold, while the weight of unspoken possibilities settled between us.

I gathered the case files and stacked them neatly, the papers rustling as I aligned the edges with unnecessary precision. "Lisa, I appreciate the warning. I really do. But I can't build my career on avoiding difficult cases because they might be dangerous."

"There's a difference between difficult and suicidal."

"Yeah. Difficult cases are the ones where the evidence is complicated. Suicidal cases are the ones where you don't have enough backup." I stood to leave, the movement causing Lisa to look up sharply. "That's why I'm not doing this alone."

"Erin Mitchell can't protect you from a federal judge with connections to organized crime."

"Maybe not," I said, shouldering my bag. "But she can help me build a case strong enough that his connections won't matter."

I turned to leave but Lisa stopped me. "What if you're wrong, Alex? What if Thatcher really is just a grieving father and Blake Costello really did kill his girlfriend?"

I turned back to face her, noting the way other diners glanced our way before quickly returning to their meals. The restaurant closed in on me, exposing me, as if the wrong ears might have overheard our conversation. "Then I'll have wasted some time investigating financial connections that turned out to be coincidental."

"And if you're right?"

"Then I'll have stopped a corrupt federal judge who killed his own daughter to protect a criminal enterprise."

"And if pursuing that gets you killed?"

I thought about Melissa, lying dead on her apartment floor. About my mother, murdered twenty years ago while investigating the same kind of network. About all the victims who'd died while their killers hid behind positions of power and influence. The weight of their deaths pressed against my chest, a reminder of what happened when good people stayed silent.

"Then at least I'll have tried to do something about it."

Outside Gracie's, I sat in my car for several minutes, reviewing Lisa's files in the dim light from the restaurant's windows. The parking lot was mostly empty, just a few scattered vehicles belonging to the evening crowd. My breath fogged the windshield as I studied the documents, the connections Lisa had found creating a pattern that was impossible to ignore.

The connections she'd found weren't proof of Thatcher's corruption, but they were threads—financial links between his rulings and the trafficking network I'd helped expose. Bank routing numbers that appeared in multiple cases, shell companies with different names but identical structures; money flows that had been protected by judicial intervention when they should have been seized as evidence.

Threads that, when pulled, might unravel something much larger than one judge's crimes.

CHAPTER SIXTEEN

"So we got new DNA results from the material under Melissa's fingernails," Erin said as we walked through the federal courthouse corridors toward Judge Thatcher's chambers. "Male DNA that doesn't match Blake or anyone in CODIS."

CODIS—the Combined DNA Index System. The FBI's database containing DNA profiles from convicted offenders, crime scenes, and missing persons. If the DNA under Melissa's nails didn't match anyone in the system, it meant her attacker either had no criminal record or had somehow avoided being entered into the database. Either way, it was another piece of evidence that didn't fit the neat narrative of Blake Costello as the obvious killer.

I adjusted my briefcase strap, my phone tucked securely in my jacket pocket with the recording app ready. "Which completely undermines our entire case against him."

"Exactly why Richardson called this morning," Erin continued. "Said his client has been patient, but now that exculpatory evidence has surfaced, he's filing a motion to dismiss. That's when Thatcher's clerk called—said the judge wanted to see us immediately about 'case developments.'"

"Exactly. Melissa clearly fought her attacker and got his DNA under her nails. If it's not Blake's DNA, then Blake didn't kill her." Erin's heels clicked against the marble floor. "Richardson's probably been sitting on this for weeks, waiting for the right moment to drop it on us."

Glancing at her, I was surprised by her matter-of-fact acceptance. "So, you're not arguing anymore? About Blake's innocence?"

"The evidence is what it is, Alex. You were right to question things. I just wish we'd gotten these results sooner."

"Don't you think it's a little odd that this report is coming out now?" I shifted my briefcase to my other hand. "DNA analysis of fingernail scrapings should have been completed weeks ago. Why are we just getting these results?"

"Maybe the lab was backed up," Erin said.

"Or maybe someone was hoping the results would get buried. Think about it, Erin—prosecutors inventing conflicts to avoid this case, FBI agents being told to keep the investigation simple, and now DNA evidence that should have been priority one gets delayed for weeks."

Erin adjusted her collar, a nervous habit I'd noticed when she was processing uncomfortable truths. "Do you think someone delayed the DNA analysis deliberately?"

"I think someone's been trying to control every aspect of this investigation from the beginning."

Erin didn't argue this time, which told me more than words could. The conspiracy theories I'd been spinning were starting to look less like paranoia and more like pattern recognition.

We reached the outer office of Judge Thatcher's chambers, where his clerk—a nervous-looking young man who kept glancing at us like we were bombs about to be set off—gestured toward the waiting area.

"His Honor will see you in a few minutes," he said, his voice barely above a whisper.

Pulling out my phone, I glanced once more at the clerk. He was deep in his own work, paying us no attention. I opened the recording app and activated it, then slipped the phone back into my jacket pocket.

"Alex," Erin said quietly, "what's our strategy here? If this DNA evidence comes in, Blake walks. That's what you've wanted all along— proof that he didn't kill her."

"True, but I want more than that. I want to know who actually killed her and why. No jury will convict Blake when someone else's DNA is literally under the victim's fingernails, but that doesn't tell us who the real killer is."

"The defense will argue Melissa scratched her real killer. It's textbook reasonable doubt."

The clerk appeared. "His Honor will see you now."

Judge Thatcher's chambers were exactly what you'd expect from a federal judge with old money—dark wood paneling, leather-bound law books, expensive furniture that belonged in a private club rather than a government building.

Thatcher sat behind a massive desk, still wearing his black robes from the morning's proceedings.

"Ms. Hayes, Ms. Mitchell," he said without looking up from the brief he was reading. "Please, sit."

Taking the chairs arranged in front of his desk, I kept my briefcase close, making sure my jacket pocket with the phone remained unobstructed.

"I understand there's been a development," Thatcher continued, finally looking up. His pale eyes fixed on me with an intensity that made my skin crawl. "Something about DNA evidence?"

Erin and I exchanged a look. How did Thatcher know about this so quickly? Richardson had only given us the results this morning.

"Your Honor," I said carefully, "while we appreciate your concern as Melissa's father, you've recused yourself from this case. Meeting with the prosecution about evidentiary matters could compromise—"

"Could compromise what, Ms. Hayes?" His voice carried an edge. "My daughter is dead. I called this meeting because I have concerns about how this case is being handled."

"Of course you do. But requesting meetings with prosecutors about specific evidentiary issues crosses ethical boundaries. You're not just a concerned father—you're a federal judge."

Thatcher's expression darkened. "Ms. Hayes, let me be direct. This DNA evidence—you need to find a way to exclude it."

The blunt statement caught me off guard. "Your Honor?"

"This DNA evidence is clearly problematic. You cannot let the defense use it to confuse the jury about Blake Costello's guilt."

Erin shifted beside me, uncrossing and recrossing her legs. "Judge Thatcher, we've only just received the results. We haven't had time to fully review—"

"Then review it quickly and find grounds for exclusion." His pale eyes bore into mine. "What's your strategy? Chain of custody? Contamination? Procedural violations?"

"Your Honor," I said, "we need to analyze the evidence thoroughly before determining our approach. If the DNA testing was properly conducted and the results are reliable—"

"The results cannot be reliable," Thatcher interrupted, his voice sharp. "Blake Costello killed my daughter. Any evidence suggesting otherwise is flawed."

"But what if the evidence shows Blake is innocent?" I pressed. "What if someone else killed Melissa?"

The change in Thatcher's demeanor was immediate and frightening. His face flushed red, and his hands clenched into fists on his desk.

"Innocent?" Thatcher's voice turned ice cold. "Ms. Hayes, Blake Costello is not innocent. He killed my daughter, and I will not have you entertaining fantasies about some mysterious killer just because of questionable DNA evidence."

"Your Honor, if the DNA doesn't match Blake—"

"Then the DNA is wrong!" He slammed his hand on the desk, making both of us flinch. "Or contaminated, or planted, or explained by secondary transfer. I don't care what technical excuse you use, but you will not allow this evidence to exonerate that boy."

The mask had slipped completely. This wasn't a grieving father seeking justice—this was something else entirely.

"You're asking us to suppress evidence that might prove a defendant's innocence," I said. "That's not just unethical—it's criminal."

"I'm asking you to do your job and convict my daughter's killer instead of chasing ghosts." Thatcher's voice took on a threatening edge. "Blake Costello is guilty, Ms. Hayes. And if you're too incompetent to prove it, perhaps someone else should be handling this case."

"Judge Thatcher," Erin interjected, her professional tone cutting through the tension, "we understand this is personal for you. But these kinds of ex parte communications about evidentiary matters are inappropriate. We should end this meeting."

Thatcher's head snapped toward her. "Are you suggesting I can't discuss my own daughter's case?"

"I'm suggesting that your emotional investment might be affecting your objectivity about the evidence."

"My objectivity?" Thatcher stood, looming over us from behind his desk. "Ms. Mitchell, my only interest is in seeing justice done. Something that seems to be in short supply in this prosecutor's office lately."

He turned back to me. "Ms. Hayes, let me give you some advice. Stop looking for complicated explanations when simple ones will suffice. Blake Costello killed my daughter because he's a violent young man who couldn't control his temper. Everything else is noise."

I felt my hand brush against my jacket pocket, ensuring the phone was still recording.

"Now, if there's nothing else," he said, "I have other matters to attend to."

We gathered our things and headed for the door.

Outside in the corridor, Erin and I walked in silence until we reached the elevator bank. Only when the doors closed did she turn to me with an expression of barely controlled fury.

"Please tell me you didn't just do what I think you did."

"What do you mean?"

"Alex." Her voice was tight with tension. "Your phone. You were recording, weren't you?"

Pulling out my phone, I stopped the recording app. The display showed seventeen minutes of captured audio.

"Are you insane?" Erin's voice was barely above a whisper. "You cannot record a federal judge without his consent. That's not just inadmissible—it's potentially criminal."

"He threatened us," I said. "He ordered us to suppress exculpatory evidence. You were there, you heard him."

"I heard a grieving father upset about DNA evidence that might let his daughter's killer go free."

"That's not what I heard." I checked to make sure the recording had saved properly. "The way he talked about that DNA evidence—he wasn't just upset. He was terrified."

"Of course he was terrified. It suggests his daughter's killer is still out there."

"Or it suggests something else entirely." The words came out before I could stop them. "What if it's his DNA under her nails?"

Erin stared at me. "Alex, you can't be serious."

"Think about it. Melissa discovered something about her father. She confronts him. There's a struggle. She scratches him, gets his DNA under her nails. He kills her and sets up Blake to take the fall."

"You're talking about a federal judge murdering his own daughter."

"I'm talking about a corrupt judge who's been protecting criminal networks for years and whose daughter discovered his crimes."

The elevator reached the ground floor, and the doors opened. As we walked toward the building's exit, Erin shook her head.

"Alex, you need to delete that recording. Right now."

I looked at my phone, at the file that might be evidence of judicial misconduct or might be career suicide.

"What if this recording proves Thatcher knows more about his daughter's death than he's admitting?"

"What if it proves you've lost all perspective? I was in that room too, Alex. I heard what you heard. But what I saw was a father desperate to see his daughter's killer punished, not evidence of murder."

I transferred the recording to a secure cloud storage account and deleted it from my phone.

"It's gone," I said, showing her the empty phone.

"Good. Because if that recording ever surfaces, it won't just destroy your career. It'll destroy any case we might have against anyone involved in this mess."

CHAPTER SEVENTEEN

I SAT at my kitchen table with Melissa's journal open in front of me, a full glass of wine at my elbow. The pages were worn from repeated handling, their edges soft from the oils of my fingers as I'd searched for answers that seemed constantly out of reach. The phone lay silent beside the journal, the recording from Thatcher's chambers locked away in cloud storage where it couldn't hurt anyone—including me.

Thatcher's words echoed in my head: *Blake Costello killed my daughter because he's a violent young man who couldn't control his temper. Everything else is noise.*

Maybe he was right. Maybe I was seeing patterns where none existed, connections that were purely coincidental. The human brain was designed to find order in chaos, to create meaning from randomness. Maybe a grieving father's desperate need to exclude DNA evidence wasn't sinister—maybe it was just denial, the inability to accept that his daughter's real killer might still be out there and that this wasn't as simple as he wanted it to be.

I flipped through the journal pages, looking for something I might have missed. The paper whispered against my fingertips, each page turn revealing another glimpse into a life cut short. Complaints about professors who assigned too much reading, excitement about law school applications, social drama that seemed earth-shattering at twenty-one but meaningless in hindsight. The handwriting was neat but hurried, the script of someone always racing to keep up with her own thoughts.

Then I found an entry I'd somehow overlooked before, dated just two weeks before her death. The ink was darker here, as if she'd pressed harder with her pen.

November 8th

Had dinner with Dad and some of his colleagues tonight. Judge Morrison, Judge Kellerman, a few others I didn't recognize. They were talking about "maintaining standards" and "protecting the integrity of the system." But the way they talked .... it felt like code for something else.

Dad keeps saying I don't understand how the world really works, that there are things beyond what you learn in textbooks. When I asked what he meant, Judge Morrison laughed and said someday I'd understand about "the old men's club that really runs things."

I used to think Dad was just a good man doing an important job. But watching him with his friends tonigh .... I'm starting to wonder if he's part of something I don't want to understand.

Blake says I'm being paranoid, that all powerful men talk like that. But Blake doesn't know what I found in Dad's foundation records. The shell companies, the offshore accounts, the money that flows through channels designed to hide its source.

What if Dad isn't the man I thought he was? What if he's part of that old men's club, and that club does things that would destroy everything I believe about justice and law?

I'm scared to find out. But I'm more scared of pretending I don't see what's right in front of me.

Closing the journal, I pushed back from the table, the chair legs scraping against the kitchen floor. The sound was harsh in the quiet house, a reminder of how alone I was with these questions. Melissa had seen it too—the sense that her father played a part in something larger, something corrupt.

But she'd also specifically mentioned shell companies and offshore accounts connected to her father's foundation. That wasn't idle speculation or overthinking—that was evidence of financial crimes. Still, what if I was reading too much into the investigation of a stressed pre-law student? What if "the old men's club" was just typical judicial networking, not evidence of a criminal conspiracy?

I walked to the bathroom and stared at myself in the mirror. The woman looking back at me had dark circles under her eyes, worry lines that hadn't been there six months ago, and the haunted expression of someone who'd been chasing ghosts for too long. My hair was pulled back in a ponytail that had started neat this morning but was now disheveled, strands escaping to frame my face. The bathroom's harsh lighting revealed every flaw, every sign of the stress that had been eating away at me since this case had begun.

James's words from our last conversation echoed in my memory: *You're letting the past control your future.*

Was that what I was doing? Had my mother's unsolved murder turned me into someone who saw conspiracies everywhere, who couldn't accept that sometimes bad things happened for simple reasons? The face in the mirror offered no answers, just the reflection of someone who'd been asking the same questions for too long.

Maybe Blake Costello really had killed his girlfriend during a domestic dispute. Maybe the DNA evidence was contaminated or degraded or explained by secondary transfer. Maybe Judge Thatcher was just a grieving father desperate to see his daughter's killer convicted, not a corrupt judge trying to cover up his own crimes.

Maybe I was the problem.

I thought about all the prosecutors who'd recused themselves from this case, claiming conflicts that didn't exist. What if they weren't scared of Judge Thatcher's power? What if they were scared of working with me, the prosecutor with a reputation for turning straightforward cases into elaborate investigations—and yes, winning them, but at what cost? My colleagues were smart, experienced lawyers who'd built successful careers by knowing when to pursue a case and when to walk away. If they were all avoiding this one, maybe the problem wasn't the case—maybe it was me.

What if Lisa's warnings about career suicide weren't about going after powerful judges? What if they were about my own pattern of self-destruction, my tendency to torch winnable cases in pursuit of shadows and speculation?

I returned to the kitchen and took a sip of the wine I'd poured earlier, the liquid catching the overhead light as it swirled in the glass. The journal sat open to Melissa's entry about the old men's club, her fears about her father's true nature. But was this evidence of corruption, or just the anxious imaginings of a young woman under stress? Law students were trained to be suspicious, to look for the loopholes and hidden meanings in everything. Maybe Melissa had simply been applying that mindset to her personal life.

My phone buzzed with a text message, the sound startling in the quiet kitchen.

Erin: *Are you okay? That meeting with Thatcher was intense. He really lost it when you mentioned the DNA.*

I stared at the message, wondering how to respond. How do you tell your colleague that you're starting to doubt your own sanity? That you're wondering if everyone who's ever accused you of seeing patterns that don't exist might be right? Erin was good at her job precisely because she was practical, focused on facts rather than theories. She'd been patient with my investigation into Thatcher's background, but I could sense her growing concern about the direction this case was taking.

I typed back: *Fine. Just thinking about the case.*

The response came quickly: *I know you want to find the truth but be careful. Thatcher seemed genuinely unhinged today.*

So Erin had noticed it too. The way Thatcher had demanded we suppress evidence, the rage when we'd suggested Blake might be innocent. That wasn't normal grief—that was something else. But acknowledging that meant accepting that my instincts might be right, and I wasn't sure I trusted myself anymore.

Closing the journal, I carried it and my wine to the living room, settling into my father's old recliner. The leather was soft and worn, molded to his shape. It still carried the faint scent of his aftershave, a reminder of weekend mornings when he'd sit here reading the newspaper while I watched cartoons on the floor beside him. The house felt too quiet, too empty, filled with the weight of questions I couldn't answer and suspicions I couldn't prove.

What if I was wrong about everything?

What if the chess piece had been sent by some random person trying to scare me, unconnected to any larger conspiracy? Online harassment was common enough; prosecutors made enemies, and some of those enemies were creative in their attempts at intimidation. What if my mother's death really was just an unfortunate accident, not the result of her investigation into trafficking networks?

What if I'd spent twenty years chasing ghosts because I couldn't accept that sometimes evil was random, meaningless, unstoppable?

I took a long sip of wine, the liquid warming my throat but doing nothing to ease the coldness that had settled in my chest. The living room was dark except for the single lamp beside my chair, casting shadows that seemed to shift and dance at the edges of my vision.

I tried to imagine what my life would look like if I stopped seeing conspiracies everywhere. If I prosecuted cases based on evidence instead of intuition, if I trusted the system instead of constantly questioning it.

Maybe I'd be happier. Maybe I'd have a normal relationship with James instead of one poisoned by my obsession with my mother's case. Maybe I'd sleep through the night without jumping at every sound, wondering if whoever killed my mother had finally come for me. Maybe I'd be the kind of prosecutor who went home at five o'clock, who didn't carry case files to bed, who could watch movies without analyzing them for clues about human nature and criminal behavior.

But then I thought about Melissa, lying dead on her apartment floor while her killer walked free. About all the victims whose cases I'd solved precisely because I hadn't accepted the obvious answers, because I'd kept digging when everyone else wanted to close the file. The trafficking ring I'd helped dismantle, the corrupt officials I'd exposed, the families who'd finally gotten justice because someone had been willing to ask uncomfortable questions.

Maybe I was paranoid. Maybe I did see patterns that didn't exist.

But what if this time, just like those other times, the patterns were real?

What if Judge Thatcher really was part of an old men's club that controlled things from the shadows, and his daughter had died because she'd discovered their secrets? What if Melissa's journal entries weren't the ramblings of a stressed college student, but the careful observations of someone who'd inherited her father's analytical mind and turned it on him?

Gulping the rest of my wine, I stared out the window at the dark street. The neighborhood was quiet, most houses showing only the blue glow of television screens behind drawn curtains. Normal people living normal lives, unburdened by the weight of unanswered questions. Somewhere out there, the truth was waiting to be found. I just didn't know if I had the courage to keep looking for it, or whether I'd finally convinced myself to stop chasing ghosts and accept the simple explanations.

The phone sat silent on the coffee table, no more messages from Erin or anyone else. The prosecutor's office was probably empty by now, everyone else having gone home to their families and their uncomplicated lives. I could join them, could choose to be satisfied with the case as presented. Blake Costello had means, motive, and opportunity. His prints were on the murder weapon. The evidence was sufficient for a conviction, even without the DNA.

But conviction wasn't the same as justice. I'd learned long ago that the legal system wasn't designed to find truth—it was designed to process cases efficiently. Sometimes, those two goals aligned, but not always. Not often.

I set down my wine glass and picked up Melissa's journal again, running my fingers over the cover. The leather was soft, expensive, the gift a father might have given to a daughter heading off to law school. Inside were the thoughts and fears of a young woman who'd seen something that frightened her, something that made her question everything she'd believed about the man who'd raised her.

Tomorrow, I'd have to decide which prosecutor I wanted to be: the one who played it safe and followed the evidence as presented, or the one who kept digging until she found answers that might destroy everything she'd worked for.

The choice should have been easy. Career survival versus professional suicide. Safety versus risk. But as I sat in my father's chair, surrounded by the ghosts of my own unresolved questions, I realized that some decisions couldn't be made with logic alone.

Sometimes you had to trust your instincts, even when everyone else was telling you they were wrong. Sometimes you had to chase the patterns, even when they led you into the darkness where truth and madness looked exactly the same.

CHAPTER EIGHTEEN

The doorbell rang at eight-thirty Friday evening, just as I was opening the takeout Chinese food and the case files. The container of kung pao chicken sat open beside me, chopsticks balanced precariously on the edge while I reviewed witness statements for the third time that day.

I wasn't expecting anyone, and unexpected visitors had taken on an ominous quality lately. Every unexpected sound, every unfamiliar car on the street, every phone call from an unknown number sets my nerves on edge.

When I peered through the peephole, my pulse quickened, not because the person on the other side was a threat, but for an entirely different reason. James stood on my front porch, overnight bag in hand and that crooked smile that had first caught my attention months ago. His hair was slightly disheveled from travel, his usually pristine appearance softened by the long day. Even tired, he looked good enough to make me forget why we'd been arguing for weeks.

I yanked open the door. "What are you doing here?"

"Hello to you too." Stepping inside, he dropped his bag, pulling me into his arms before I could protest. The familiar scent of his cologne mixed with stale coffee and airplane air, a combination that somehow managed to comfort me. "I told you I was coming to Houston this weekend."

"You said maybe. Your case—"

"Can survive without me for forty-eight hours." His mouth found mine, cutting off further argument.

The kiss tasted like missed opportunities and unspoken words, like all the conversations we'd avoided and all the space that had grown between us. His hands tangled in my hair, and for a moment I let myself sink into the familiar comfort of his touch. When we broke apart, I was breathless, my carefully constructed walls threatening to crumble.

"James, I'm glad you're here, but—"

"But nothing. We need to talk, and I need to see you." He glanced around the living room, taking in the scattered files and empty wine glasses. Case documents covered every available surface—coffee table, couch, even the floor beside my father's old recliner. My father knew the routine when my cases got big like this. He usually moved to working on things outside. "When's the last time you left this house for something that wasn't work-related?"

"I leave the house plenty."

"For court. For crime scenes. For meetings with victims' families." He moved to the couch and started gathering case files, his movements deliberate but gentle, as if he was trying not to disturb some carefully constructed order. "When's the last time you did something just for yourself?"

Watching him stack the papers, I tried to remember. The question should have been easy to answer, but my mind came up blank. "Last weekend I went to the grocery store."

"That doesn't count."

"I bought ice cream. That was for me."

James set down the files and turned to face me fully. Even after the long flight from D.C., he looked good—sharp suit slightly rumpled, tie loosened, dark hair mussed in a way that made me want to run my fingers through it. But there was something in his expression that hadn't been there before, a weariness that went beyond travel fatigue.

"Alex, I'm worried about you."

"You flew across the country to tell me that?"

"No, I flew across the country because I miss you. Because our relationship is falling apart and I want to fix it." He stepped closer, close enough that I could see the fine lines around his eyes, the small scar on his chin from a childhood accident he'd told me about on our second date. "And because every time we talk, you sound more disconnected from everything except this case."

"This case is important."

"They're all important to you. Every victim, every injustice, every conspiracy you think you've uncovered." His voice softened, carrying the weight of months of frustration and concern. "I love you for it, but it's also what's killing us."

I moved to the kitchen, needing distance and activity. The takeout containers sat abandoned on the counter, the smell of ginger and soy sauce now making me vaguely nauseous. "Want some wine? I have that Pinot Noir you like."

"Alex, don't change the subject."

"I'm not. I'm being hospitable." I opened the bottle with more force than necessary, the cork popping out with a sharp sound that echoed in the quiet kitchen. "You want to fix our relationship? Let's start by having a normal evening. No case talk, no analysis of my psychological state."

James followed me to the kitchen, his footsteps heavy on the hardwood floor. "Is that what you think this is?"

"That's exactly what this is." I poured two glasses, the wine catching the overhead light as it splashed against the glass, spots flying onto the countertop. My hands were steadier than I'd expected, muscle memory taking over even as my mind raced. "You show up unannounced because you're concerned about my mental health. You start cleaning up my files like I'm incapable of managing my own space. You lecture me about work-life balance while your own case is so consuming you can barely return my calls."

"That's not fair."

"No? You missed my last three calls because you were in depositions. You cancelled our weekend in Galveston because of trial prep. And now you want to talk about my work habits?"

We stood in my kitchen, the island between us creating a barrier. James set down his wine glass and ran his hands through his hair, a gesture I'd seen him make countless times when he was frustrated with a case, a judge, a witness who wouldn't cooperate.

"Tell me about the case," he said finally. "Really tell me. What's happening that has you so convinced there's a larger conspiracy?"

Gulping down half of my wine, I told him about the prosecutors who'd lied about conflicts to avoid the case, their excuses so transparent that even Callahan had seemed embarrassed by them. I told him about FBI Agent Morrison being told to keep the investigation simple, about how the federal agents had seemed more interested in closing the case quickly than finding the truth.

I told him about Judge Thatcher's suspicious knowledge of evidence that hadn't been officially disclosed, his desperate attempts to exclude DNA results that might exonerate Blake, his threatening behavior in chambers when I'd pushed back against his rulings.

I told him about Melissa's journal entries, her growing suspicions about her father's business dealings and the foundation that served as a front for money laundering operations. Not to mention the financial irregularities Lisa had uncovered, and the shell companies connected to trafficking networks I'd helped expose just months ago.

I told him about the chess piece that had appeared on my doorstep, about the growing sense that everyone involved in this case was being manipulated by someone who remained several steps ahead of us all.

James listened without interrupting, his expression growing more concerned with each detail I shared. He leaned against the counter, wine glass forgotten, his full attention focused on my words. But I could see something shifting in his face as I talked, a kind of professional distance replacing the personal concern.

"Alex," he said when I finished, "do you hear yourself?"

"What do you mean?"

"You're describing a conspiracy involving federal judges, FBI agents, defense attorneys, and crime lab technicians. You think a sitting federal judge murdered his own daughter and is now orchestrating an elaborate frame-up of her boyfriend." His voice was careful, measured, the tone he used when cross-examining witnesses whose credibility he wanted to undermine.

"When you put it like that—"

"It sounds exactly like what it is. A conspiracy theory built on speculation and coincidence."

The words hit me with unexpected force, partly because I'd been thinking the same thing just hours earlier. "So you think I'm paranoid."

"I think you're brilliant and dedicated and so focused on finding patterns that you sometimes create them where they don't exist." James moved closer, his voice gentle but firm. "I think your mother's unsolved murder has left you unable to accept that sometimes bad things happen for simple reasons."

"This isn't about my mother."

"Everything is about your mother. Every case you take, every injustice you fight, every conspiracy you uncover—it's all about trying to solve a twenty-year-old murder that may not be solvable."

Turning away from him, I stared out the kitchen window at my darkened backyard. The motion sensor light had activated when a cat wandered through the garden, casting harsh shadows across the lawn before clicking off again. "You think I should just give up. Stop looking for answers."

"I told you before that I think you should stop letting a dead woman write your story."

I spun around to face him, anger immediately flaring hot. The wine glass in my hand trembled, and I set it down hard on the counter.

My voice took on a hard edge as I said, "Don't you dare. Don't you dare reduce my mother's murder to some psychological hang-up that's ruining my life."

"That's not what I meant—"

"That's exactly what you meant. You think I'm chasing ghosts because I can't process grief. You think I'm damaged and obsessed and incapable of seeing cases clearly."

"I think you're in pain. And I think that pain is driving you to see connections that might not exist."

"The connections exist, James. The financial links between Thatcher's foundation and the trafficking network are real. The prosecutors avoiding this case are real. The DNA evidence someone—a federal judge—desperately wants excluded is real."

"But your interpretation of what they mean—"

"Is the only interpretation that makes sense of all the evidence."

We stood across from each other in my kitchen, the distance between us now feeling unbridgeable. James's expression was pained, like he was watching someone he loved destroy herself and couldn't figure out how to stop it. The kitchen felt claustrophobic suddenly, the walls pressing in.

"You asked me to tell you about the case," I said, my voice sharp. "I did. And now you're using it against me."

"I'm trying to understand—"

"No, you're trying to diagnose me. There's a difference."

James rubbed his face with both hands, exhaustion evident in every line of his body. "What do you want from me, Alex? Do you want me to tell you you're right? That Judge Thatcher is a corrupt murderer, and you're the only one brave enough to expose him? Do you want me to encourage this investigation even though I think it's going to destroy your career and possibly get you killed?"

"I want you to trust my judgment."

"I want to," James said. "But your judgment has been compromised by twenty years of unresolved grief."

"My judgment solved the Pierce case," I replied, jabbing a finger in his direction. "My judgment exposed Judge Leland's corruption. My judgment has put away dozens of criminals who everyone else thought were untouchable."

"And it's also isolated you from everyone who cares about you." He set down his wine glass with a sharp click against the granite. "When's the last time you had a conversation that wasn't about work? When's the last time you went on a date that didn't get interrupted by case-related phone calls?"

I opened my mouth to respond, but I couldn't. The silence stretched between us as I tried to remember the last time we'd had a normal evening together, the last time I'd prioritized our relationship over whatever case was consuming my attention. The last time James and I had gone out without work intruding had been during our trip to Austin. Before the chess piece, before this case, before everything had gotten complicated.

"That's what I thought," James said quietly. "Alex, I love you. But I can't keep watching you disappear into these investigations. I can't keep feeling like I'm competing with dead people for your attention."

"So what are you saying?"

"I'm saying we both work too much. We both let cases consume us. But at least I know when to walk away. At least I can separate my professional life from my personal obsessions." He paused, choosing his words carefully. "You can't. And until you can, we don't have a future."

The words hung in the air between us, heavy with finality. James's expression was pained but resolute, like he'd been building up to this conversation for months. I could see the effort it was costing him to say these things, the way his hands clenched and unclenched at his sides.

"Is that what you want?" I asked him, my voice hollow. "To end this?"

"I want you to choose," he said. "Between chasing your mother's ghost and building a life with me."

"That's not a fair choice."

"It's the only choice. Because right now, you can't do both."

I stared at him, this man I might have loved, might have built a future with. He was smart, successful, attractive–everything I should want in a partner. But he was asking me to abandon the one thing that had driven me for twenty years, the quest for answers that had shaped every decision I'd made since I was eight years old.

I crossed my arms, a defensive gesture I couldn't stop. "I can't just stop, James. This is who I am."

"I know. And that's the problem."

He finished his wine and set the glass on the counter with careful precision, as if he was already distancing himself from the domestic intimacy of sharing a drink in my kitchen. "I'm going to get a hotel room. Give you some space to think."

"You don't have to leave."

"Yeah, I do." He paused at the kitchen doorway, his overnight bag still sitting by the front door. "I hope you find what you're looking for, Alex. I really do. But I can't keep waiting for you to come back to me when I know you never really left that night twenty years ago."

Following him to the living room, I watched as he picked up his bag. The gesture was final, decisive, the movement of someone who'd already made up his mind. "James, wait—"

"I'll call you tomorrow. We can talk then, when we've both had time to think."

He kissed my forehead, a gesture that felt more like goodbye than see-you-later, and walked out into the night.

After he left, I sat alone in my kitchen with the half-empty wine bottle and the weight of his words pressing down on me. The house felt different now, emptier, as if his brief presence had reminded me of how isolated I'd become. The takeout containers still sat on the counter, the food long since gone cold, but I couldn't bring myself to clean them up.

James was asking me to choose between the life I'd built around finding my mother's killer and the possibility of a future with him. An ultimatum disguised as concern, a demand that I abandon the one thing that had given my life meaning since I was a child.

The choice should have been easy. Love versus obsession. Future versus past. But as I sat there in the silence, listening to the house settle around me, I realized it was the hardest decision I'd ever faced.

Because what if he was right? What if I really was letting a dead woman write my story, allowing twenty-year-old grief to dictate every choice I made? What if my pursuit of justice had become something else entirely, a compulsion that was destroying everything good in my life?

And what if the story she was writing was leading me toward a truth that would destroy everything I had left?

I poured myself another glass of wine and stared out at the empty street. The night was quiet, suburban Houston settling into its evening rhythm. Somewhere nearby, James would be checking into a hotel, probably relieved to have finally said the things he'd been thinking for months. Judge Thatcher would sleep peacefully in his mansion, secure in the knowledge that his secrets were safe.

My mother's killer would continue to run free, still breathing, still living a life that should have ended twenty years ago.

I finished my wine and stood, my reflection in the kitchen window showing a woman at a crossroads.

Some stories were worth finishing, no matter what they cost to write.

CHAPTER NINETEEN

MONDAY MORNING HIT me like a freight train. I'd spent the weekend replaying my conversation with James, alternating between anger at his ultimatum and doubt about my own judgment. By the time I reached the office, I'd perfected a mask of professional competence that I hoped would fool everyone, especially Erin.

Yet the moment I walked into the conference room we'd commandeered for trial prep, she glanced up from her files and frowned.

"Rough weekend?" she asked, taking in my appearance.

"Something like that." I set down my coffee and briefcase, avoiding her gaze. "Where are we with witness prep?"

Erin turned back to her notes. "I've got David Chen coming in this afternoon to go over his testimony about Blake's gaming alibi. The roommate is scheduled for tomorrow, and I'm still trying to pin down the neighbor who heard raised voices."

I pulled out my legal pad and started making notes, grateful for the distraction. "What about the forensics experts?"

"Dr. Martinez from the crime lab is confirmed for Thursday. She'll walk through the blood spatter analysis and the DNA evidence." Erin paused. "Assuming we decide to present the DNA evidence."

We both sat in silence for a beat. The DNA under Melissa's fingernails that didn't match Blake was the kind of evidence that could destroy our case—or force us to acknowledge we were prosecuting the wrong person.

"We present it," I said finally. "We can't hide exculpatory evidence just because it complicates our narrative. Richardson's clearly going to bring it up. Better for us to address it head on."

"Even if Thatcher's pushing us to exclude it?"

"Especially because Thatcher's pushing us to exclude it."

Erin made a note on her legal pad before tapping her pen to the paper. "Callahan wants to see us in his office at ten. Something about 'case coordination.'"

I checked my watch. We had forty minutes to review our cross-examination strategy before facing whatever Callahan had to say about our handling of the case.

"Let's run through Blake's cross," I said, spreading crime scene photos across the conference table. "I want to focus on the inconsistencies in his timeline, the lies about the gaming alibi, and his knowledge of Melissa's research."

"What about his family's connections?" Erin asked. "The threats Melissa wrote about in her journal?"

"We have to approach that carefully. I don't want to get into conspiracy territory without solid evidence to back it up."

The words felt strange in my mouth, a concession to James's warnings about seeing patterns everywhere. But maybe being more cautious wasn't a bad thing. Maybe sticking to provable facts instead of following every suspicious thread was the smart approach.

"That's ... unexpected," Erin said, studying me. "Usually, you're the one pushing to explore every angle."

I didn't look up at her. "I'm trying to be more focused. Stick to what we can prove in court."

She didn't seem convinced, but before she could press further, her phone buzzed with a text message.

"David Chen wants to reschedule. Something about being uncomfortable with his testimony." She set her phone on the table with a clunk. "That's the third witness who's tried to change their statement this week."

I met her eyes with concern. "What do you mean?"

"The neighbor suddenly isn't sure about the timing. Melissa's roommate is now claiming she might have been mistaken about when she last saw the laptop. And now David is getting cold feet about contradicting Blake's alibi."

I sucked in a sharp breath. "Someone's gotten to them."

"Or they're just nervous about testifying in a high-profile case."

I wanted to believe that. Wanted to accept that simple explanation instead of seeing threats and manipulation everywhere. But the pattern was too obvious to ignore.

"Erin, how many federal cases have you worked where multiple witnesses suddenly developed memory problems?"

"Not many," she admitted. "But this case is different. Judge's daughter, media attention, political pressure—"

"Political pressure from who?"

Before she could answer, there was a knock on the conference room door. Cynthia poked her head in.

"Mr. Callahan would like to see you both in his office now."

We gathered our materials and made our way down the hall. Callahan's office had the kind of organizational system that made everything look perpetually busy but under control. I aspired to emulate it.

"Close the door," Callahan said, settling behind his desk.

Erin shut the door and we took the chairs across from him. Callahan opened one of his files and pulled out what looked like printouts of emails.

"I've been getting calls," he said without preamble. "About this case. About your investigation methods. About concerns that you're pursuing theories without sufficient evidence."

"Calls from who?" I asked.

He glared at me. "People who matter. People who are concerned that a high-profile case is being turned into a fishing expedition for unrelated corruption allegations."

"We're following the evidence—"

"Are you? Because from what I'm hearing, you're investigating Judge Thatcher's financial dealings, questioning FBI investigative decisions, and developing theories about judicial corruption that have nothing to do with Blake Costello's guilt or innocence."

"The financial dealings are directly related to Melissa's murder," I said. "She was killed because she discovered her father's involvement in money laundering."

"According to who? A college student's journal entries? Speculation based on shell company connections that could be entirely coincidental?"

Callahan leaned forward, his expression serious. "Alex, I've supported your unconventional approaches in the past because they've gotten results. But this case is different. This case has implications beyond a single murder prosecution."

"What kind of implications?"

"The kind that can destroy careers and reputations based on unfounded allegations." He pulled out another file. "I'm reassigning primary responsibility for this case."

I felt the hair on the back of my neck stand up. A flush of heat spread across my face as the implications sank in.

"What?"

"Erin will take lead. You'll remain as second chair, but all major decisions go through her. And both of you will focus strictly on proving Blake Costello's guilt or innocence. No tangential investigations, no financial deep dives, no conspiracy theories."

"You can't—"

"I can, and I am. Alex, you're too close to this case. Your judgment is compromised."

I stared at him, trying to process what was happening. "My judgment has resulted in successful prosecutions—"

"Your judgment has also resulted in complaints from multiple sources about the direction of this investigation. I'm doing this to protect the integrity of the case and, frankly, to protect you from yourself."

Callahan's expression was sympathetic but firm, like a doctor delivering bad news he couldn't change.

"The decision is final," he said. "Erin leads, you follow, and both of you stick to the evidence that's actually relevant to this case."

We left Callahan's office in silence, walking back to our conference room like mourners leaving a funeral. I felt humiliated, angry, and worst of all, uncertain about whether Callahan might be right.

Erin turned to me. "Alex—"

"Don't." I raised my hand. "Whatever you're about to say, just don't."

I sat down at the conference table and tried to focus on the witness files, but the words blurred together. Everything I'd worked for, every instinct I'd developed over years of prosecution, was being questioned by everyone around me.

"I didn't ask for this," Erin said quietly.

"I know."

"And I don't necessarily agree with it."

I looked up at her. "But?"

She locked eyes with me. "But maybe he has a point about staying focused. Maybe we should concentrate on Blake's guilt or innocence instead of trying to solve every related crime."

"Even if Blake's just a pawn in something larger?"

Erin nodded. "Even if. Because proving he's a pawn still requires proving he didn't kill Melissa. And we can't do that if we're distracted by theories about judicial corruption."

She was right. I hated that she was right. Maybe the smart approach was to focus on the murder case in front of us instead of chasing larger conspiracies.

I pulled up the shared drive on my laptop to review our trial preparation files. The folder labeled "Costello Cross-Examination Strategy" was empty.

"Erin, did you move the cross-exam files?"

"No, why?"

I refreshed the page, hoping it was just a server glitch. The folder was still empty, but the modification date showed it had been accessed an hour ago.

My blood ran cold, skin erupting with goosebumps.

"Someone deleted our entire cross-examination strategy."

Erin came around the table to look at my screen. "Are you sure you saved it to the right folder?"

"I'm sure. I worked on it all weekend." I checked the deleted files folder, the backup drives, even my local computer. Nothing. Three days of work, gone.

"Could have been an IT glitch," Erin said, but her voice lacked conviction.

"Or someone with access to our shared drives wanted to sabotage our trial preparation."

"Alex, you're doing it again. Looking for complicated explanations when simple ones make more sense."

I turned in my chair to face her. "Simple explanations don't account for witnesses changing their stories, supervisors reassigning case responsibilities, and critical files mysteriously disappearing."

"And complicated explanations don't always reflect reality."

We looked at each other, the gulf between us growing wider with each exchange. Erin wanted to focus on the provable facts. I couldn't shake the feeling that someone was orchestrating every setback we encountered.

"I'll recreate the cross-examination strategy," I said finally. "It'll take a few days, but I remember most of it."

"We'll work on it together. I mean, I'm supposed to be leading now, right?" Erin's voice carried a note of irony. "And Alex? Whatever's going on with you outside of work, whatever's making you seem so on edge—maybe you should deal with that before we go to trial."

I nodded, not trusting myself to speak. Because the truth was, I didn't know how to separate my personal doubts from my professional instincts. I didn't know if I was seeing real threats or creating them out of my own paranoia.

All I knew was that someone had deleted three days of work, and I was the only one who thought that wasn't a coincidence.

CHAPTER TWENTY

I FOUND Dad in his workshop Sunday evening, sanding a piece of oak that would eventually become a bookshelf. The rhythmic scraping sound comforted me, a steady counterpoint to the chaos in my head. He looked up when I entered, taking in my expression.

"You look like you could use a beer," he said, setting down the sandpaper.

"I could use several beers. And maybe a new career."

Wiping his hands on a rag, he gestured toward the folding chairs he kept in the corner of the garage. "That bad?"

I settled into one of the chairs and accepted the beer he pulled from a small refrigerator tucked behind his workbench. The workshop smelled of wood shavings and motor oil, like weekend afternoons when I was a kid, watching him build furniture with the same methodical patience he'd brought to police work.

I took a swig of the beer, letting it cool my throat. "Jury selection starts tomorrow."

"Are you ready?" Dad asked.

"I don't know. Last week, I thought I was. Now I'm not even sure I should be in that courtroom."

Dad pulled up the other chair and sat facing me. "What happened last week?"

I told him. About Callahan reassigning me to second chair, the criticism from everyone that I was pursuing conspiracy theories instead of focusing on Blake's guilt or innocence. About the witnesses who'd changed their stories and the trial prep files that had mysteriously disappeared.

"Sounds like someone's trying to sabotage your case," he said.

"Or everyone's right that I'm paranoid and seeing patterns that don't exist."

"Those aren't mutually exclusive," Dad said, tilting his bottle toward me. "You can be paranoid and right."

I took another long sip, letting my shoulders settle. "James thinks I'm letting Mom's death turn me into someone who can't accept simple explanations for anything."

"James said that?"

"Among other things. He came here Friday night." I stared at the beer bottle in my hands. "We had a fight. A bad one."

Dad was quiet for a moment. "You want to talk about it?"

I traced the condensation on the bottle with my thumb, organizing my thoughts. "He thinks I'm obsessed. With Mom's case, with finding conspiracies everywhere, with turning every prosecution into a personal crusade." The words came out fast, like I'd been holding them back for days. "He said I have to choose between chasing Mom's ghost and building a life with him."

"What did you tell him?"

"Nothing. He left before I could figure out what to say."

Dad leaned back in his chair, studying me. "Do you love him?"

"I thought I did. But I don't know if I love him or if I love the idea of having someone who understands the work we do."

"Those are different things."

"Yeah, I'm starting to figure that out."

We sat in comfortable silence for a few minutes, listening to the distant sound of traffic and the neighbor's dog barking.

"Dad," I said, "what if James is right? What if I am so focused on finding Mom's killer that I can't see cases clearly anymore?"

"Are you asking me as your father or as a cop?"

I considered for a moment. "Both."

He took a sip of his beer. "As your father, I think you're one of the strongest, most dedicated people I know. As a cop, I think your instincts are usually right, even when everyone else thinks you're crazy."

"But?"

"But I also think grief can make us see connections that aren't there. I spent years convinced that every case I worked might somehow lead back to your mother's killer. Most of the time, I was wrong."

"Most of the time," I repeated. "But not always."

"No, not always." He met my eyes directly. "Alex, what does your gut tell you about this case? Not your theories about judicial corruption or trafficking networks. Just the basic question: did Blake Costello kill Melissa Thatcher?"

I thought about Blake's lies, his inconsistent timeline, his knowledge of things he shouldn't have known. But especially the DNA evidence beneath Melissa's fingernails that didn't match him at all.

"I think he was there when she died. I think he knows who killed her. But I don't think he struck the fatal blow."

The corner of Dad's mouth lifted. "That's a hell of a theory to take into a murder trial."

"I know. And if I'm wrong, Blake walks free while the real killer is never caught."

"And if you're right?"

"Then someone's been manipulating this case from the beginning to make sure Blake takes the fall for a crime he didn't commit."

Dad finished his beer and set the bottle on his workbench. "You know what I learned in twenty-five years of police work?"

I shook my head. "What?"

"Sometimes the system protects the wrong people. Sometimes good cops and good prosecutors get pressured to look the other way when powerful people are involved. And sometimes the only thing standing between justice and a cover-up is one person willing to ask uncomfortable questions."

"Even when asking those questions destroys your career?"

"Especially then."

Tears pricked at my eyes, though I wasn't sure if they were from relief or fear. "I'm scared, Dad. That I'm wrong about everything. That

I'm right. And most of all, that tomorrow I'm going to walk into that courtroom and not know who I can trust."

"Trust yourself. Trust Erin. And remember that your mother would be proud of you for fighting for the truth, even when it's hard."

"What if the truth is that I've been chasing shadows for twenty years?"

"Then at least you'll know. And you can stop running and start living."

He stood and moved to his workbench, picking up the piece of oak he'd been sanding. "You know why I build furniture?"

"You've been doing this since before you retired," I said, remembering childhood weekends in this very workshop.

He chuckled at that. "True. But it means more now. Because when you're building something, you can see exactly what you're working with. The wood doesn't lie to you. It doesn't have hidden agendas or ulterior motives. It's just what it is."

"Must be nice."

"Yes, it is. But it's also boring as hell." He smiled. "People are complicated, Alex. They lie, they scheme, they protect secrets that sometimes need protecting and sometimes don't. Your job isn't to make them simple. Your job is to find the truth despite the complications."

"And if the truth gets me killed?"

"Then I'll spend the rest of my life hunting down whoever hurt you." His voice was matter-of-fact, like he was discussing the weather. "But I don't think it'll come to that. I think you're smarter and more careful than your mother was."

"She wasn't careful enough."

"No, she wasn't. But she was brave enough to try. And so are you."

His words settled over me. My mother had been brave—brave enough to pursue dangerous truths, even when it cost her everything. And here I was, twenty years later, following in her footsteps. The question was whether I'd learned enough from her mistakes to survive what she hadn't.

I finished my beer and stood to leave. At the workshop door, I turned back.

"Dad?" He looked at me and nodded to continue. I had to force the words out from the back of my throat. "What if I lose this case? What if everything I've worked for falls apart?"

"Then you'll figure out what comes next," he said. "You always do."

I stood in the doorway and blinked at him. "That's it? That's your advice?"

"Well, plus one more thing."

"What's that?"

"Win or lose, don't let anyone convince you that caring too much is a weakness. The world needs prosecutors who give a damn about justice, even when it's inconvenient."

Smiling, I left the workshop, walking back to the house feeling lighter than I had in weeks.

My phone buzzed with a text message as I reached the front door. My heart skipped a beat when I read James' name. *Good luck tomorrow. I know you'll do the right thing.*

Staring at the message for a long moment, I then deleted it without responding. Tomorrow was about finding justice for Melissa Thatcher. Not about choosing between my past and my future.

Tomorrow was about discovering whether twenty years of chasing my mother's ghost had prepared me to catch a killer, or whether I'd been running in circles the entire time.

CHAPTER TWENTY-ONE

THE COURTHOUSE STEPS were crowded with reporters and camera crews by seven-thirty Monday morning, three weeks after Callahan had reassigned the case. I pushed through the crowd with my head down, ignoring the shouted questions about "the judge's daughter's murder" and "Blake Costello's innocence claims."

The media attention had intensified after someone leaked details about the DNA evidence that didn't match Blake. Every day brought new headlines speculating about wrongful prosecution and mysterious killers, turning what should have been a straightforward domestic violence case into a public spectacle.

Inside the federal courthouse, security had been doubled. Metal detectors moved slowly, and every bag was searched thoroughly. The atmosphere felt more like a high-security, political event than a murder trial.

"You ready for this?" Erin asked as we made our way to Judge Patricia Henley's courtroom. She'd been carrying herself differently since Callahan made her lead prosecutor—more confident, decisive. The change suited her even as it still upset me.

"As ready as anyone can be for a circus," I replied, shifting my trial bag to my other shoulder.

Judge Henley had a reputation for running tight proceedings. No grandstanding, no media theatrics, just efficient legal process. I hoped that would work in our favor, given the public attention this case had attracted.

We entered the courtroom to find it already packed. The gallery was filled with reporters, legal observers, and curious citizens who'd managed to get seats. I spotted Becca Thatcher in the third row, looking pale and nervous in a black dress that made her seem even younger than her fifteen years.

Judge Henley took the bench precisely at nine o'clock. Despite her small stature and silver hair, her commanding presence filled the room, causing the crowd to quiet down of their own accord.

"Ladies and gentlemen," Judge Henley began, her voice carrying throughout the packed courtroom. "We're here for jury selection in the matter of United States v. Blake Costello. I want to make something very clear from the outset. This is a murder trial, not a media event. I will not tolerate disruptions, outbursts, or attempts to turn these proceedings into entertainment."

She looked directly at the gallery. "Anyone who cannot conduct themselves appropriately will be removed immediately. Is that understood?"

A murmur of agreement rippled through the crowd.

"Very well. Bailiff, please bring in the jury pool."

Sixty potential jurors filed into the courtroom, looking around with the mixture of curiosity and apprehension that comes with civic duty. Judge Henley began the preliminary questioning—basic information about employment, family status, prior jury service.

Then came the crucial questions about pretrial publicity.

"How many of you have heard about this case in the media?" Judge Henley asked. Nearly every hand went up. "How many of you have formed an opinion about Mr. Costello's guilt or innocence based on what you've heard or read?"

About half the hands stayed up.

The judge looked down at her notes, then back up at the potential jury. "Juror number fourteen, what have you heard about this case?"

A middle-aged woman in a blue blazer shifted in her seat. "That the victim was a federal judge's daughter. That there's DNA evidence that doesn't match the defendant. The news has been saying the prosecution might have the wrong person."

My stomach tightened. The leaked DNA evidence was already poisoning the jury pool, making them doubt our case before we'd even presented it.

Judge Henley nodded. "Based on what you've heard, have you formed an opinion about whether Mr. Costello is guilty?"

"I ... I think there's probably more to the story than we're being told."

"That's an honest answer. Can you set aside what you've heard and decide this case based solely on the evidence presented in this courtroom?"

"I'm not sure I can, Your Honor."

"Thank you for your honesty. You're excused."

The process continued for two hours. Judge Henley dismissed seventeen potential jurors for cause—those who'd already decided Blake's guilt or innocence, people with connections to law enforcement, people who admitted they couldn't be impartial given the case's notoriety.

Then we reached the individual questioning phase.

Juror number twenty-three was a retired police officer who seemed perfect for the prosecution—law and order mindset, experience with domestic violence cases, the kind of person who would trust law enforcement testimony. When Erin questioned him, he made it clear he believed victims deserved justice.

"I've seen too many cases where abusers escalate to murder," he said, looking directly at Blake with obvious disapproval.

I expected Richardson to challenge him for cause or use a peremptory strike. Instead, he accepted the juror without question.

Juror number thirty-one was even more problematic for the defense. A middle-aged woman who'd survived an abusive marriage and clearly sympathized with domestic violence victims.

"Young women today need to know that the system will protect them," she said firmly. "Too many men think they can hurt women without consequences."

Again, Richardson accepted her, barely asking any follow-up questions.

The pattern continued through the afternoon. Jurors who were obviously favorable to the prosecution made it through selection, and Richardson wasn't challenging any of them. It was as if he'd been instructed to accept a prosecution-friendly jury despite representing a defendant facing murder charges.

During a brief recess, I pulled Erin aside in the hallway outside the courtroom.

"Something's off with this jury selection," I said quietly.

"What do you mean?"

"Richardson isn't challenging anyone. We're getting jurors who are obviously pro-prosecution—the retired cop, the domestic violence survivor, the victim's rights advocate. Any competent defense attorney would be using peremptory strikes on these people."

Erin glanced around to make sure we weren't being overheard. "Maybe he's saving his challenges for worse jurors."

"Or maybe someone told him not to fight this jury selection. Maybe he's been instructed to let us have a prosecution-friendly panel."

Erin shook her head. "That doesn't make sense. Why would the defense want a jury that's biased against their client?"

The pieces suddenly clicked into place. Thatcher's desperate insistence that we convict Blake. His fury when we'd mentioned the DNA evidence. Richardson's sudden appearance as Blake's high-powered attorney.

"Because Judge Thatcher wants Blake convicted. He doesn't care if Blake's innocent—he just needs someone to take the fall for his daughter's murder. And somehow, he's gotten to Richardson."

"Alex, that's a serious accusation—"

"Think about it. Thatcher pressured us to exclude the DNA evidence. Now Blake's own attorney is sabotaging jury selection. It all points to someone orchestrating a conviction regardless of guilt."

"Even if that's true, there's nothing we can do about it."

"We could object. Point out to Judge Henley that Richardson's not adequately representing his client's interests."

"We can't object against ourselves. If we're getting a favorable jury, we take it. We don't sabotage our own case because we think the defense attorney is being incompetent."

"What if it's not incompetence?" I couldn't keep the edge out of my voice. "What if Richardson is throwing jury selection because someone wants Blake convicted?"

"Then that's Richardson's problem," Erin said. "Not ours. Our job is to present the evidence to whatever jury we get."

"Even if we know Blake might be innocent?"

"We don't know that. We know there's DNA evidence that complicates things, but Blake could still be guilty. Maybe he had help. Maybe the DNA is from earlier in the day. There are explanations."

We returned to the courtroom for the final phase of selection. Richardson continued to accept jurors who should have been terrible for the defense, while we gratefully took advantage of his apparent incompetence.

By five o'clock, we had our jury: twelve people and four alternates who seemed unusually sympathetic to law enforcement and hostile to claims of domestic violence.

"This jury's going to convict him," I whispered to Erin as Judge Henley dismissed the panel for the day.

"Maybe that's what Richardson wants."

"Why would a defense attorney want his client convicted?"

Erin's eyes snapped to mine. "Maybe because he knows something we don't. Maybe Blake told him he's guilty, and Richardson figures a conviction on the evidence is better than whatever else might come out at trial."

As we packed up our materials, I caught sight of Becca Thatcher in the gallery. She was watching the jury file out with an expression I couldn't read—hope, fear, or something else entirely.

Outside the courthouse, the media circus was in full swing. Reporters shouted questions about jury selection, about the leaked DNA evidence, about whether we still believed Blake was guilty despite the new developments.

Erin repeated, "No comment," as we pushed through the crowd.

But I found myself wondering what I really believed anymore. Did I think Blake killed Melissa? The DNA evidence said no. But his lies, his presence at the scene, his knowledge of details he shouldn't have known all pointed to involvement.

Maybe the truth was more complicated than guilt or innocence. Maybe Blake knew who killed Melissa but was too scared to say. Maybe he'd helped cover it up. Maybe we were prosecuting the right person for the wrong reasons.

Or maybe we were about to help convict an innocent man because the real killer had the power to orchestrate the perfect frame.

CHAPTER TWENTY-TWO

THE COURTROOM WAS PACKED beyond capacity when Judge Henley took the bench Tuesday morning. Every seat in the gallery was filled, reporters lined the walls, and the overflow crowd had been moved to a separate room with closed-circuit television. The weight of all those eyes felt oppressive, but one person's gaze made my skin crawl.

Judge Henry Thatcher sat in the front row directly behind the prosecution table. His presence felt more like surveillance than grief.

An hour before the proceedings began, Erin and I had met in the conference room to finalize our strategy.

"I still think you should do the opening," Erin had said. "You know this case better than anyone."

"Callahan made you lead prosecutor. And he was clear—no conspiracy theories, no financial investigations. Just the murder."

"Which is exactly why you should do it. You'll stick to the facts because you know what's at stake if you don't." She'd pushed the notes across the table. "Besides, I'll be right there if you need backup."

Now, standing before the jury, I questioned that decision.

"Ladies and gentlemen of the jury," Judge Henley began, "you'll now hear opening statements. These are not evidence, but rather each side's outline of what they expect the evidence to show. Ms. Mitchell, you may proceed."

Erin stood. "Your Honor, Ms. Hayes will be delivering our opening statement."

Judge Henley nodded, and I rose, walking to the lectern with the weight of the moment pressing down on me. Twelve jurors looked back at me expectantly. A prosecution-friendly panel that Richardson had inexplicably allowed us to seat.

I thought back to this morning's written order from Judge Henley regarding the DNA evidence. Despite our motion to exclude it—a motion Thatcher had pressured us to file—Judge Henley's ruling had been clear: "The DNA evidence recovered from under the victim's fingernails is clearly relevant and was properly collected and tested. The motion to exclude is DENIED. The defense may present this evidence, and the jury shall determine what weight to give it." We'd received the order at seven AM, giving us barely enough time to adjust our strategy.

Keep it simple, I told myself. Domestic violence. Escalation. Murder. Just like Callahan ordered.

I faced the jurors and spoke. "Members of the jury, this case is about a young woman whose life was cut short by the man who claimed to love her. Melissa Thatcher was twenty-one years old, a college senior with her whole life ahead of her. She'd been accepted to Georgetown Law School. She was intelligent, beautiful, and full of promise."

I clicked a remote, and Melissa's photograph appeared on the courtroom's large screen. Young, blonde, smiling—the kind of picture that made jurors want justice. I moved away from the lectern, establishing eye contact with each juror. This was the story they expected to hear, the narrative that fit the evidence we could prove.

"But Melissa was also trapped in an increasingly dangerous relationship with the defendant, Blake Costello. What started as romance became control. Control became abuse. And abuse became murder.

"The evidence will show that on the night of November 22nd, Blake Costello killed Melissa Thatcher in her apartment near campus. This wasn't an accident. This wasn't self-defense. This was the deliberate murder of a young woman by her abusive boyfriend."

Behind me, I could feel Thatcher's stare boring into my back. Was this the story he wanted me to tell? The simple explanation that avoided any mention of foundations or corruption?

"Blake Costello was possessive and controlling. Melissa's journal, which you'll see as evidence, documents months of escalating abuse. Jealousy when she talked to other men. Anger when she made plans without him. Physical violence when she tried to assert her independence."

I clicked to the next slide—a timeline of the relationship's deterioration.

"The evidence will show that Blake's behavior became increasingly erratic in the weeks before Melissa's death. He monitored her movements, questioned her activities, demanded to know where she was at all times. Friends will testify that Melissa was afraid—of Blake's temper, his jealousy, and what he might do.

"On November 22nd, that fear became reality. Blake went to Melissa's apartment that evening. What happened next was captured in the physical evidence—signs of a struggle, blood spatter patterns consistent with blunt force trauma, a young woman who fought for her life and lost.

"After killing Melissa, Blake attempted to cover his tracks. He left the scene without calling for help. He constructed an elaborate lie about his whereabouts, claiming he was playing video games with a friend when he was actually committing murder. When confronted with evidence that contradicted his story, he changed his account. These are not the actions of an innocent man. These are the actions of someone trying to escape responsibility for murder."

I paused, forcing myself to maintain eye contact with the jurors despite my growing discomfort with the case I was presenting.

"The defense will try to confuse you with technical arguments about DNA evidence. They'll suggest that foreign DNA found under Melissa's fingernails proves someone else killed her. But DNA can be transferred in many ways—through secondary contact, contamination during evidence collection, or the chaos of a violent struggle. Don't let technical distractions obscure the clear evidence of Blake's guilt."

The words tasted like ash in my mouth. I was asking the jury to dismiss evidence that might exonerate the defendant, and every instinct I'd developed over years of seeking justice rebelled against it.

"Blake Costello had motive—his increasingly violent need to control Melissa. He had opportunity, having been at her apartment the night she died. He had means—the physical evidence shows Melissa was killed by blunt force trauma, not requiring any special weapon or expertise."

I clicked to my final slide—a photograph of Melissa laughing with friends at a college party, alive and happy in a moment frozen in time.

"Melissa Thatcher should be alive today. She should be preparing for law school, building a career, creating a life free from fear and violence. Instead, she's dead because Blake Costello decided that if he couldn't control her completely, he would kill her."

I returned to the prosecution table, feeling hollowed out by the performance I'd just given. I'd argued the case exactly as Thatcher and Callahan wanted—simple domestic violence, no mention of Melissa's research or what she'd discovered.

Richardson approached the jury box with the confidence of a defense attorney who'd been doing this for decades. He was perfectly groomed, expensive suit immaculate.

"Ladies and gentlemen, the prosecution just painted a very clear picture. Domestic violence, escalating abuse, murder. It's a story we've all heard before, and it's compelling precisely because it's familiar."

He smiled at the jurors, establishing the kind of casual rapport that came naturally to experienced trial lawyers.

"But familiar stories aren't always true stories. And the prosecution's account has some very serious problems that they're hoping you won't notice."

Richardson walked closer to the jury box, his tone becoming more serious.

"First, let's talk about what the prosecution doesn't have. They don't have a murder weapon. They have no eyewitness to this alleged crime. They don't even have a confession from my client. What they have is speculation about domestic violence and a young man who made poor decisions after finding someone he loved already dead."

He paused, letting that statement sink in.

"Blake Costello is not a perfect young man. He'll be the first to admit that his relationship with Melissa Thatcher had problems. They argued, sometimes loudly. He was jealous and possessive—character flaws he's struggled with and tried to address. But being a flawed boyfriend does not make someone a murderer."

Richardson moved to stand near Blake, placing a protective hand on his client's shoulder.

"The evidence will show that Blake went to Melissa's apartment that night hoping to reconcile their relationship, not to end her life. What he found there traumatized him so deeply that he made the worst decision of his life—he panicked and left without calling for help."

Blake sat motionless, his young face pale and drawn. He looked exactly like what he was—a scared kid in way over his head.

Richardson's voice took on a tone of righteous indignation. "The prosecution talks about DNA evidence as if it's meaningless, something to be dismissed as contamination or secondary transfer. But as Judge Henley ruled just this morning, this evidence is admissible and relevant. We will present evidence—evidence the prosecution has had for weeks—showing substantial DNA under Melissa's fingernails. DNA that shows she fought her attacker, and that attacker was not Blake Costello."

"If Blake had killed Melissa in the violent struggle the prosecution describes, where is his DNA under her nails? Where are the defensive wounds on his hands and arms? Where is any physical evidence connecting him to this crime beyond his admitted presence at the scene?"

He gestured toward our table, where Erin and I sat trying to maintain neutral expressions.

"The prosecution asks you to convict Blake Costello based on lies he told after finding Melissa dead. But consider this: if you discovered someone you loved brutally murdered, if you panicked and made terrible decisions in the worst moment of your life, wouldn't your story have inconsistencies too?"

Richardson's voice softened, becoming almost paternal. He returned to stand beside Blake, his hand again on his client's shoulder.

"Blake Costello did not kill Melissa Thatcher. The evidence will show that he's a young man who made catastrophic errors in judgment after discovering a tragedy he couldn't comprehend. The evidence will show that while Blake was lying to protect himself from suspicion, the real killer was walking free.

"Melissa Thatcher deserves justice. But justice isn't served by convicting an innocent man simply because he was in the wrong place at the wrong time and made poor decisions afterward. The evidence will show that Blake Costello is guilty of many things—being a difficult boyfriend, lying to police, showing terrible judgment in a crisis. But murder is not one of them."

Richardson sat down, and Judge Henley addressed the jury about the lunch recess. As the courtroom began to empty, I felt Thatcher's eyes on me again. When I finally turned to look at him directly, he was smiling—a satisfied expression that made my blood run cold.

During the lunch break, Erin and I reviewed our witness list in a small conference room down the hall from the courtroom.

"Richardson just made the DNA evidence the centerpiece of his defense," Erin said. "I thought Thatcher wanted it excluded."

"Maybe he couldn't make that happen. Or maybe Richardson decided to use it anyway." I rubbed my temples. "Either way, we need to be ready to address it."

"We stick to the plan. Secondary transfer, contamination, the possibility that Melissa had someone else's DNA under her nails from earlier in the day."

"Even though we both know that's unlikely?"

Erin set down her legal pad and looked at me directly. "Alex, we present the case we have. If the jury thinks the DNA creates reasonable doubt, they'll acquit. That's how the system works."

As we walked back to the courtroom for the afternoon session, I caught sight of Thatcher in the corridor. He was talking quietly with Richardson—a brief exchange that ended when they noticed me watching.

When Thatcher approached, his expression was pleased.

"Excellent opening statement, Ms. Hayes. Focused, professional, exactly what this case needed."

"Thank you."

"Much better than chasing conspiracy theories about judicial corruption," he said. "My daughter deserves a straightforward presentation of the facts."

"We'll present all the relevant evidence, Judge Thatcher."

"I'm sure you will. Though I do hope the defense's focus on DNA evidence won't confuse the jury about the obvious truth—that Blake Costello killed my daughter."

He walked away, leaving me standing in the courthouse corridor with the uncomfortable certainty that despite Richardson's strong opening, Thatcher still seemed confident about the outcome.

CHAPTER TWENTY-THREE

Wednesday morning brought the methodical work of building a murder case through forensic evidence. The courtroom had settled into the rhythm of testimony—witnesses sworn in, exhibits marked, technical details explained to twelve citizens who'd rather be anywhere else.

Dr. Elena Martinez took the witness stand with the confidence of someone who'd testified in hundreds of trials. As the lead forensic pathologist for Harris County, she'd performed Melissa's autopsy and could walk the jury through the clinical details of death.

"Dr. Martinez," Erin said from the lectern, "you performed the autopsy on Melissa Thatcher on November 24th, correct?"

"Yes. The body was brought to our facility the morning after it was discovered."

"Based on your examination, what was the cause of death?"

"Blunt force trauma to the head. Specifically, a depressed skull fracture in the temporal region that caused significant intracranial bleeding."

Erin clicked a remote, and a diagram of a skull appeared on the courtroom screen. Several jurors shifted in their seats but remained focused.

"Can you describe the nature of this injury?"

"The victim sustained a severe blow to the left side of her head, consistent with impact from a blunt object. The force was sufficient to fracture the skull and cause fatal brain hemorrhaging."

"In your opinion, could this injury have been caused by falling and striking a coffee table?"

Dr. Martinez shook her head. "Unlikely. The angle and force of impact suggest the victim was standing when struck. A fall would typically produce different injury patterns."

Richardson was taking notes but didn't object. So far, the testimony supported our theory of intentional violence rather than accidental death.

"Dr. Martinez, were you able to determine an approximate time of death?" Erin asked.

"Based on rigor mortis, body temperature, and environmental factors, I estimate death occurred between 8:00 and 10:00 PM on November 22nd."

The timeline was crucial. Blake's gaming alibi showed him offline from 7:15 to 9:00 PM—a window that perfectly encompassed the estimated time of death.

"Thank you, Doctor. No further questions."

Richardson approached the witness stand with a measured pace, having cross-examined forensic experts countless times.

"Dr. Martinez," he said, "you mentioned that time of death estimates can vary depending on environmental factors. What was the temperature in the victim's apartment that night?"

"According to police reports, approximately 72 degrees Fahrenheit."

"And how does temperature affect the accuracy of your time estimate?"

"Warmer temperatures can accelerate decomposition and rigor mortis, potentially affecting our calculations."

"So your estimate of 8:00 to 10:00 PM could be off by how much?"

Dr. Martinez hesitated. "Potentially an hour in either direction."

Chills erupted on my neck. Richardson was chipping away at the precision of our timeline, creating room for doubt about when exactly Melissa had died.

"So death could have occurred as early as 7:00 PM or as late as 11:00 PM?" Richardson asked.

"That's within the margin of error, yes."

"Thank you, Doctor."

The concession wasn't devastating, but it lessened the significance of Blake's alibi. Richardson had effectively expanded the window of death to include times when Blake might have been gaming.

Our next witness was Detective Sarah Kim, the lead investigator who'd processed the crime scene. She took the stand with the no-nonsense demeanor of a veteran cop who'd seen everything.

"Detective Kim," I said, taking over the questioning, "you arrived at Melissa Thatcher's apartment on the morning of November 23rd?"

"Yes, at approximately 9:30 AM, about fifteen minutes after the 911 call."

"Can you describe what you observed?"

"The victim was lying in the living room near an overturned coffee table. There was blood on the floor and spatter patterns on the nearby wall. The apartment showed signs of a struggle."

I clicked to crime scene photographs—the sanitized versions that showed the scene without Melissa's body.

"What did the blood spatter patterns tell you about what happened?"

"The patterns suggested the victim was struck while standing," Detective Kim said. "The blood drops on the wall were consistent with blunt force trauma, not a fall."

Richardson was already on his feet. "Objection. The witness isn't qualified as a blood spatter expert."

"Sustained," the judge replied. "Detective Kim, please limit yourself to your observations rather than interpretations."

I nodded and adjusted my approach. "Detective Kim, did you observe anything unusual about the scene?"

"The living room showed signs of cleanup in certain areas. Some blood appeared to have been wiped away, and items seemed to have been moved after the initial incident."

"What made you think items had been moved?" I asked.

"Blood transfer patterns that didn't match the final positions of furniture. And the victim's laptop was missing, though her roommate confirmed she always kept it on the kitchen counter."

The missing laptop was significant—it suggested someone had taken potential evidence from the scene.

"Did you find any signs of forced entry?" I asked.

Detective Kim shook her head. "No. The apartment door was unlocked when police arrived, but there was no damage to locks or door frames."

"Suggesting the victim knew her attacker?"

Richardson objected before I could finish. "Leading the witness, Your Honor."

"Sustained. Rephrase, Ms. Hayes."

I nodded and continued on. "What conclusions, if any, did you draw from the lack of forced entry?"

"Either the victim let her attacker in, or the attacker had access to the apartment."

I felt the significance of the testimony settling with the jury. No forced entry, signs of staging, missing laptop—all evidence that pointed to someone Melissa knew and trusted.

"Thank you, Detective. No further questions."

Richardson's cross-examination was surgical, picking apart small details without challenging the core narrative.

"Detective Kim, you mentioned Mr. Costello had a key to Ms. Thatcher's apartment, correct?"

"According to the victim's roommate, yes."

"So he wouldn't have needed to force entry?"

"Correct."

"And the cleanup you observed—could that have been done by someone trying to help the victim rather than hide evidence?"

Kim hesitated. "It's possible, but unlikely given the patterns we observed."

"But possible?"

"Yes."

Richardson was creating reasonable doubt without directly contradicting our evidence. Each small concession added up, making our case seem less certain than we'd presented it.

Our final witness of the day was David Chen, Blake's gaming partner, who'd eventually admitted that Blake was offline during the crucial window. David looked nervous as he was sworn in, clearly uncomfortable with his role in destroying his friend's alibi.

"Mr. Chen," Erin began, "you're a friend of the defendant?"

David's voice was barely audible. "We were friends. Are friends."

"On November 22nd, were you playing online games with Blake Costello?"

"We started playing around five PM. But Blake logged off around seven-fifteen and didn't come back online until after nine."

"How certain are you of those times?"

"Very certain. I was keeping track because we were trying to complete a specific mission that required coordination."

Erin nodded. "Did Mr. Costello tell you why he was logging off?"

"He said he had to go somewhere but would be back soon."

"And when he returned to the game?"

David shifted, tilting his head down. "He seemed upset. Distracted. He asked me to say we'd been playing together all evening if anyone asked."

"Did you agree to that?"

David nodded. "At first, yes. I thought I was helping a friend. But when I realized it was about a murder investigation …"

Erin let the silence hang for a moment. "What changed your mind about lying for Blake?"

"I couldn't be part of covering up something like that," David said. "And I started thinking about that girl, about her family. It wasn't right."

Erin returned to the prosecution table, and Richardson rose for cross-examination.

"Mr. Chen," he began, "Blake didn't tell you he'd committed a crime, did he?"

"No."

"He didn't confess to murder or ask you to help hide evidence?"

"No."

"For all you knew, he might have had any number of innocent reasons for wanting an alibi?"

David shrugged. "I guess so."

"Thank you."

Richardson's brevity was strategic. By keeping his cross short and focused, he'd highlighted that David had no actual knowledge of Blake committing a crime—just that Blake had asked for an alibi. It reinforced his opening theme that Blake had made poor decisions after finding Melissa dead, not that he'd killed her.

As court recessed for the day, I felt cautiously optimistic about how the evidence was playing with the jury. The forensic testimony supported our theory of intentional violence, the crime scene evidence suggested staging and cover-up, and David's testimony destroyed Blake's alibi.

But Richardson's cross-examinations had been skillful, creating small doubts without directly challenging our narrative. And throughout the day, I'd caught glimpses of Judge Thatcher in the gallery, watching everything with intense focus, as if monitoring a performance.

"How do you think it went?" Erin asked as we packed up our materials.

"The evidence is landing," I said, slipping a file folder into my bag. "The jury seems engaged. But Richardson's good—he's not trying to prove Blake's innocence, just creating enough doubt to muddy the waters."

"That's his job."

"I know." I paused for a moment. "But he's not fighting as hard as he should be."

Erin glanced around and lowered her voice. "Maybe he knows something we don't. Maybe Blake confessed to him."

"Or maybe someone told him not to fight too hard."

"We need to focus on the evidence, not theories about what Richardson may or may not be doing."

Tomorrow we'd continue building our case against Blake Costello. But with each witness, with each piece of evidence, I felt more certain that we were prosecuting someone who might not have committed the murder—even if he knew more about it than he was saying.

CHAPTER TWENTY-FOUR

THURSDAY MORNING'S pretrial motion hearing felt more like a chess match than a legal proceeding. Judge Henley had cleared the courtroom of everyone except counsel, the court reporter, and bailiff. The jury wouldn't hear these arguments, but the outcome would determine how much of Melissa's story we could tell.

Richardson had filed a motion to exclude the journal entries immediately after I'd referenced them in opening statements. Now we had to defend their admissibility against his challenge.

Erin stood at the lectern with Melissa's journal in her hands. "Your Honor, the prosecution opposes the defense motion to exclude the victim's journal. These entries are admissible under Federal Rules of Evidence 803(3) and 807—the state-of-mind exception and residual hearsay exception."

Judge Henley adjusted her reading glasses. "What specific entries are you seeking to introduce, Ms. Mitchell?"

"Entries documenting the victim's fear of the defendant, her awareness of escalating violence in their relationship, and her state of mind in the weeks before her death."

Richardson rose from his seat. "Your Honor, the defense objects to any journal entries. These are classic hearsay statements that don't fall under any recognized exception. The victim's out-of-court statements about my client are prejudicial and unreliable."

I bit my tongue, forcing myself to remain silent while Erin handled the argument. This was her case now, and her decision on how aggressively to push for the journal's admission.

"The entries we're seeking to admit fall squarely within the state-of-mind exception," Erin continued. "They demonstrate the victim's mental state and emotional condition, not to prove the truth of any alleged acts."

Judge Henley opened the journal and began reading through the marked passages. The courtroom was silent except for the soft rustle of pages and the click of the court reporter's machine.

"Ms. Mitchell, I'm looking at the entries you've marked. Some of these appear to be direct accusations against Mr. Costello. How do you propose to get around the hearsay prohibition?"

"Your Honor, these entries demonstrate Melissa Thatcher's state of mind—that she believed herself to be in danger, that she was experiencing fear. We're not offering them as proof that specific events occurred."

It was a fine legal distinction, but an important one. The journal entries couldn't be used to prove Blake had hit Melissa, but they could show that Melissa believed he had, and that she'd been afraid of him.

I shifted in my seat, the irony not lost on me. Here I was, helping to build a case against someone I didn't believe had killed Melissa. But Callahan had made it clear—pursue the case against Blake or lose my job. And maybe if Blake was convicted of a murder he didn't commit, it would force the real story into the light eventually.

Richardson stepped forward. "Your Honor, the prejudicial impact of these entries far outweighs any probative value. The jury will inevitably use them to conclude that Mr. Costello is violent, regardless of limiting instructions."

Judge Henley continued reading, occasionally making notes. I watched her expression for any hint of how she was leaning, but her judicial poker face revealed nothing.

"I'm particularly concerned about this entry from November 18th," she said, reading from the journal. "'Blake grabbed me by the throat today. Actually grabbed my throat and squeezed until I couldn't breathe. Said this was his last warning about the research project.'"

My heart sank. That was one of our strongest entries for showing Blake's attempts to stop Melissa's investigation—though for our simplified domestic violence case, it was just evidence of escalating violence.

"Your Honor," Richardson said, "that entry is exactly why this journal should be excluded. It's a specific accusation of assault that my client has no opportunity to rebut or explain. It's fundamentally unfair."

"And this entry from November 20th," Judge Henley continued. "'Someone's been following me... Blake says I'm being paranoid. But then he asked if I'd told anyone about my research.' This goes well beyond state of mind into speculation about third parties."

I clenched my jaw. The judge was focusing on exactly the entries that revealed what this case was really about—not domestic violence but silencing someone who'd discovered dangerous truths.

"Your Honor," Erin said, "those entries demonstrate the victim's psychological state in her final days."

"They also introduce unsubstantiated claims about research projects and third-party threats unrelated to the defendant's alleged actions." Judge Henley closed the journal and looked at both legal teams. "I'm going to allow limited portions of this journal under the state-of-mind exception, but with significant restrictions."

I held my breath, waiting for the ruling that would determine how much of Melissa's story the jury would hear.

"The court will admit entries that describe the victim's emotional state, her feelings about the relationship, and general expressions of fear or concern. However, I'm excluding any entries that make specific accusations of physical violence, references to research projects or third-party threats, and entries that appear to be attempts to document events for potential legal proceedings."

The ruling wasn't surprising—I'd seen enough evidence hearings to know judges erred on the side of caution with hearsay. But it still felt like a betrayal of Melissa's truth.

"Specifically," she continued, "the court excludes the November 18th entry about physical assault, the November 20th entry about surveillance, and the November 22nd entry about research and threats. These entries are either too prejudicial or venture into areas beyond the victim's state of mind."

Richardson looked pleased but not surprised. Of course, he'd expected this ruling—any experienced defense attorney would have.

"The entries that may be admitted include general expressions of relationship dissatisfaction, emotional distress, and non-specific concerns about the defendant's behavior. Ms. Mitchell, you'll need to redact the excluded portions before presenting the journal to the jury."

"Thank you, Your Honor," Erin said, disappointment evident in her tone.

"Thank you, Your Honor," Richardson echoed, his tone much more satisfied.

As the hearing ended and we gathered our materials, frustration burned in my chest. Not because I wanted Blake convicted—I still believed he hadn't killed Melissa. But because the judge had just ensured the jury would never hear the real reason Melissa had died. They'd never know about her investigation, about the threats to silence her, about the conspiracy she'd been close to exposing.

In the hallway outside the courtroom, I waited until we were out of earshot before speaking.

"That ruling just gutted our ability to show motive," I said quietly.

"Alex—"

"Not Blake's motive. The real killer's motive. Without those entries about her research and the threats, the jury will never understand why someone wanted her dead."

"The jury doesn't need to understand that," Erin said, exasperated. "They need to determine if Blake Costello killed her."

"Based on an incomplete picture of what was really happening."

"Based on the admissible evidence." Erin stopped walking and faced me directly. "Look, I know you think Blake's innocent. I'm starting to think that too. But our job is to present the case and let the jury decide."

"Our job is to seek justice."

"Which we're doing by presenting all the admissible evidence, including the DNA that doesn't match Blake. If he's innocent, the jury will see that."

Back in the courtroom, Erin presented the sanitized version of Melissa's journal to the jury. The entries we were allowed to introduce painted a picture of relationship strain and emotional distress, but nothing that explained why someone might have wanted Melissa dead.

"This entry from October 15th reads: 'Blake and I had another fight today. Sometimes I feel like I can't breathe in this relationship,'" Erin read aloud.

"And from November 10th: 'I don't know how much more of this I can take. Blake gets so angry when I try to have my own life, my own interests.'"

Relationship problems without context. Generic enough to support our domestic violence theory without revealing the specific threats Melissa had documented.

Richardson's cross-examination was perfunctory, barely challenging the admitted entries. Why would he fight evidence that made his client look like a difficult boyfriend rather than someone involved in silencing a dangerous investigation?

As the court recessed for lunch, I felt the frustration of presenting half-truths. Melissa's journal had been her attempt to document the truth about what was happening to her. But the version the jury heard was a pale shadow of that truth, sanitized to fit a narrative that had nothing to do with why she'd really died.

Judge Thatcher was waiting in the corridor as we left the courtroom, his expression pleased and calculating.

"Excellent handling of the journal evidence," he said to Erin. "Very professional, very focused on the relevant issues."

"Thank you, Judge Thatcher."

He turned to me. "I hope you're learning the importance of staying focused on provable facts rather than chasing speculation, Ms. Hayes."

"I'm learning a lot about how the system works," I replied.

"Good. Because the system works best when prosecutors focus on the evidence rather than conspiracy theories that can't be proven."

The truth about why Melissa Thatcher had died was being systematically excluded from her own murder trial. And there was nothing I could do about it without losing my career—and any chance of eventually exposing what really happened.

CHAPTER
TWENTY-FIVE

Becca Thatcher looked even younger than her fifteen years as she walked to the witness stand Friday afternoon. She wore a simple black dress that made her pale skin appear almost translucent, and her hand shook as she placed it on the Bible to be sworn in. The courtroom felt different with her presence—quieter, more solemn, as if everyone recognized they were about to hear from someone whose world had been shattered.

"Please state your name for the record," Erin said gently from the lectern.

"Rebecca Marie Thatcher. But everyone calls me Becca."

"And Melissa Thatcher was your sister?"

"Yes." Becca's voice was barely audible, and Judge Henley asked her to speak up.

"Yes," she repeated, louder this time. "Melissa was my big sister."

Erin approached the witness stand slowly, her demeanor softer than it had been with any previous witness. Examining a teenage victim's sibling required delicate handling—too aggressive, and you'd alienate the jury; too gentle and you wouldn't get the testimony you needed.

"Becca, I know this is difficult, but I need to ask you about your sister's relationship with the defendant, Blake Costello."

Becca nodded, glancing briefly at Blake before looking away. He sat motionless at the defense table, his young face drawn and pale.

"How long had Melissa been dating Blake?"

"About eight months. Since last spring."

"Did you have opportunities to observe them together?"

"Yes. Blake came to our house for dinner sometimes, and I saw them together when he picked Melissa up or dropped her off."

"What did you observe about their relationship?"

Becca shifted in her chair, clearly uncomfortable. "At first, it seemed normal. Blake was polite, charming. My parents liked him."

"But did that change over time?"

"Yes. By the summer, things felt different. Melissa seemed ... smaller when she was around him. Like she was trying not to upset him."

"Can you give us an example?"

"One time at dinner, Melissa mentioned a friend from school—just something casual about studying together. Blake got this look on his face—his jaw clenched, his eyes narrowed, and he went completely still. Then he started asking all these questions about who the friend was, why they were studying together, whether it was necessary. Melissa got quiet and didn't mention the friend again."

I watched the jury as Becca spoke. Several of them—particularly the domestic violence survivor and the victims' rights advocate—were leaning forward, clearly engaged with her testimony.

"Did you observe physical interactions between Blake and your sister that concerned you?" Erin asked carefully.

"Objection," Richardson said, rising from his chair. "Leading the witness."

"I'll rephrase," Erin said before the judge could rule. "Can you describe any physical interactions you observed between Blake and your sister?"

"A few times," Becca said. "He would grab her arm when they were talking, grip her really tight like he was trying to control where she went. And once I saw him push her against our car when he thought no one was looking."

"When was this?"

"Maybe six weeks before she died. They were arguing about something in our driveway, and Blake grabbed her shoulders and shoved her back against the car. When he saw me watching from the window, he let go and acted like nothing happened."

The testimony was powerful—concrete examples of physical aggression. It fit perfectly with the case Thatcher wanted us to present, even though I knew it was only part of the story. Blake's violence had been about stopping Melissa's investigation, not simple domestic abuse.

"Becca, did your sister ever talk to you about her relationship with Blake?"

"Sometimes. Especially toward the end."

"What did she tell you?"

Becca hesitated for a moment, her gaze dropping to her hands. "She said Blake was getting possessive, that he wanted to know where she was all the time. She said he didn't like her college friends and was trying to get her to stop hanging out with them."

"Did she seem afraid of him?"

"Objection," Richardson said. "Calls for speculation about the victim's state of mind."

"I'll allow it," Judge Henley ruled. "The witness can testify about her observations of her sister's demeanor."

"Yes," Becca said, her voice growing stronger. "She was definitely afraid. Especially the last week."

"Can you tell us about that final week?" Erin asked, her voice soft.

Becca's composure began to crack, tears welling in her eyes. "She was jumpy, nervous. She kept checking her phone and looking over her shoulder. She asked me not to tell our parents if Blake called the house looking for her."

"Did Blake call the house looking for her?"

"Yes, several times. He said she wasn't answering her phone and wanted to know if she was home. When I told him she wasn't, he asked if I knew where she'd gone and who she was with."

The picture Becca was painting was textbook stalking behavior, the kind that ended in violence.

"Becca, did your sister say anything to you about why she was afraid?"

Becca nodded. "She said Blake was angry about some school project she was working on. She said he wanted her to drop it, but she couldn't because it was for a grade."

My pulse quickened. Through her sanitized testimony, Becca was alluding to Melissa's research—the investigation that might have gotten her killed.

"Did she tell you what this school project was about?" Erin asked.

"She said it was about how government works, about people in power. She seemed really interested in it but also scared."

Richardson was on his feet. "Objection. Hearsay."

"Sustained. The jury will disregard the victim's statements about her school project."

But the damage was done. The jury had heard that Melissa was working on something involving "people in power" that made Blake angry enough to demand she stop.

"Becca," Erin continued, "I need to ask you about the last time you saw your sister alive."

The question broke something in Becca's composure. Tears started flowing freely, and she took several deep breaths before answering.

"It was the morning of November 22nd. She'd come back home for a few days, but she was leaving to return to school, and I was getting ready for my own classes."

"How did she seem that morning?"

"Scared. Really scared. She hugged me longer than usual and told me she loved me. She said..." Becca broke into quiet sobs, punctuated with the occasional sniff.

"Take your time," Erin said gently.

Sympathy radiated from the jury as Becca took a few moments to gain her composure before continuing. "Melissa said if anything happened to her, I should remember that she was trying to do the right thing. She was trying to help people."

The courtroom was silent except for the sound of Becca's quiet sobs. Several jurors wiped their own eyes.

"No further questions," Erin said quietly.

Richardson approached the witness stand with obvious reluctance. Cross-examining a grieving teenager required extraordinary care—one wrong move, and you'd turn the jury completely against your client.

"Becca, I'm very sorry for your loss," he began, his voice gentle and respectful. "I know how difficult this must be for you."

"Thank you."

"You loved your sister very much, didn't you?"

"Yes."

"And you want whoever hurt her to be held responsible?"

"Yes."

"That's completely understandable," Richardson said. "When someone we love is taken from us, we want answers, we want justice."

Richardson was walking a careful line—acknowledging Becca's grief while setting up the argument that her testimony might be colored by her desire for revenge.

"Becca, you were fifteen when your sister died, and you're still fifteen now, correct?"

"Yes."

"At fifteen, you were naturally closer to your sister than to her boyfriend, right? She was your family. Blake was just someone she was dating."

Becca shrugged. "I guess so."

"And when you saw interactions between Blake and Melissa, you might have interpreted them through the lens of wanting to protect your big sister?"

"Objection," Erin said. "Argumentative."

"Sustained."

Richardson adjusted his approach. "Becca, when you saw Blake grab Melissa's arm or push her against the car, did you ever see Melissa fight back or tell him to stop?"

"No, but—"

"And you never saw Melissa with any injuries—bruises, cuts, anything like that?"

"No."

"So while you interpreted Blake's behavior as aggressive, Melissa herself never indicated to you that she felt physically threatened?"

"She told me she was scared of him."

"But she never said he'd hit her or hurt her physically?"

Becca hesitated. "Not exactly."

"And regarding your sister's state of mind—you're telling us what you observed, not necessarily what was actually happening, correct?"

"I... yes."

"So you can't tell this jury whether Blake had legitimate concerns about your sister's activities, or whether those concerns had anything to do with her death?"

"I... no, I can't."

Richardson was skillfully undermining Becca's testimony without attacking her. He was painting her as a grieving sister who might have misinterpreted normal relationship dynamics through the lens of tragedy.

"Becca, you want justice for your sister, don't you?"

"Yes."

"And if Blake didn't kill Melissa, if someone else hurt her, you'd want that person to be caught and punished, right?"

"Yes, of course."

"So your testimony today isn't about Blake specifically—it's about wanting answers, wanting someone to be held responsible for your sister's death?"

Becca opened her mouth but couldn't find the right words immediately. Then she said, "I just want the truth."

Richardson nodded. "Thank you, Becca. No further questions."

As Becca stepped down from the witness stand, she looked directly at Blake for the first time during her testimony. The expression on her face was unreadable—sadness, anger, confusion.

"Your Honor," Erin said, standing as Becca left the courtroom, "the prosecution rests."

Judge Henley checked her watch. It was only 3:30 in the afternoon, but the emotional impact of Becca's testimony seemed to have drained everyone in the courtroom.

"Given the nature of today's testimony and the late hour," Judge Henley said, "we'll recess until Monday morning. The defense may begin presenting their case at that time."

As the jury filed out, I felt a mixture of satisfaction and unease about how our case had played. Becca's testimony had been powerful, painting a clear picture of escalating abuse and control. But Richardson's cross-examination had been skillful, raising questions about whether a grieving teenager's perceptions could be trusted.

More troubling was what Becca's testimony had revealed about Melissa's final days—the fear, the secrecy, the statement that Melissa was "trying to do the right thing" and "help people." Even in the sanitized version we'd been allowed to present, hints of the larger truth kept breaking through.

"Strong finish," Erin said as we packed up our materials. "Becca was a compelling witness."

"She was," I replied. "But Richardson handled her well. He made her seem sympathetic without making Blake seem guilty."

"That's the best he could do with that testimony. No defense attorney wants to attack a victim's teenage sister."

As we left the courtroom, I noticed Judge Thatcher wasn't in his usual spot in the gallery. For the first time since the trial began, he'd missed a day of testimony. I wondered if hearing his younger daughter describe his eldest's final days had been too much even for him.

Or if he'd simply heard enough to know that everything was proceeding according to plan. We'd presented a case stripped of any reference to Melissa's real discoveries, focused solely on domestic violence. If Blake was convicted, the truth about why Melissa died would be buried with him.

Monday would bring the defense case, and Richardson's continued reluctance to fight as hard as he should. The question was whether the DNA evidence would be enough to create reasonable doubt, or whether the jury would convict based on the compelling but incomplete story we'd told them.

Either way, justice for Melissa Thatcher remained frustratingly out of reach.

CHAPTER TWENTY-SIX

THE WEEKEND HEADLINES had dissected Becca's testimony with surgical precision. "VICTIM'S SISTER: 'SHE WAS TRYING TO HELP PEOPLE'" and "THATCHER MURDER: MORE QUESTIONS THAN ANSWERS" dominated the morning news cycle. The courtroom buzzed with anticipation as Richardson began presenting his defense.

His first witness was Dr. Patricia Vance, a forensic psychologist who specialized in analyzing crime victims' mental states. She took the stand with the polished confidence of an expert witness who'd testified hundreds of times.

"Dr. Vance," Richardson began, "you've reviewed materials related to Melissa Thatcher's psychological state in the months before her death, correct?"

"Yes. I've examined her medical records, portions of her personal journal, interviews with family and friends, and academic records from the university."

"Based on your review, what conclusions did you reach about Ms. Thatcher's mental state?"

I tensed, knowing where this was heading. Richardson was about to attack Melissa's credibility by painting her as emotionally unstable.

"Ms. Thatcher exhibited signs of significant anxiety and stress in the months preceding her death. Her journal entries show increasing paranoia, social isolation, and what appears to be delusional thinking about surveillance and threats."

"Can you elaborate on what you mean by delusional thinking?"

"Her writings include claims about being followed, beliefs that unnamed powerful people were threatening her, and an obsessive focus on conspiracy theories involving judicial corruption. These are classic symptoms of anxiety-induced paranoia."

My stomach lurched. Dr. Vance was taking Melissa's legitimate fears—the very real threats she'd documented—and reframing them as mental illness.

"In your professional opinion," Richardson said, "was Ms. Thatcher's perception of threats and danger reliable?"

"It's unlikely," Dr. Vance replied. "Individuals experiencing high levels of anxiety often misinterpret normal events as threatening. A car behind them becomes surveillance, a casual comment becomes a threat, coincidental events become evidence of conspiracy."

"Could Ms. Thatcher have misinterpreted normal relationship conflicts with Mr. Costello as abuse?"

"Objection," Erin said, rising from her chair. "Calls for speculation."

"I'll allow it," Judge Henley ruled. "The witness may answer based on her professional expertise."

Dr. Vance cleared her throat. "It's certainly possible. Anxiety disorders can cause individuals to catastrophize normal relationship dynamics. What might be a typical disagreement or expression of concern could be perceived as controlling or threatening behavior."

Richardson walked closer to the jury box, ensuring they were following every word. "Dr. Vance, did you find evidence that Ms. Thatcher was seeking treatment for her anxiety?"

"She had consulted with the university counseling center on several occasions. The records indicate she was experiencing significant stress related to academic pressure and relationship concerns."

"Would someone in Ms. Thatcher's psychological state be prone to making poor decisions or putting herself in dangerous situations?"

"Yes. Individuals with severe anxiety often make impulsive choices, particularly when they believe they're under threat. They might take unnecessary risks or confront situations they should avoid."

I sucked in a breath. Richardson wasn't just attacking Melissa's credibility—he was suggesting her death might have resulted from her own poor judgment rather than deliberate murder.

"Thank you, Doctor. No further questions."

Erin's cross-examination was aggressive, but Dr. Vance was unflappable.

"Dr. Vance," Erin began, "you never actually examined Ms. Thatcher while she was alive, did you?"

"No, that's correct."

"So your diagnosis of her mental state is based entirely on records and third-party accounts?"

"Yes, which is standard practice in forensic psychology when direct examination isn't possible."

"And you're aware that Ms. Thatcher was an excellent student, maintained strong friendships, and was accepted to Georgetown Law School?"

"Yes, but academic success doesn't preclude anxiety disorders. In fact, high-achieving individuals often experience significant stress."

"Dr. Vance, if Ms. Thatcher's fears about surveillance and threats were actually based in reality, would that change your assessment of her mental state?"

"Objection," Richardson said. "Hypothetical question assumes facts not in evidence."

"Sustained."

"No further questions."

Dr. Vance's testimony was having its intended effect. I could see it in the jurors' faces—doubt creeping in about whether Melissa's fears had been real or imagined.

Richardson's next witness was Dr. Michael Torres, a forensic pathologist who offered an alternative interpretation of Melissa's injuries.

"Dr. Torres, you've reviewed the autopsy report and crime scene evidence in this case?"

"Yes, I have."

"Do you agree with the medical examiner's conclusion that Ms. Thatcher's injuries were consistent with intentional homicide?"

"Not necessarily. The injury pattern could also be consistent with accidental trauma—perhaps a fall during an altercation that wasn't intended to be fatal."

"Could these injuries have resulted from Ms. Thatcher falling and striking her head?"

"It's possible," Dr. Torres said. "The location and nature of the skull fracture are consistent with impact against a hard surface during a fall."

"Could you explain your reasoning?"

Dr. Torres pulled up a diagram on the courtroom screen. "The fracture pattern shows a single point of impact with radiating cracks. This is consistent with the head striking a stationary object, rather than being struck by a moving weapon. Additionally, the angle suggests the victim was falling when impact occurred."

"In your opinion, could this have been an accident?"

"Based purely on the physical evidence, yes. During a struggle or heated argument, someone could have pushed Ms. Thatcher, causing her to fall and strike her head fatally."

Erin's cross-examination challenged Dr. Torres's conclusions, but he held his ground, creating enough reasonable doubt about intent to muddy our murder charge.

By the end of the day, I felt like we were watching our case dissolve in real time. Richardson had taken everything we'd argued—Melissa's fears, her journal entries, even her death—and reframed it as the tragic result of mental illness and poor judgment rather than deliberate murder.

That evening, Erin and I worked late in the conference room, preparing for the next day's testimony and trying to salvage our case.

"We're losing them," I said, reviewing my notes from the jury's reactions. "Dr. Vance's testimony was devastating. She made Melissa sound like a paranoid conspiracy theorist whose fears weren't based in reality."

"Which is exactly what Richardson intended," Erin said. "He's not trying to prove Blake's innocence—he's trying to prove that Melissa's death was tragic but not criminal."

"The DNA evidence still doesn't match Blake. How is Richardson going to explain that?"

"Richardson will probably argue that it supports his theory. If Melissa was acting erratically, putting herself in dangerous situations, she might have encountered someone else shortly before her death."

I rubbed my temples, feeling a headache building. "So according to the defense, Melissa was mentally ill, her fears were imaginary, and her death was either accidental or the result of her own poor judgment."

"It's a coherent narrative. And it doesn't require the jury to believe Blake is innocent—just that he's not guilty of intentional murder."

"Which is what I've been thinking all along," I said quietly. "That Blake didn't actually kill her. But now Richardson's using that doubt to let him walk completely free."

"Richardson will argue that Blake panicked after finding her dead or accidentally injured. That he made terrible decisions but didn't commit murder."

I stared at the crime scene photos spread across the conference table. Melissa looked so young, so vulnerable. The idea that her legitimate fears were being dismissed as mental illness made my stomach turn.

"Erin, we both know Melissa's fears were based in reality. She discovered something about her father's foundation, about judicial corruption. That's what got her killed, not some imaginary paranoia."

"But we can't prove that in court," Erin said. "Not with the evidence we're allowed to present."

The irony wasn't lost on me. For weeks I'd been told to stop chasing conspiracies, to focus on the simple domestic violence case. Now that conspiracy was the only thing that could save our prosecution, and we had no way to introduce it.

"What about Blake's testimony?" I asked. "If he takes the stand, we can cross-examine him about his knowledge of Melissa's research, his family's connections—"

"*If* he takes the stand," Erin said. "Richardson might decide the psychological defense is strong enough without risking Blake's testimony."

We worked until nearly midnight, preparing cross-examination strategies and rebuttal arguments. But it felt like we were rearranging deck chairs on the Titanic. Richardson had successfully reframed the entire case, turning our victim into an unreliable narrator and our murder into a tragic accident.

As we finally packed up to leave, Erin voiced what we were both thinking. "We might lose this case."

"I know."

"How do you feel about that?"

I considered the question. A month ago, I'd been convinced Blake hadn't killed Melissa—that he was being set up to take the fall for someone else. Now, watching him potentially walk free while the real killers remained hidden, I wasn't sure which outcome would be worse.

"I feel like we're failing Melissa," I said. "Not by potentially losing the case against Blake, but by never telling the real story of why she died."

"Sometimes the real story isn't something you can prove in court."

"And sometimes that's exactly what the real killers are counting on."

As we left the courthouse, the media was still camped outside despite the late hour. Camera crews and reporters who sensed a story bigger than a simple murder trial, who'd picked up on the undercurrents of conspiracy and cover-up that we'd been forced to suppress.

"Ms. Hayes!" a reporter called out. "Do you still believe Blake Costello is guilty?"

I pushed past without answering, but the question echoed in my head as I drove home through the empty Houston streets. Did I believe Blake was guilty? Or was I just hoping someone would be held accountable for Melissa's death, even if it wasn't the right person for the right reasons?

CHAPTER TWENTY-SEVEN

Tuesday's session began with Richardson dropping a bombshell. He approached Judge Henley's bench with a thick file folder and the confident stride of a lawyer about to deliver a knockout punch.

"Your Honor, the defense moves to admit Defense Exhibit 47—a psychiatric evaluation of the victim conducted by the university counseling center six weeks before her death."

My stomach dropped. We'd known about Melissa's visits to the counseling center from witness interviews, but the actual records had been sealed under doctor-patient privilege. Somehow Richardson had gotten them unsealed.

"Your Honor," Erin said, rising quickly, "the prosecution objects. These records are protected by doctor-patient privilege and are highly prejudicial."

"Mr. Richardson," Judge Henley said, "on what grounds are you seeking to admit sealed psychiatric records?"

"The privilege was waived when the prosecution introduced the victim's journal entries and presented testimony about her state of mind. Once her mental condition became an issue in the case, these records became relevant and admissible."

It was a clever legal argument, and I could see Judge Henley considering it. By using Melissa's journal to show her fears and state of mind, we'd inadvertently opened the door to other evidence about her psychological condition.

"Furthermore," Richardson continued, "these records directly contradict the prosecution's portrayal of the victim as a reliable narrator of events. They show someone suffering from severe anxiety, paranoid ideation, and delusional thinking."

"Your Honor," Erin argued, "even if privilege was waived, the prejudicial impact of these records far outweighs any probative value. The jury will use this information to blame the victim for her own death."

Judge Henley reviewed the file for several long minutes while the courtroom waited in tense silence. When she finally looked up, her expression was apologetic but resolute.

"The court finds that by introducing evidence of the victim's state of mind through her journal entries and witness testimony, the prosecution has waived doctor-patient privilege as it relates to her mental health. The records are admissible."

This was a devastating blow. Richardson had just gained access to Melissa's most private thoughts—her fears, her anxieties, her struggles with the pressure of discovering her father's crimes. All of it would now be twisted to make her seem unreliable and mentally unstable.

"However," Judge Henley continued, "I'm limiting their use to general mental health issues. Specific details about family relationships or personal trauma remain protected."

It was a small consolation, but not nearly enough to offset the damage Richardson was about to inflict.

The defense called Dr. Rebecca Liu, the university counselor who'd treated Melissa in her final weeks. She took the stand reluctantly, clearly uncomfortable about testifying regarding her former patient.

"Dr. Liu," Richardson began, "you met with Melissa Thatcher on four occasions between September and October of last year?"

"Yes, that's correct."

"What was the nature of her concerns during these sessions?"

Dr. Liu shifted in her seat, adjusting her glasses before answering. "Ms. Thatcher was experiencing significant anxiety related to academic pressure and family expectations. She reported feeling overwhelmed by the responsibility of living up to her family name."

"Did she express any concerns about threats or danger to her personal safety?"

Dr. Liu glanced at the prosecution table before answering. "She mentioned feeling like she was being watched or followed, but these concerns appeared to be manifestations of her anxiety rather than based in reality."

"Did you recommend any treatment for her condition?"

"I suggested she consider anti-anxiety medication and regular counseling sessions. She was resistant to medication but agreed to continue therapy."

"In your professional opinion, was Ms. Thatcher's perception of threats and danger reliable?"

"Based on my observations, Ms. Thatcher was experiencing anxiety-related paranoia. Her fears seemed disproportionate to any actual danger she faced."

"No further questions."

Richardson had destroyed Melissa's credibility in less than ten minutes, using her own therapist to paint her as mentally unstable and unreliable.

Erin's cross-examination tried to minimize the damage. "Dr. Liu, isn't it true that many of Ms. Thatcher's sessions focused on academic stress rather than these supposed paranoid fears?"

"Yes, academic pressure was a primary concern."

"And she was functioning well enough to maintain excellent grades and gain admission to Georgetown Law School?"

"That's correct."

"So despite whatever anxiety she was experiencing, she was still a high functioning, intelligent young woman?"

"Yes, absolutely."

"No further questions."

But the damage was done. The jury now had professional confirmation that Melissa's fears might have been imaginary.

During the lunch recess, Erin and I retreated to a small conference room to discuss damage control. We'd barely closed the door when it burst open again.

Judge Thatcher stood in the doorway, his face flushed with anger and his eyes blazing with fury. He stepped inside and slammed the door behind him.

"What the hell do you think you're doing?" he demanded.

Erin held up her hands. "Judge Thatcher, you can't—"

"I can't what? I can't be concerned that you're destroying my daughter's reputation? That you're letting that defense attorney turn her into some kind of paranoid lunatic?"

"Sir," I said, trying to keep my voice calm, "we're doing everything we can to present Melissa's story accurately."

His face was tomato red, veins bulging at his temples. "Are you? Because it looks like you're letting Richardson walk all over you. You're supposed to be prosecuting Blake Costello for murder, not participating in character assassination of the victim."

Thatcher moved closer, towering over us with barely controlled rage. "Melissa wasn't crazy. She wasn't paranoid. She was a smart, capable young woman who got in over her head with dangerous people."

Erin and I exchanged glances before I asked, "What dangerous people?"

"Blake and his family connections. The people who wanted her to stop asking questions about things that didn't concern her."

"Judge Thatcher, all this time you've been telling us not to focus on conspiracies. You've repeatedly said we should stick to the simple explanation, that everything else was 'noise.'" My voice sharpened. "Now you're telling us there was a conspiracy involving Blake's family?"

Thatcher's expression hardened. "I never told you there wasn't a conspiracy, Ms. Hayes. I told you to focus on convicting Blake Costello. Because he killed my daughter."

"But you specifically said—"

"I said you needed to focus on provable facts instead of chasing theories you couldn't substantiate in court." His voice rose, becoming more aggressive. "I've been a federal judge for thirty years. I know where cases fail. I know what juries will accept and what they'll dismiss as fantasy."

Erin crossed her arms. "Judge Thatcher—"

"I'm not going to let my daughter's murder case get turned around on me when the killer is sitting right there in that courtroom." Thatcher moved closer. "Blake Costello murdered Melissa. Everything else is distraction."

The phrase "turned around on me" echoed what I'd noticed in our first meeting—his odd way of talking about his daughter's death, as if it were more about him than her. Not turned around on the case or turned around on justice. Turned around on him personally.

"What things, Judge Thatcher?" I pressed. "What else is distraction?"

Thatcher's expression shifted, as if he'd said more than he intended. "Her research project. The academic work that Blake was so determined to shut down."

"But why would Blake's family care about an academic research project?"

"Because some families have secrets they'll kill to protect. Because some people think they're above the law and will eliminate anyone who threatens to expose them."

The words felt calculated, like he was feeding us a narrative he'd prepared.

"Judge Thatcher, if you have evidence that Blake's family was involved in threatening Melissa, we need to know about it."

"I don't have evidence. I have suspicions. The same ones Melissa had before they killed her."

"They?"

"Blake and whoever was pulling his strings. The people who decided my daughter knew too much and needed to be silenced."

Thatcher moved to the window, staring out at the courthouse plaza. "She called me the night she died, you know. Around seven o'clock. Said she was scared, that she'd discovered something that could destroy people's lives. She said Blake had been threatening her, trying to get her to stop her research."

My pulse quickened. "What did she tell you she'd discovered?"

"She said she'd found evidence of money laundering through charitable foundations. Financial connections between judges and criminal enterprises. She said she was going to expose it all, regardless of who got hurt."

"And what did you tell her?"

Thatcher turned back to us, his expression pained. "I told her to be careful. I told her that some secrets are dangerous to know. I said …" He paused, his voice dropping to almost a whisper. "I said she wasn't ready for that world. That it would eat her alive if she didn't stay quiet."

The words echoed in my mind. I'd read that exact phrase in Melissa's journal, but I'd assumed she was describing something Blake had said. Now I realized she'd been quoting her father. Her own father had been trying to silence her research.

"Judge Thatcher," I said slowly, "are you saying you advised your daughter to abandon her investigation?"

He looked away again. "I was trying to protect her. I knew what kind of people she was dealing with, what they were capable of."

"What kind of people?"

"Powerful people. People with connections to organized crime, to trafficking networks, to corruption that reaches the highest levels of the judiciary."

"Was she researching your charitable foundation?"

Thatcher's expression became guarded. "I've said too much already. The point is, you need to focus on convicting Blake Costello. He's the one who killed my daughter, either on his own or on orders from his family."

"But if there's a larger conspiracy—"

"Focus on what you can prove!" Thatcher's voice rose to nearly a shout, his earlier admission about conspiracies apparently forgotten. "Blake Costello killed my daughter. That's what matters. Do your jobs."

He stormed out of the conference room, leaving Erin and me staring at each other in stunned silence.

"Did you hear what I heard?" I asked.

"That he completely contradicted everything he's been telling us for weeks?"

"That, and the way he said the case couldn't get 'turned around on him.' Not on justice, not on the truth—on himself."

Erin was already gathering her files. "We need to get back to court. The jury's waiting."

"Erin, he just admitted that Melissa was investigating his foundation. That he told her to stay quiet about it."

"Which we can't use because it's not evidence. It's hearsay from an emotional conversation."

"But that quote from Melissa's journal—'He said I wasn't ready for his world. That it would eat me alive if I didn't stay quiet.' I always assumed she was talking about Blake."

"She could have been talking about anyone."

"But Thatcher just used those exact words. He admitted telling her to stay quiet about her research."

Erin paused at the door. "What are you suggesting?"

"I'm suggesting that maybe Blake was just a pawn all along. Maybe the person who wanted Melissa silenced was her own father."

"Which is what you suspected from the beginning," Erin said quietly. "Remember? After that first meeting with Thatcher, you said something felt off about him."

"And everyone told me I was being paranoid, seeing conspiracies where none existed."

"Maybe we all should have listened to your instincts."

Walking back to the courtroom, I watched Judge Thatcher take his usual seat in the front row. His expression had returned to its typical mask of judicial composure, but now I saw it differently. Not grief, but calculation. Not a father seeking justice, but a man ensuring his secrets stayed buried.

The real killer might have been sitting twenty feet away this entire time, watching us prosecute someone else for his crime.

CHAPTER TWENTY-EIGHT

I SAT at my kitchen table with Melissa's journal open to the entry that had been haunting me since Thatcher's outburst. The words stared back at me, now carrying a different voice.

He said I wasn't ready for his world. That it would eat me alive if I didn't stay quiet.

For weeks, I'd assumed Melissa was writing about Blake. The controlling boyfriend who wanted her to drop her research, who escalated to violence when she refused to comply. But hearing Thatcher use those exact words this afternoon had shifted everything.

The pronouns were ambiguous throughout the journal—always "he said" or "he warned," never specifying who. I'd filled in the blanks with my assumptions, but now those assumptions felt dangerously wrong.

I flipped through the journal pages, looking for other entries with fresh eyes. It was all so much clearer: Melissa's growing fear, her sense that powerful people wanted her silenced, her belief that "sometimes the people who are supposed to protect you are the ones you need to run from."

The front door opened and closed, followed by the familiar sound of Dad's work boots on the kitchen tiles.

"You're home early," he said, glancing at the journal spread across the table. "How'd court go today?"

"Badly," I said. "The defense got Melissa's psychiatric records admitted. Made her look paranoid and like her fears weren't based in reality."

Dad poured himself coffee from the pot I'd left warming and settled into the chair across from me. "But you don't think that's true."

"I think she was documenting real threats from real people. People who wanted her research to disappear."

"People close to her?"

The question caught me off guard. "What makes you say that?"

"The way you're reading that journal. Like you're seeing it differently than before." Dad took a sip of coffee. "Plus, you've got that look."

"What look?"

"The look you get when pieces start falling into place in ways you didn't expect. Usually involving someone the victim should have been able to trust."

I set down the journal and rubbed my temples. "Dad, I've suspected Thatcher from the beginning. Remember? After our first meeting, I told you something felt off about him."

"I remember. But suspecting and knowing are different things."

"Today he said something that changed suspicion to certainty. He claimed Melissa called him at seven PM the night she died, scared about her research. But he used the exact phrase from her journal—told her she wasn't ready for his world, that it would eat her alive if she didn't stay quiet."

"Could be coincidence," Dad said. "Could be he was repeating what she told him someone else had said."

"Could be. But there's something else." I pulled out my phone and scrolled to the case timeline. "Thatcher said she called him, but I haven't seen any phone records showing an outgoing call from Melissa at that time."

"You think he was lying about the phone call?"

"I think he was lying about a lot of things," I said. "Every time I've mentioned investigating conspiracy or corruption, he's steered me away from it. Every time evidence pointed to larger involvement, he's pushed me to focus solely on Blake."

Dad leaned back in his chair. "Twenty-five years as a cop taught me that the person who's most eager to control an investigation usually has something to hide."

"But he's a federal judge." I leaned back too. "What kind of man kills his own child?"

"The kind who values power more than family. The kind who sees people as problems to be solved rather than human beings to be protected." Dad's voice grew grim. "I've seen it before, Alex. Not often, but I've seen it."

"How do I prove it? How do I prove a federal judge murdered his daughter without destroying my career and possibly getting myself killed?"

"Carefully. With solid evidence. And with people you trust watching your back."

I thought about Erin's reaction in the conference room, her growing realization that my instincts about Thatcher had been right all along. About Agent Morrison, who'd seemed genuinely concerned when he learned about evidence his team hadn't seen.

"Dad, if I'm right about this, it means we're currently prosecuting an innocent man while the real killer sits in the courtroom every day, watching us perform exactly as he scripted."

"And if you're wrong?"

I thought for a moment. "Then I'm a prosecutor who's lost all perspective and is seeing conspiracies where none exist."

Dad finished his coffee and set the mug on the table. "You know what your mother would say if she were here?"

"What?"

"She'd say trust your instincts, but verify everything. Don't let anyone convince you that caring about the truth is a weakness." He stood and moved toward the sink. "But she'd also say be smart about how you pursue it. Don't give them reasons to eliminate you the way they eliminated her."

The comparison made my chest tight. "You think that's what happened to Mom? Someone eliminated her because she got too close to the truth?"

"I think your mother was investigating corruption that reached powerful people. And I think those people decided she was a threat that needed to be removed." Dad turned back to face me. "If you're right about Thatcher, you need to be more careful than she was."

After Dad went to bed, I sat alone with Melissa's journal and my growing certainty that we'd been prosecuting the wrong person. When I'd first read these entries after finding the journal at Becca's house, I'd seen them through the lens of domestic violence. Now they read as a daughter's growing horror at discovering her father's crimes.

But certainty wasn't evidence. And accusations against a federal judge required more than intuition and circumstantial connections.

I pulled out my laptop and began searching for Melissa's phone records from November 22nd. If Thatcher was lying about the seven PM phone call, that lie might be the thread that unravels everything else.

The records showed incoming and outgoing calls throughout the day, but no outgoing call to her father's number at seven PM. In fact, the last outgoing call from Melissa's phone was at 3:47 PM to a classmate about a study group.

Which meant Thatcher had lied about his daughter calling him in fear. But why lie about that specific detail unless he was creating an alibi for being in contact with her that evening?

Unless he hadn't needed to call her, because he'd already been there.

CHAPTER TWENTY-NINE

THE NEXT MORNING, I watched Judge Thatcher from across the courthouse lobby as he finished a conversation with another federal judge. He carried himself with the practiced ease of someone who'd spent decades navigating these halls, but I noticed something I'd missed before—the way his eyes constantly scanned the room, cataloging faces, assessing threats.

The behavior of someone with secrets to protect.

As court recessed for lunch, I made my excuse to Erin about needing to make phone calls and slipped out through a side exit. Thatcher was already walking down the courthouse steps, his expensive suit perfectly tailored, his silver hair catching the afternoon sunlight.

I followed at a distance, grateful for the lunch crowd that provided cover as he made his way down Main Street. Three blocks from the courthouse, he turned into a small park where office workers ate lunch on scattered benches.

Thatcher found an isolated bench near a fountain and pulled out his phone, along with a pack of cigarettes from his jacket pocket. I positioned myself behind a large oak tree about fifty yards away, close enough to observe but far enough to avoid detection.

He lit the cigarette with practiced motion, took several deep drags while conducting what appeared to be an intense phone conversation.

His body language was tense, aggressive—not the demeanor of a grieving father, but of someone conducting business.

After ten minutes, he ended the call and finished the cigarette, dropping the butt beside the bench before crushing it under his shoe. He looked around once—a quick, paranoid scan of his surroundings—then walked back toward the courthouse.

I waited until he was completely out of sight before approaching the bench. The cigarette butt lay among fallen leaves. It was a long shot—DNA from saliva could degrade quickly, and chain of custody would be a nightmare. But if it matched what was under Melissa's fingernails...

I pulled out a tissue and carefully picked it up, sealing it in a small evidence bag I'd brought from the office.

Back at the courthouse, I found Erin reviewing notes for the afternoon session.

"Where did you go?" she asked without looking up.

"Made some calls about other cases," I lied smoothly. "How long until we're back in session?"

"Twenty minutes. Richardson's calling his psychiatric expert this afternoon."

Perfect. That would give me time to make another call.

I stepped into the hallway and dialed Lisa's number.

"Cooper."

"Lisa, it's Alex. I need a favor. A big one."

"What kind of favor?"

"The kind that requires your forensic lab connections and absolute discretion."

There was a pause, the sound of Lisa closing a door in the background. "What are you into now?"

"I have a DNA sample that needs to be compared against evidence from an active case." I glanced around the hallway, lowering my voice. "Rush job, off the books."

"Whose DNA?"

"I can't tell you that over the phone. Can you meet me after court today?"

"Off the books DNA testing isn't something I do lightly."

"This could be the break that solves Melissa Thatcher's murder. The real break."

Another pause, longer this time. "What aren't you telling me about this case?"

"Everything," I admitted. "But I will tonight if you help me with this."

Her breathing crackled against the phone speaker. "Fine. Meet me at the lab at seven. And Alex? This better be worth risking my career over."

The afternoon session dragged as Richardson's psychiatric expert testified about Melissa's supposed mental instability. I tried to focus on the testimony, on preparing cross-examination questions, but my mind kept drifting to the cigarette butt sealed in the evidence bag in my briefcase.

If the DNA under Melissa's fingernails matched her father's, it would prove he'd been in physical contact with her during a struggle. Close enough to leave genetic material. Close enough to kill.

When court finally recessed at five-thirty, I caught up with Erin in the hallway.

"I need to handle something tonight," I said. "Can you cover the prep session with tomorrow's witnesses?"

"Alex, we need to—"

"I know. Just give me tonight. Tomorrow everything might be clearer."

Erin studied my face with growing concern. "What's going on?"

Shifting my weight, I gripped my briefcase tighter. "I'm following a lead. If it pans out, it changes everything about the case."

She folded her arms, narrowing her eyes. "What kind of lead?"

"The kind I can't discuss until I know if it's real."

Erin's expression hardened. "Alex, when we took this case, you promised me you wouldn't go off on your own pursuing conspiracy theories. You promised we'd work together."

"I know—"

"And now you're running off on some secret investigation without telling me what you're pursuing or why."

"Erin, I need one night. Just give me one night to confirm something."

"Confirm what? I'm supposed to be lead prosecutor on this case, but you're treating me like I can't be trusted."

I could see the hurt in her eyes, the frustration of being shut out of something that might be crucial to our case. "It's not about trust," I told her. "It's about protecting you if this goes sideways."

"Protecting me from what?" Her voice rose slightly, then dropped as she remembered we were in a public hallway.

"From being associated with unauthorized investigative methods that could destroy both of our careers if I'm wrong."

Erin stared at me for a long moment. "And if you're right?"

"If I'm right," I said, "then tomorrow we'll know who really killed Melissa Thatcher."

She shook her head, clearly torn between professional responsibility and personal loyalty. "I don't like this. I don't like being kept in the dark about my own case."

"And I'm sorry for that. But I need you to trust me on this one."

"Fine," she said finally, her voice tight with frustration. "But tomorrow morning, before court starts, you tell me everything. Whatever this lead is, whatever you discover tonight, I need to know before we put Blake on the stand."

"I promise."

"You better." Her eyes hardened on mine. "Because if this blows up our case, it's on both of us."

At seven o'clock, I met Lisa at the Harris County Medical Examiner's forensic laboratory. The building was mostly empty except for security guards and a few technicians working the night shift. Lisa led me through a maze of corridors to a DNA analysis lab.

"Okay," she said, closing the door behind us. "Show me what you've got."

I pulled out the evidence bag containing the cigarette butt. "I need this compared against DNA evidence from under Melissa Thatcher's fingernails."

Lisa took the bag and examined it under a magnifying lamp. "Whose cigarette is this?"

"Someone who might have killed her."

She glared up at me. "That's not an answer."

I remained neutral. "It's the only answer I can give you right now. Can you run the comparison?"

Lisa seemed to be weighing the risks. "If this comes back to bite me, if anyone finds out I ran unauthorized DNA analysis..."

"No one will find out," I said. "And if I'm right, this evidence could expose a killer who's been manipulating the entire investigation."

"And if you're wrong?"

"Then I'm a paranoid prosecutor who wasted your time and endangered your career."

Lisa's undergrad had been in forensic science before she went to law school, and she'd maintained friendships with the lab techs through years of prosecuting cases together. She knew who would help off the books and who would report straight to their supervisors. Now I was asking her to cash in those relationships on my hunch.

She sighed and moved to a computer terminal. "The DNA profile from under the victim's fingernails is already in the system. I can extract DNA from this cigarette and run a comparison, but it'll take hours."

"How many?"

"Six, maybe eight. I can have results for you first thing in the morning."

A bolt of panic ran through my chest. "I need them tonight. Before court starts tomorrow."

She looked at me with both concern and exasperation. "That's not how DNA analysis works. The extraction process alone takes—"

"What if we expedite everything?" I asked, feeling my eyes widen. "What if we cut corners on protocol?"

Lisa stared at me. "You want me to compromise the integrity of the analysis?"

"I want you to give me preliminary results that tell me whether it's worth pursuing this lead further. If it's a match, we do a full analysis with proper protocols. If it's not, we forget this ever happened."

Lisa looked at the cigarette butt again, then at the determination in my eyes. "Three hours. I can give you preliminary results in three hours, but they won't be admissible in court."

"I'm not planning to use them in court. I'm planning to use them to get a confession."

At eleven PM, Lisa called my cell phone, her voice breathless.

"It's a match."

My heart skyrocketed. "Are you sure?"

"Preliminary analysis shows significant DNA markers in common between the cigarette sample and the evidence from under the victim's fingernails. Full analysis would be needed for court presentation, but the basic markers align." She paused. "Alex, whose DNA is this?"

I stood in my living room, staring out at the dark street, hands shaking. "That cigarette belonged to Judge Thatcher."

The silence on the other end of the line stretched for several seconds.

"Jesus Christ, Alex. A federal judge's DNA is under his own daughter's fingernails?"

"That's exactly what I'm telling you."

"This is... this is huge. If a federal judge killed his daughter—"

"If a federal judge killed his daughter, then he's been manipulating this entire prosecution to frame an innocent man. And anyone who gets too close to proving that might end up as dead as Melissa Thatcher."

Lisa was silent for a few more moments. Her voice was quiet when she asked, "What are you going to do with this information?"

There was only one thing I could do.

"I need to present it in court. Can you get the full analysis finished by tomorrow morning? Something that would be admissible as evidence?"

"The timing will be close, but I'll try my best. I'll have to work through the night, cut some corners on documentation, but I might be able to get you preliminary court-ready results by eight AM."

Relief flooded my system. "That would give me just enough time to file a motion before court starts."

"But if this goes public, if it comes out that a federal judge murdered his own daughter..."

"This stays between us until I figure out how to proceed safely."

I hung up and stared out my living room window at the dark street beyond. Tomorrow Blake Costello would take the stand in his own defense, maintaining his innocence while the real killer sat in the front row of the courtroom.

But now I had evidence. DNA proof that Judge Henry Thatcher had been involved in his daughter's death. The cigarette butt was the smoking gun I needed. Now I had to figure out how to fire it without destroying everything in the blast.

CHAPTER THIRTY

AT MIDNIGHT, I sat in my car outside the address I'd found in our case files—Agent Morrison's apartment complex in northwest Houston. I'd seen it listed as his contact information in the FBI's initial reports. Now I debated whether what I was about to do would save an innocent man or destroy both our careers. The DNA evidence was compelling, but it needed corroboration. I needed proof that Judge Thatcher had been at Melissa's apartment the night she died.

Morrison answered his door in a T-shirt and sweatpants, clearly annoyed at being woken up.

He rubbed his eyes, squinting against the hallway light. "Ms. Hayes? What the hell are you doing here at midnight?"

"I need to talk to you," I said. "It's about the Thatcher case."

"Can't this wait until morning? I have a six AM briefing—"

"By morning it might be too late. Blake takes the stand tomorrow."

He glanced around the parking lot, then stepped aside with obvious reluctance. "Five minutes."

His apartment was sparse, functional—the kind of place where someone who worked too many hours caught a few hours of sleep between cases.

"This better be good," he said, gesturing toward a barstool at his kitchen counter. "And it better be worth you somehow finding my home address."

I pulled out a copy of the preliminary DNA results Lisa had given me. "Agent Morrison, I have evidence that Judge Henry Thatcher was present at his daughter's murder scene."

Morrison's expression shifted from annoyance to sharp attention. "What kind of evidence?"

"Judge Thatcher's DNA under Melissa's fingernails. The same evidence your team said didn't match Blake Costello."

He took the report and read it carefully, his jaw tightening with each line. "Where did you get this?"

"I can't tell you that. But I can tell you it's legitimate."

"Ms. Hayes, this is ... if this is accurate, it changes everything about our investigation."

"I know. And I need your help to corroborate it."

Morrison set down the report and looked at me. "What kind of help?"

"Cell tower data for Judge Thatcher's phone on November 22nd," I said. "Security camera footage from the area around Melissa's apartment. Anything that can place him near the scene during the time of death."

"You're asking me to conduct surveillance on a federal judge based on DNA evidence I can't verify and obtained through methods you won't disclose."

"I'm asking you to verify whether a potential suspect was at the scene of a crime."

Morrison stood and paced to his kitchen window. "Do you understand what you're suggesting? If Judge Thatcher killed his daughter, it means he's been manipulating our investigation from the beginning. It means everything we've done, every piece of evidence we've collected, might be compromised."

"Which is why we need independent verification."

"And if I access his cell records without a warrant, anything we find gets thrown out of court." He turned back, crossing his arms. "Fourth Amendment violations don't disappear just because the suspect is guilty."

My heart sank. "So you can't help me."

Morrison turned back to face me. "I didn't say that. I said accessing his records without a warrant would be problematic."

"Then how—"

"There are ways to access publicly available information that don't require warrants," he said. "Traffic cameras are maintained by the city. Security footage from businesses is often available through cooperative requests. Cell tower data... that's trickier."

I leaned forward. "What are you saying?"

Morrison sat back down at the counter, drumming his fingers on the surface. "I'm saying that if a concerned citizen provided me with credible evidence that a federal judge might be involved in his daughter's murder, I'd have an obligation to investigate through proper channels."

"Which takes time we don't have," I said. "Blake takes the stand in the morning."

Morrison was quiet for a long moment, clearly weighing his options. "What you're asking me to do could end my career if it goes wrong."

"And an innocent man goes to prison if we do nothing."

He looked at me steadily. "You're certain Blake didn't kill her?"

"I'm certain Judge Thatcher was involved in her death. Whether Blake was coerced, manipulated, or completely innocent, I don't know yet. But I know he didn't act alone."

Morrison picked up the DNA report again. "This evidence—can it be authenticated in court?"

"If it needs to be, yes."

"And you're planning to use it tomorrow?"

"If I can corroborate it with location evidence showing Thatcher was at the scene."

Morrison stood and moved to a desk in the corner of his living room. He pulled out his laptop and brought it back to the counter.

"What are you doing?" I asked.

"I'm checking publicly available traffic camera data from the city database. As a federal agent investigating a murder case, I have access to this information through proper channels."

Adrenaline shot through me. "And if you find something?"

"If I find evidence that Judge Thatcher was in the vicinity of his daughter's apartment on the night she died, I'll have to decide whether that information is relevant to our investigation."

His fingers moved quickly across the keyboard, navigating through the city's traffic monitoring system. After twenty minutes, he turned the laptop toward me.

"Traffic camera at the intersection of Main and Fifth," he said, "two blocks from Melissa's apartment. November 22nd, 7:47 PM."

The image showed a silver Mercedes sedan with a license plate that was clearly visible.

"Is that—?"

"Judge Thatcher's car. Registered in his name, traveling in the direction of his daughter's apartment complex."

My pulse quickened. "Can you get footage from closer to the apartment?"

"I can try. But even if I find more evidence placing him at the scene, it doesn't prove he killed her."

"Combined with the DNA evidence, it establishes opportunity and physical contact. And he claimed she called him at seven—if he was already driving there at 7:47, the timeline doesn't work."

Morrison continued working, pulling up camera feeds from various intersections and businesses near Melissa's apartment. After another hour, he had constructed a timeline showing Thatcher's car arriving in the area at 7:47 PM and leaving at 9:23 PM.

"He was there for over an hour and a half," I said.

"Long enough to kill his daughter and stage the scene to look like domestic violence."

Morrison closed the laptop and rubbed his eyes. "Ms. Hayes, I need to think about this. What you're showing me … it's explosive. If it becomes public that I helped build a case against a federal judge..."

"I understand the risks."

"Do you?" He leaned forward, looking at me with concern. "Because if we're wrong, if there's an innocent explanation for this evidence, both our careers are over. And if we're right, if Judge Thatcher really did kill his daughter, he might not hesitate to eliminate anyone who threatens to expose him."

The weight of his words settled over me. My mother had been eliminated for getting too close to the truth. Now I was following the same path.

"So what do you want to do?" I asked.

Morrison looked at the DNA report one more time. "I need to think about this. Sleep on it. Weigh the risks against what's right."

"Morrison—"

"By eight AM tomorrow, you'll have your answer about what I'm going to do. If I decide this evidence is worth pursuing, you'll know. If I decide it's too dangerous..."

"Then Blake goes to prison for a crime he didn't commit."

"Maybe," he said, moving toward the door. "Or maybe we're seeing patterns that don't exist."

The doubt in his voice deflated my certainty. "I understand."

"I hope you do. Because if I decide to help you tomorrow, there's no going back for either of us."

I stood to leave, uncertainty pressing down on me. Morrison hadn't committed to helping, hadn't promised the evidence would be available. He'd simply said I'd have my answer by morning.

"Agent Morrison, whatever you decide, I want you to know I appreciate you listening."

"Don't thank me yet," he said, his voice dropping low. "Tomorrow, you'll either have the evidence you need, or you'll be facing a federal judge's wrath alone. Either way, there's no turning back from what you've set in motion."

CHAPTER THIRTY-ONE

I ARRIVED at the courthouse Thursday morning with my nerves stretched tight as piano wire. Eight o'clock came and went with no word from Morrison. Eight-fifteen passed without a call from Lisa. By eight-thirty, as Erin and I made our way to the courtroom, I was checking my phone every thirty seconds.

"Alex, you're making me nervous," Erin said as we settled at the prosecution table. "What's going on? You promised you'd tell me everything this morning."

"I'm still waiting for confirmation that what I have to say is reliable," I told her. "If it comes through, it could change our entire approach to Blake's testimony."

Erin's voice was tight with frustration. "What kind of confirmation?"

"Evidence that might prove Blake didn't act alone."

Erin's eyes narrowed. "Blake is about to take the stand. I need to know what you're planning."

"I'm planning to cross-examine him based on the evidence we have. If additional evidence becomes available during his testimony, I'll adjust accordingly."

"That's not an answer."

Before I could respond, Judge Henley entered the courtroom, and Blake Costello was called to the witness stand. He looked even younger than his twenty-one years, pale and nervous in a navy suit that made him appear more like a scared college student than an accused murderer.

Richardson approached his client with the gentle demeanor of a father figure rather than a defense attorney.

"Blake," he said. "I know this is difficult, but I need you to tell the jury about your relationship with Melissa Thatcher."

Blake's voice was barely audible. "We'd been together for eight months. She was ... she was amazing. Smart, passionate about everything she cared about. I loved her."

"How would you describe your relationship in the early months?"

"Happy. Normal college relationship stuff. We'd study together, go to parties, spend weekends at each other's apartments. Her family liked me; my family liked her."

"When did things begin to change?"

Blake's hands gripped the sides of the witness box, knuckles whitening. "Around October. Melissa started working on this research project for her pre-law thesis. It was supposed to be about judicial ethics, something like that."

"How did this project affect Melissa?"

"At first she was excited about it. She said she was uncovering interesting connections, that her professor was impressed with her work. But then she started getting ... obsessed."

Richardson nodded sympathetically. "What do you mean by obsessed?"

"She'd spend all night on her laptop, following links and reading documents. She'd print out pages and pages of financial records and court cases." Blake's voice cracked slightly as he continued. "She stopped hanging out with friends, stopped coming to parties. Everything became about the research."

I noticed several jurors leaning forward, engaged by Blake's apparent sincerity. The domestic violence survivor in particular seemed to be reassessing her initial impressions.

"Did Melissa share details of her research with you?"

"Some. She said she was finding evidence of corruption in the judicial system. Money laundering through charitable foundations, judges making decisions that benefited criminal organizations." Blake's voice grew stronger. "She believed she'd uncovered this massive conspiracy involving trafficking and corruption."

Richardson stepped closer to the witness box, his expression concerned. "What was your reaction to these claims?"

"I was worried about her. She wasn't sleeping, wasn't eating regularly. She'd get these wild theories about being followed or watched. I thought the research was making her paranoid."

"Did you encourage her to continue this research?"

"No. I tried to get her to focus on other classes, to take breaks from the project." Blake ran a hand through his hair, a gesture that made him look even younger. "I suggested she talk to someone about the anxiety it was causing her."

"How did Melissa respond to your concerns?"

"She got angry. Said I didn't understand what she'd discovered, that I was trying to silence her just like everyone else. She started accusing me of not supporting her work."

My phone vibrated against the table. A text from Morrison: *Still reviewing. Need more time.* My stomach tightened. Without corroboration, Blake's testimony was painting him as a concerned boyfriend, not a co-conspirator.

"Blake," Richardson continued, "did your concerns about Melissa's research lead to arguments between you?"

"Yes. Especially in the last few weeks," Blake replied. "She was convinced that powerful people wanted to stop her from finishing the project. She said her phone was being tapped, that cars were following her."

"Did you believe these concerns were real?"

Blake looked down at his hands. "I thought she was scaring herself. Reading too much into coincidences. I mean, she was a college student researching government corruption—who would really care that much about her school project?"

"How did these arguments affect your relationship?"

"They were tearing us apart. Melissa started pulling away from me, saying I was part of the problem because I wouldn't validate her fears. She'd accuse me of trying to control her or silence her research."

Richardson let the testimony sink in before continuing. "Blake, I need to ask you about some difficult topics. Did you ever become physical during these arguments?"

Blake's composure cracked slightly. "A few times I ... I grabbed her arm when she was trying to walk away from me during an argument. I never meant to hurt her; I was just trying to get her to listen."

"Did you ever strike Melissa or hurt her intentionally?"

"No. Never. I know grabbing her was wrong, and I felt terrible about it. But I never hit her or tried to hurt her."

Richardson's voice softened with compassion. "In the weeks before Melissa's death, how would you describe her state of mind?"

"She was terrified," Blake said, genuine sadness overtaking his expression. "Convinced that someone was going to hurt her because of her research. She'd call me at all hours, saying she heard noises outside her apartment or saw the same car parked on her street."

"What did you do when she called with these concerns?"

"I'd go over to her place, check the locks, look around outside. I never saw anything suspicious, but I wanted her to feel safe."

The narrative Blake was constructing felt too perfect, too carefully designed to explain away every piece of evidence against him. He was admitting just enough wrongdoing to seem honest while painting Melissa as increasingly unstable.

"Blake," Richardson said, his tone shifting to address the crucial night, "tell the jury about November 22nd. What were your plans that day?"

"I had classes in the morning," Blake said, "then I was supposed to meet David for our usual gaming session. But around seven, I started thinking about Melissa. We'd had a bad fight the day before, and I felt guilty about how I'd handled it."

"What did you decide to do?"

"I logged off the game and decided to go see her. I wanted to apologize for not being more supportive of her project, to try to work things out between us."

"What time did you arrive at Melissa's apartment?"

"Around eight-thirty. I had a key, but when I got to the door, it was already unlocked."

"Was that unusual?"

Blake nodded. "Very. Melissa was always careful about locking her door, especially lately with all her fears about being watched."

"What did you do when you found the door unlocked?"

"I called her name as I went inside. When she didn't answer, I got worried. I thought maybe she'd stepped out quickly and forgotten to lock up."

Richardson paused, allowing the tension to build. "Tell the jury what you found when you entered the living room."

Blake's voice broke. "She was on the floor. There was blood everywhere. The coffee table was overturned, books scattered around."

"What was your first reaction?"

"I ran to her, knelt down beside her. I tried to find a pulse, tried to see if she was breathing. But her skin was already getting cold." Tears started flowing down Blake's face. "I kept saying her name, begging her to wake up, but she was gone."

Richardson gave his client a moment before asking, "Blake, did you cause Melissa's injuries?"

"No. When I found her, she was already dead. Whatever happened to her happened before I got there."

"What did you do after you realized Melissa was dead?"

Blake wiped his eyes with the back of his hand. "I panicked. I couldn't think straight. All I could think about was how this would look—the boyfriend with a history of arguments finding the body. I knew people would assume I killed her."

"So what did you do?"

"I left. I got in my car and drove home as fast as I could. I sat in my driveway for maybe an hour, trying to figure out what to do."

"Who did you call first?"

"My father. I told him what I'd found, how scared I was. He told me to call you immediately."

"Did your father tell you to lie to the police?"

"No. He just said I needed legal representation before I talked to anyone about what happened."

"Blake, why didn't you call 911 when you found Melissa?"

Blake's shoulders sagged with apparent regret. "I should have. I know that now. It was the worst decision of my life, and I'll regret it forever. But I was terrified and not thinking clearly."

"Looking back, do you wish you'd done anything differently?"

"Everything. I wish I'd been more supportive of Melissa's research, even if I thought it was making her paranoid. I wish I'd taken her fears more seriously. I wish I'd called 911 the moment I found her." Blake looked directly at the jury. "But most of all, I wish I'd been able to protect her from whatever happened to her that night."

Richardson paused, letting Blake's emotional testimony resonate. I watched the jury's faces—several were clearly moved by his apparent remorse. The retired police officer maintained his skepticism, but even the domestic violence survivor seemed less certain of Blake's guilt.

"Blake, did you kill Melissa Thatcher?"

Blake straightened in his seat, meeting Richardson's gaze directly. "No. I loved her. Even with all our problems, even when she was pursuing research that scared me, I would never hurt her. Never."

"Thank you, Blake. No further questions."

I felt my phone buzz and checked it quickly. A text from Lisa: *Running late. Results in 30 minutes.*

Thirty minutes might be too late if I had to start my cross-examination immediately.

Judge Henley looked at our table. "Ms. Hayes, cross-examination?"

I stood, still hoping my phone would ring with the evidence I needed. Blake looked at me with the expression of someone who knew his fate was about to be decided.

"Your Honor," I said, my voice holding conviction, "may I have a moment to confer with co-counsel?"

Judge Henley nodded once. "You may."

I leaned over to whisper to Erin. "Can you stall for a few minutes?"

She whispered back, "How am I supposed to stall?"

"Object to something. Ask for a sidebar. Anything to buy me time."

Erin looked at me like I'd lost my mind, but she stood. "Your Honor, before cross-examination begins, the prosecution would like to approach for a sidebar."

Judge Henley waved us forward, clearly annoyed. "What is it, Ms. Mitchell?"

"Your Honor, we'd like to request a brief recess to review our cross-examination strategy in light of the defendant's testimony."

Judge Henley's expression hardened. "Absolutely not. You've had weeks to prepare for this moment. Proceed with your cross-examination, or I'll hold you both in contempt."

We returned to our table, my face burning with embarrassment and frustration. I had to cross-examine Blake without the evidence that might prove his involvement with Judge Thatcher. I'd have to rely on intuition, on the inconsistencies in his story, on the hope that I could break him through pure force of will.

CHAPTER
THIRTY-TWO

JUDGE HENLEY LOOKED at our table expectantly. "Ms. Hayes, cross-examination?"

I stood on unsteady legs, my mind racing through possible approaches without the evidence I'd been counting on. Blake looked at me from the witness stand, his eyes red from crying but his expression defiant.

"Your Honor, I need a moment to organize my materials."

"Proceed, counselor."

I approached the witness stand, buying time by shuffling through papers that suddenly felt meaningless. Without the DNA evidence or Morrison's location data, I was flying blind.

"Mr. Costello, you testified that you arrived at Melissa's apartment at approximately eight-thirty PM on November 22nd, correct?"

"Yes."

"And you found the door unlocked?"

"That's right."

"Which you said was unusual for Melissa?"

"Very unusual," Blake said, his voice raw from emotion. "She was always careful about security."

I was stalling, hoping something would come to me, some angle that might break through his story. But Blake seemed confident, prepared for standard cross-examination questions.

"Mr. Costello, when you found Melissa on the floor, you said you checked for a pulse?"

"Yes, I tried to help her."

"Did you move her body at all?"

"I ... I might have touched her shoulder, her neck. I was trying to see if she was alive."

"Did you move anything else in the apartment?"

Blake hesitated. "I don't think so. I was in shock."

"You don't think so, or you didn't?"

"I was in shock," he repeated. "I can't remember every detail."

I was losing him, and I could feel the jury's attention drifting. Without concrete evidence to challenge his story, I sounded like I was fishing for inconsistencies that might not exist.

"Mr. Costello, you testified that you immediately called your father after finding Melissa. Why your father and not 911?"

"I told you, I panicked. I wasn't thinking clearly."

"But you were thinking clearly enough to drive home safely?"

"Objection," Richardson called. "Argumentative."

"Sustained."

I was floundering, and everyone in the courtroom could see it. Blake's story was holding together under my unfocused questioning, and I had no ammunition to break through his defenses.

The courtroom doors opened with a soft whoosh, and I glanced back from my position at the lectern to see Lisa Cooper walking quickly down the center aisle, followed closely by Agent Morrison. She carried a manila folder, each step carrying palpable urgency. Morrison took a seat in the back row.

"Your Honor."

Judge Henley said sharply, "who is this person approaching the well of the court during cross-examination?"

Lisa froze midstep, realizing her breach of protocol.

"Your Honor," Erin said quickly, rising from the prosecution table, "this is Lisa Cooper from the District Attorney's office. She appears to have urgent information relevant to this case."

"Ms. Mitchell, this is highly irregular—"

"Your Honor," I said, "may I have a moment to confer with

counsel?"

Judge Henley's face showed clear displeasure. "Ms. Hayes, you're in the middle of cross-examination."

Lisa had reached the prosecution table and handed the folder to Erin, who glanced at its contents and her eyes widened. She stood and approached the lectern where I stood.

"Your Honor," Erin said, "the prosecution has just received critical evidence that directly relates to the defendant's testimony. We request permission to approach the bench."

Judge Henley frowned. "What kind of evidence?"

"DNA and location evidence that was not available until this morning, Your Honor."

Richardson was on his feet immediately. "Objection! Your Honor, I demand to see any evidence the prosecution intends to use. This is a clear violation of discovery rules."

"Your Honor," I said, "under Federal Rule 16, the prosecution has a continuing duty to disclose evidence as it becomes available. I request to approach the bench with defense counsel."

Judge Henley let out an exasperated breath, then motioned us forward. "Approach."

At the sidebar, Judge Henley, Richardson, Erin and I huddled together. Erin shot me a look that mixed shock with barely controlled anger—I'd clearly blindsided her with evidence in her own case.

"Your Honor," Erin said, taking control as lead prosecutor despite her obvious surprise, "we've just received DNA and location evidence that was not available until this morning."

Judge Henley and Richardson reviewed the DNA results and traffic camera photos while I stood slightly behind Erin, my hands clasped tightly in front of me to hide their trembling.

"This is explosive evidence," Judge Henley said quietly. "Mr. Richardson, have you seen any of this before?"

"Absolutely not, Your Honor. This is trial by ambush." Richardson looked flustered. "And these traffic camera photographs—the prosecution cannot authenticate these without proper foundation."

"Your Honor," I said, glancing toward the gallery where Morrison sat, "Agent Morrison of the FBI is present in the courtroom. He compiled this traffic camera evidence and can authenticate it."

"That doesn't matter," Richardson said desperately. "The prosecution cannot just call witnesses in the middle of cross-examination—"

"Counselor, I have to say, I'm surprised by your objection." Judge Henley studied the documents again, then looked at Richardson with a puzzled expression. "This evidence isn't prejudicial to your client at all—quite the opposite. It suggests someone else was present during the crime. Most defense attorneys would be celebrating evidence like this."

Richardson shifted his weight and avoided eye contact with either me or the judge. He acted like a man looking for any excuse to object to evidence that should exonerate his client.

Like a man under threat.

"Mr. Richardson?" Judge Henley pressed. "Do you wish to maintain your objection to evidence that appears to support your client's defense?"

Richardson glanced toward the gallery, toward Judge Thatcher, then back at the evidence. His jaw worked silently for several seconds before he spoke.

"No, Your Honor," he said. "I withdraw my objection to the evidence."

"Very well." Judge Henley faced Blake and said, "Mr. Costello, please step down temporarily. The court will hear brief authentication testimony from Agent Morrison."

Blake looked confused and terrified as he left the witness stand. In the gallery, Judge Thatcher sat perfectly still, his face a marble mask of judicial composure. But I noticed his hands gripping the armrests of his seat, knuckles white with tension.

Morrison was called to the stand and quickly authenticated the photographs and timeline. Judge Thatcher's car had been near the apartment complex from 7:47 PM to 9:23 PM—well before Blake had claimed to have arrived. Lisa followed, establishing the chain of custody for the DNA evidence.

"Thank you, Ms. Cooper. The DNA analysis and traffic camera evidence will be admitted as Prosecution Exhibits 84 and 85." Judge

Henley looked at Blake. "Mr. Costello, please retake the stand. Ms. Hayes, you may continue your cross-examination."

I approached Blake with the admitted evidence in hand, knowing I now had the weapons I needed to break his story and blow this case wide open. Behind me, I could feel Erin's eyes boring into my back—we would have words later about my methods, but for now, the truth took precedence.

"Mr. Costello," I said with renewed confidence, "you testified that when you arrived at Melissa's apartment, no one else was there, correct?"

He nodded. "That's right."

"And you found her already dead?"

"Yes."

"Mr. Costello, I'm going to show you what's been marked as Prosecution Exhibit 84." I handed him a photograph from Morrison's traffic camera collection. "Do you recognize this intersection?"

Blake studied the photo. "It's near Melissa's apartment complex."

"And do you recognize this vehicle?" I pointed to Thatcher's Mercedes in the image.

Blake's face paled. "I ... it looks like a silver Mercedes."

"The timestamp shows 7:47 PM on November 22nd. Do you know whose car this is?"

He shook his head and cleared his throat. "I don't know."

"Mr. Costello, this is Judge Henry Thatcher's vehicle. Melissa's father's vehicle. Were you aware he was in the area that night?"

Blake's eyes darted to Richardson, then to Judge Thatcher in the gallery. "I ... no, I wasn't aware of that."

"Mr. Costello, you testified that you may have touched Melissa while checking for signs of life, correct?"

"Yes."

"So, your DNA might be found on her body?"

"Possibly."

"But DNA found under her fingernails would indicate she fought with her attacker, wouldn't it?"

A bead of sweat formed on Blake's forehead. "I suppose so."

"Mr. Costello, I'm going to show you Prosecution Exhibit 85—DNA analysis results from material found under Melissa's fingernails." I handed him the document. "This analysis shows a match to DNA collected from Judge Henry Thatcher. Melissa's father."

The courtroom erupted in gasps and murmurs. Blake stared at the document, his hands shaking.

"Mr. Costello, if Judge Thatcher's DNA was found under his daughter's fingernails, and traffic cameras show his car approaching the scene well before you arrived, what does that suggest to you?"

"I ... I don't know."

"Let me rephrase," I said, avoiding the objection I could feel Richardson preparing. "Can you explain how Judge Thatcher's DNA could be under his daughter's fingernails if you found her alone and already dead?"

Blake's breaths came in short and shallow. He stuttered once more, his hands shaking. "I don't know what it suggests."

I kept my voice firm. "Mr. Costello, you've testified under oath that you found Melissa already dead and that you were alone in the apartment. But the evidence shows that Judge Thatcher was there during the time of her death. Were you lying about being alone?"

Blake's composure was cracking. "I told you what I remembered."

"Or were you protecting Judge Thatcher?"

"No, I—"

"Mr. Costello, what really happened when you arrived at that apartment?"

Blake looked desperately at Richardson, at Judge Thatcher, then back at me. The weight of the evidence was crushing his carefully constructed story.

"I told you," he said, looking into my eyes. "I found her dead."

"The evidence says otherwise," I replied. "The evidence says Judge Thatcher was there, and that Melissa fought with her killer, whose DNA does not match yours." I silently pleaded with him, allowing my voice to soften. "What really happened?"

Blake was on the verge of panic, his whole body shaking. "I can't ... I don't ..."

"Mr. Costello, did Judge Thatcher kill his daughter?"

"Objection!" Richardson was on his feet. "Calls for speculation!"

"Overruled," Judge Henley said, more like a bewildered bystander. "The witness may answer."

Blake let out soft sobs and said, "I didn't know what he was going to do. I swear I didn't know."

"What didn't you know, Blake?"

He swallowed. "When Judge Thatcher called me that night, he said Melissa was in trouble. That she'd gotten involved with dangerous people because of her research, and he needed my help to convince her to stop before something happened to her."

"So you went to the apartment that night knowing Judge Thatcher would be there?"

Blake nodded through his tears. "He told me to come at eight-thirty. Said he was going to talk to her first, try to reason with her as her father. If that didn't work, maybe hearing it from both of us would make her understand how serious this was."

I tilted my head. "But that's not what you found when you got there, was it?"

"No." Blake's voice was barely a whisper. "When I got there, I heard shouting from inside. I used my key to get in, and I saw ... I saw him hitting her. She was on the ground, and he was standing over her, and there was blood."

The courtroom was dead silent except for Blake's sobbing. In my peripheral vision, I saw Judge Thatcher rise slowly from his seat in the gallery, his face a mask of cold fury. Several people in nearby seats instinctively leaned away from him.

"What did you do?" I asked Blake.

"I yelled at him to stop," he said. "Asked him what he was doing. But she wasn't moving. She was just lying there." Blake looked directly at the jury, several of whom had tears in their eyes. The domestic violence survivor covered her mouth with her hand. "He'd killed her. Melissa Thatcher's own father had killed her."

Behind me, I heard a sharp intake of breath from Erin. When I glanced back, she was staring at Judge Thatcher with dawning horror.

I gripped the edges of the lectern, my knuckles white with tension. "And then what happened?"

"He grabbed me by the shirt and said if I ever told anyone what I'd seen, he'd destroy my entire family. He said he had connections everywhere—police, prosecutors, judges. He said he could make my parents lose their jobs, could get my little sister kicked out of school, could ruin everyone I cared about."

"What did Judge Thatcher tell you to do?"

"He said we had to make it look like a break-in gone wrong, or like she'd fallen during a fight." Blake swallowed, his voice growing stronger, speaking months' worth of hidden truths. "He made me help him move things around, clean up some of the blood. He took her laptop because it had all her research on it."

"And Judge Thatcher promised you wouldn't be charged?"

"He said if I stuck to the story about finding her dead, if I never mentioned he was there, he'd make sure I was protected. He said I might get arrested—that it would look suspicious if I wasn't—but that he had connections in the prosecutor's office. He said the case would be handled properly, that I'd never actually be convicted."

Blake's voice broke completely. "He said if I kept quiet and played my part, everything would work out. But if I ever said a word about what really happened, he'd make sure my whole family paid the price."

I stared at Blake, then at Judge Thatcher in the gallery. Thatcher sat perfectly still, his face a mask of cold calculation.

I looked back at the broken young man before me, terrified for his life. "Mr. Costello, are you testifying that Judge Henry Thatcher murdered his own daughter and then threatened your family to force your cooperation in covering it up?"

"Yes." Blake looked directly at Judge Thatcher. "He killed Melissa because she found out about his crimes. And he made me help him cover it up by threatening everyone I love."

The courtroom exploded in chaos. Judge Henley banged her gavel, bailiffs moved toward Judge Thatcher, and reporters rushed for the exits.

But all I could focus on was Blake Costello, finally telling the truth about the night Melissa Thatcher died—and the father who had murdered her and manipulated everyone else to cover his tracks.

CHAPTER THIRTY-THREE

THE CHAMBERS of Judge Patricia Henley felt smaller than usual with six people crammed inside. The court reporter sat in the corner, her machine clicking rapidly as she captured every word of what would undoubtedly become a pivotal moment in legal history.

Judge Henley removed her black robes and hung them carefully on a wooden stand, revealing a crisp white blouse. Her expression was full of controlled fury that came from decades of managing courtrooms. Richardson sat across from Erin and me, his expensive suit wrinkled, his usual composure completely shattered. Behind him, a younger associate from his firm frantically took notes, even though no one was speaking yet.

Erin sat rigidly beside me, radiating tension. We hadn't spoken directly since the DNA evidence had been introduced—there hadn't been time in the chaos that followed Blake's testimony. Now, sitting in these chambers, I could feel her anger like heat from a fire.

The judge settled behind her desk and looked at each one of us. "Ladies and gentlemen, in thirty years on the bench, I have never witnessed testimony quite like what just occurred in my courtroom."

Richardson was already reaching for his briefcase. "Your Honor, the defense moves immediately for a mistrial. Mr Costello's testimony has fundamentally altered the nature of this case. The jury has now heard explosive allegations against a sitting federal judge that go far beyond the scope of this murder trial."

"Your Honor," Erin interjected, "the defendant's testimony was responsive to proper cross-examination. We didn't elicit these statements, nor did you object to them, Mr. Richardson. Mr. Costello volunteered this information when confronted with evidence."

"Evidence that was sprung on the defense and the court without proper notice," Richardson countered, his voice rising. "This entire line of questioning was based on DNA analysis and traffic camera footage that we'd never seen before today."

Judge Henley held up a hand for silence. "Mr. Richardson, let's address your concerns one at a time. First, regarding the DNA evidence—my ruling allowing its admission was correct. The prosecution has a continuing duty to disclose evidence as it becomes available, and they fulfilled that obligation this morning."

"But Your Honor, the prejudicial impact—"

"The prejudicial impact favors your client, counselor. Evidence suggesting someone else committed the crime typically helps the defense." Judge Henley's expression sharpened. "Which brings me to a more troubling question: why is defense counsel objecting to evidence that supports his client's innocence?"

Richardson's face flushed red. "Your Honor, I'm simply concerned about proper procedure—"

"Mr. Richardson." Judge Henley's voice carried the weight of judicial authority. "I've been watching your conduct throughout this trial. Your jury selection strategy was puzzling. You accepted jurors who were clearly biased *against* your client. Your cross-examinations have been perfunctory at best. And now you're objecting to evidence that could exonerate Mr. Costello. I'm beginning to wonder whether you're adequately representing your client's interests."

The room went silent except for the court reporter's machine. Richardson glanced at his associate, then back at Judge Henley, clearly struggling for a response.

"Your Honor, I've been providing zealous advocacy within the bounds of—"

"Have you?" Judge Henley leaned forward. "Because it looks like you've been more concerned with managing this case than winning it. And given Mr. Costello's testimony about promises made by Judge Thatcher, I'm starting to understand why."

My pulse quickened as the implications became clear. Judge Henley was thinking the same thing I was—that Richardson had been compromised from the beginning, possibly taking direction from Judge Thatcher about how to handle the defense.

"Your Honor," I said carefully, "the prosecution believes Mr. Costello's testimony is credible and materially relevant to this case. If he was coerced into participating in a cover-up, that changes the nature of his culpability."

"Agreed. Which brings us to the question of how to proceed." Judge Henley opened a legal pad and began making notes. "Mr. Richardson, your motion for mistrial is denied. However, given the extraordinary circumstances that have emerged, I'm prepared to consider other options."

"What kind of options?" Erin asked.

"The defendant has essentially confessed to being an accessory after the fact while implicating a federal judge in the actual murder. The prosecution may wish to consider whether the current charges are appropriate, or whether amended charges better reflect the evidence."

Richardson looked panicked. "Your Honor, any change in charges would require starting over completely—"

"Not necessarily. Federal Rule of Criminal Procedure 7 allows for amendment of charges during trial if it doesn't prejudice the defendant's substantial rights." Judge Henley looked directly at Richardson. "And given that reduced charges would benefit your client, I fail to see how he could be prejudiced."

I exchanged a glance with Erin. Judge Henley was offering us a way to adjust the charges to reflect Blake's actual role—accessory after the fact instead of murder. It would be a much lighter sentence and would acknowledge that he'd been coerced.

"Your Honor," Erin said, "we'd need time to consider our options and consult with our supervisors about potential charge amendments."

"Of course. However, we also have the immediate question of what to do about Judge Thatcher." Judge Henley's expression darkened. "If

Mr. Costello's testimony is accurate, we have a sitting federal judge who committed murder and manipulated the judicial process to cover it up."

"That's beyond the scope of this trial," Richardson said quickly.

"Is it?" Judge Henley stood and moved to her window, looking out at the courthouse plaza where media crews were undoubtedly setting up for breaking news reports. She looked back at Richardson. "If Judge Thatcher orchestrated a conspiracy that included your client, it's directly relevant to Mr. Costello's culpability."

"Your Honor," I said, "what's the court's position on continuing with this trial while these allegations are being investigated?"

"My position is that justice requires us to take all evidence into account. If that means exposing corruption within the judiciary, so be it. However, I'm also concerned about the safety of the witnesses and attorneys involved in this case."

Judge Henley was acknowledging what we all knew but hadn't said aloud—that Judge Thatcher had already threatened Blake's family, and people who threatened sitting federal judges sometimes ended up dead.

"I'm ordering enhanced security for all parties involved in this trial, effective immediately," Judge Henley said. "I'm also referring Mr. Costello's allegations about Judge Thatcher to the FBI for investigation. And I'm issuing a gag order—no one in this room discusses these proceedings with the media until further notice."

Richardson's associate was scribbling notes frantically. "Your Honor, what about the jury? They've heard Mr. Costello's testimony. How do we proceed with deliberations when the case has fundamentally changed?"

"The jury will deliberate on the charges as filed, based on all admitted evidence. If the prosecution chooses to file amended charges, we'll address that separately." Judge Henley returned to her desk. "But Mr. Richardson, I want to be very clear about something: if I discover that you've been taking direction from Judge Thatcher or anyone else about how to represent Mr. Costello, I'll refer you to the bar association for disciplinary action and order new counsel for your client. What your colleagues across the table here decide to do with that information is up to them."

Richardson's face went pale. "Your Honor, I've always acted in my client's best interests—"

"We'll see. Court will resume tomorrow morning at nine AM. I expect all parties to be prepared to proceed professionally and ethically, regardless of the extraordinary circumstances." Judge Henley's tone held no room for negotiation. "And counselors, I suggest you all be very careful over the next few days. If Mr. Costello's testimony is accurate, there are powerful people who won't want this investigation to continue."

Walking out of chambers, I felt the weight of what we'd unleashed. Blake's confession had blown open a conspiracy that reached to the very heart of the federal judiciary. But exposing the truth about Judge Thatcher's crimes would make us all targets.

In the hallway outside chambers, Richardson hurried past us without making eye contact. His associate followed like they were fleeing a crime scene.

"That was interesting," Erin said quietly as we walked toward the elevators.

"That was Richardson realizing his career might be over," I replied. "Judge Henley knows he's been compromised. The question is whether he was working for Thatcher voluntarily or whether he was threatened too."

Erin looked at me. "What do you think?"

I thought about Richardson's puzzling trial strategy, his failure to challenge prosecution-friendly jurors, his reluctance to fight evidence that should have helped his client.

"I think Judge Thatcher has been pulling strings from the beginning. Richardson, the jury selection, maybe even the timing of when evidence became available—all of it orchestrated to create the illusion of a fair trial while ensuring Blake would be convicted."

"Until Blake finally told the truth."

"Until Blake realized that Thatcher's promises were lies and decided to save himself."

CHAPTER THIRTY-FOUR

THE JURY HAD BEEN out all day yesterday and for six hours so far today. More than enough time for the media circus outside to triple in size, and for Judge Thatcher to disappear from his usual gallery seat. Despite Blake's explosive testimony Judge Henley had denied Erin's emergency motion for immediate arrest, ruling that while Blake's testimony provided probable cause, the proper procedure was for law enforcement to investigate and obtain a formal arrest warrant based on evidence beyond a co-defendant's testimony. Whether an arrest would ever be made, we didn't know.

When the bailiff finally announced that the jury had reached a verdict, the courtroom filled with an electric tension that made the air feel thick and difficult to breathe. Blake sat at the defense table between Richardson and his associate, his young face pale and drawn. He'd aged years in the past twenty-four hours.

Judge Henley entered with her usual measured pace, but I caught the tension in her shoulders, the way her eyes swept the packed gallery before settling on the jury box.

"Ladies and gentlemen of the jury, I understand you'd like to communicate with the court?"

The foreman, a middle-aged insurance adjuster who'd seemed sympathetic to our case throughout the trial, stood with a piece of paper that seemed to shake slightly in his hands.

"Yes, Your Honor. We've been deliberating for over twenty-three hours total, and we are unable to reach a unanimous verdict on any of the charges."

"I see," Judge Henley said. "Have you taken multiple votes on each count?"

"We have, Your Honor. We've voted seven times on the murder charge and five times on the lesser included offenses. We remain deadlocked."

"And do you believe further deliberation might result in a unanimous verdict?"

The foreman shook his head firmly. "No, Your Honor. The divisions are too deep. We are at an impasse."

Judge Henley nodded grimly. "Will the defendant please rise."

Blake stood on unsteady legs, Richardson's hand on his shoulder in what might have been support or restraint.

"Ladies and gentlemen of the jury, it appears you are unable to reach a verdict. This sometimes happens in complex cases with conflicting evidence."

She turned to address the full courtroom. "The jury is unable to reach a unanimous verdict. I hereby declare a mistrial on all charges."

My fingers tightened around my pen until my knuckles went white. The jury had been torn between believing Blake's explosive confession about Judge Thatcher and suspecting he was still lying to save himself. Some had clearly been convinced by his testimony about coercion and threats. Others must have thought his story was just another manipulation.

It was the worst possible outcome. No closure, no justice, no resolution.

"Ms. Mitchell," Judge Henley said, "given the mistrial, the government has ninety days to decide whether to retry this case. Mr. Costello will remain in custody pending that decision, or the prosecution may file a motion for bail reconsideration."

I looked at Erin, who looked as stunned as I felt. "Your Honor, we'll need to consult with our supervisors about how to proceed."

"Very well. Court is adjourned."

The gavel fell with a finality that echoed in my chest. Blake was led away in handcuffs, his head down, his fate still hanging in the balance. Richardson gathered his materials, looking like a man who'd dodged a bullet but wasn't sure the shooter had run out of ammunition.

"A hung jury," Erin said quietly as the courtroom began to empty. "Twenty-three hours of deliberation and they couldn't decide whether to believe Blake's story."

"Half the jury thought he was telling the truth about Thatcher," I said. "The other half thought he was still lying to save himself."

"Or maybe some of them were influenced by things that had nothing to do with the evidence."

I knit my brows together. Had Judge Thatcher's connections reached into the jury room? Had some jurors been approached, threatened, or bought?

"Ms. Hayes?"

I turned to see Special Agent Morrison approaching our table. His expression was grim.

"Agent Morrison. I assume you heard the verdict?"

"I did. And I wanted you to know that Judge Thatcher was arrested earlier this morning at his home. Federal charges for obstruction of justice, conspiracy, and pending DNA confirmation, murder."

The news should have felt like victory, but something in Morrison's tone suggested otherwise. Blake could face retrial now, which meant Thatcher would have months to eliminate witnesses, destroy evidence, or disappear entirely.

"But?"

Morrison sucked in a breath. "He posted bail two hours later. Federal judge, no flight risk, strong ties to the community. Magistrate judge set it at two million dollars."

I nearly stumbled back into my seat. "Two million dollars bail for a murder charge?"

"The magistrate judge was Robert Kellerman. He and Thatcher have been colleagues for fifteen years."

My stomach dropped, the knots tying tighter. "So Thatcher's free, pending trial."

"Free and very angry, according to my sources. The arrest warrant was sealed, but word travels fast in legal circles."

"Agent Morrison," Erin said, "are you suggesting we're in danger?"

"I'm suggesting you both be very careful about where you go and who you trust. Men like Thatcher don't go down quietly, especially when they have nothing left to lose."

Morrison left us standing in the nearly empty courtroom. Outside, we could hear the media frenzy building—reporters shouting questions, camera crews setting up for live broadcasts, the carnival atmosphere that surrounded high-profile legal cases.

"We need to get out of here before the circus finds us," Erin said, gathering her files. "Side exit?"

I nodded, and we made our way through the courthouse corridors, taking a route that would avoid the main lobby where reporters were undoubtedly waiting. The marble halls echoed with our footsteps, the sound somehow amplified by everything that had just unfolded.

We didn't speak until we reached the parking garage, the concrete structure providing a buffer from the chaos outside. Erin stopped walking and turned to face me, her expression a mixture of exhaustion and something like regret.

"Alex, I owe you an apology."

"For what?"

"For not believing you. For dismissing your instincts about this case." She set down her briefcase and leaned against a concrete pillar. "You kept saying something felt wrong about Blake's story, about the way evidence was being presented, about Judge Thatcher's behavior. And I kept telling you to focus on the facts we could prove."

"You were doing your job," I said. "You were being a good prosecutor."

"No, I was being a safe prosecutor. There's a difference." Erin ran her hand through her hair, disturbing the professional composure she'd maintained throughout the trial. "You were willing to ask uncomfortable questions even when everyone else—even when I wanted simple answers. You pushed for DNA evidence that exonerated our defendant. You recorded Thatcher threatening us in chambers."

"That recording probably isn't admissible—"

"That's not the point. The point is that you saw what the rest of us missed or chose to ignore." She met my eyes directly. "If you hadn't pushed, Blake would have been convicted of murder while the real killer walked free."

Some of the tension left my shoulders. Having Erin acknowledge what I'd been feeling for months—that something fundamental was wrong with this case—meant more than I'd expected.

"I still don't know if the conspiracy necessarily connects to my mother. But I do think there's a network of corruption that reaches higher than we want to admit." I said the words slowly, as if testing them out.

So many people had told me that I was seeing things where they didn't exist, letting a dead woman write my story. Even after yesterday's explosive revelation, it left me wondering if they were all right.

"The chess piece. The trafficking connections from your previous cases. The way multiple prosecutors recused themselves from this case without real conflicts." Erin was quiet for a moment. "Alex, what if you've been right about more than just this case?"

"What do you mean?"

"What if the pattern you've been seeing—corrupt judges protecting criminal networks—is real? What if your mother really was killed because she got too close to exposing it?"

"I don't know," I said honestly. "But I know that Judge Thatcher killed his daughter to protect secrets worth killing for. And I know that someone has been manipulating this case to make sure Blake took the fall."

"The jury selection. Richardson's inexplicable trial strategy. The way evidence kept appearing at convenient moments." Erin nodded slowly. "It does feel orchestrated."

"So where does this leave us?" I asked.

Erin chewed the inside of her cheek for a moment. "It leaves us with a choice. We can treat this as an isolated case—one corrupt judge who killed his daughter and manipulated one trial. Or we can accept that this might be part of something larger."

My heart skipped a beat. "And if it is part of something larger?"

"Then we decide whether we're prosecutors who play it safe or prosecutors who pursue justice wherever it leads."

"Even if it's dangerous?"

"Especially if it's dangerous. Because if a federal judge's daughter can be killed to protect their secrets, what does that say about the system we've sworn to serve?"

I looked at Erin—really looked at her—and saw someone who'd been fundamentally changed by what we'd experienced. The safe, by-the-book prosecutor was still there, but underneath was someone who'd seen how corruption could manipulate justice itself.

"Morrison was right about being careful," I said. "If we're right about this network, they won't hesitate to eliminate threats."

"Then we'll have to be smarter than your mother was. More careful about who we trust and how we proceed."

"Blake Costello is facing retrial while Judge Henry Thatcher walks free on bail," I said. "That's not justice."

"No, it's not," Erin said. "But maybe it's not the end of the story either."

CHAPTER THIRTY-FIVE

THE FEDERAL BUILDING hummed with an electric undercurrent of tension. Conversations stopped abruptly when I passed groups of attorneys in the hallway. Clerical staff avoided eye contact. Even the security guards at the entrance seemed to watch me with new interest, their gazes following my movement through the metal detectors.

Word traveled fast in legal circles, and Judge Henry Thatcher's arrest had sent shockwaves through the entire justice system.

Erin and I rode the elevator to the fifth floor in silence, both of us processing the weight of what we'd unleashed. We'd exposed a sitting federal judge as a murder suspect. The implications rippled far beyond our case.

"Hayes." Callahan's voice cut through the elevator doors as they opened. He stood in the hallway outside his office, arms crossed, looking like a man who'd been fielding phone calls all morning. "My office. Now."

I exchanged a glance with Erin, who gave me an encouraging nod before heading toward her own office. The walk down the corridor felt longer than usual, every door I passed representing another attorney who probably had opinions about what I'd done to their carefully ordered world.

Callahan's office smelled like stale coffee and stress. He'd rolled up his sleeves and loosened his tie—sure signs that the day's pressure had already taken its toll. His desk was covered with case files, legal briefs, and what looked like printouts of news articles.

"Close the door," he said.

I settled into the chair across from his desk.

"Hell of a trial," he said finally, leaning back in his chair and studying my face. "Hell of a verdict."

"A hung jury isn't exactly a victory."

"Isn't it?" Callahan picked up a newspaper clipping and slid it across the desk. The headline read: FEDERAL JUDGE ARRESTED IN DAUGHTER'S MURDER. "Because from where I'm sitting, it looks like you just brought down one of the most powerful men in the federal judiciary."

I scanned the article, noting how the reporter had focused on Blake's explosive testimony about coercion and cover-ups. The story painted Judge Thatcher as a corrupt judge who'd killed his own daughter to protect his secrets, then manipulated the legal system to frame an innocent man.

"I followed the evidence. When Blake confessed to being coerced—"

"You followed your instincts, and they turned out to be right." Callahan set down his coffee mug and rubbed his jaw. "I owe you an apology, Alex. I was wrong to demote you to second chair. I was trying to manage political pressure instead of trusting one of my best prosecutors to do her job."

The admission caught me off guard. "You were trying to protect the office."

"I was trying to protect myself. And in doing so, I nearly let you prosecute an innocent kid who just got in way over his head while the real killer walked free." His expression grew more serious. "Your instincts about this case were solid from the beginning. The problem is how you acted on them."

"What do you mean?"

He chuckled. "I mean that exposing judicial corruption requires finesse, not a sledgehammer. You got the right result, but you also set off alarms throughout the entire federal judiciary." Callahan gestured toward a stack of pink message slips on his desk. "I've been fielding calls all morning from judges, senators, and DOJ officials who want to know how we let this happen."

I shifted forward in my seat, my spine straightening with indignation. "How we let what happen?"

"How we let a federal prosecutor expose a sitting judge in open court without warning, without coordination, without considering the broader implications." Callahan stood and began pacing behind his desk, his movements agitated. "Alex, what you discovered about Thatcher is important. Critical, even. But the way you exposed it has created a crisis of confidence in the entire federal judiciary."

"Because people might start questioning whether other judges are corrupt?"

"Because people might start believing that the entire system is compromised. That they can't trust federal courts, federal prosecutors, federal law enforcement." He turned back to face me. "Whether that's true or not, the perception becomes reality if we're not careful."

Anger rose in my chest, hot and immediate. "So we should have covered it up? Let Blake get convicted of murder to protect the system's reputation?"

"We should have found a way to expose Thatcher's crimes without burning down public confidence in the process. There are protocols for investigating judicial corruption, channels that exist to handle these situations quietly and effectively."

"Quietly enough that the corruption never sees daylight?"

Callahan's expression hardened. "Effectively enough that justice gets served without destroying the institutions that make justice possible in the first place."

The conversation was taking a different turn than I'd expected.

"Are you saying there was a better way to have handled this?"

"I'm saying that effective prosecutors learn how to work *within* the system to achieve justice, not just expose wrongdoing. There's a difference between being right and being effective." He returned to his desk and sat down. "You were right about Thatcher. But now he's free on bail, posted by a foundation with connections we don't understand, while the entire federal judiciary circles the wagons."

I crossed my arms. "So what should I have done differently?"

"Built the case quietly. Coordinated with the Public Integrity Section from the beginning. Made sure we had enough evidence to prevent bail being granted." Callahan leaned forward. "The goal isn't just to expose corruption, Alex. It's to make sure the corrupt actually face consequences."

I sat with that for a moment, recognizing the truth in his words even as they frustrated me. He was right—I'd been so focused on exposing the truth that I hadn't thought strategically about what would happen after. Now Thatcher was free, with time and resources to build his defense or potentially flee. If I'd been more patient, more methodical, we might have been able to keep him in custody.

"You're saying I should have played politics," I said slowly.

"I'm saying you should have been strategic. There's a difference between compromising your principles and being smart about how you achieve them."

I nodded. "What happens now?"

"Now you learn how to look behind the veil without tearing it down completely." Callahan pulled out a file from his desk drawer. "The Public Integrity Section is taking over the Thatcher investigation. They have resources and authority that we don't. Your job is to support that investigation when asked, but not to run your own parallel inquiry."

I gripped the armrests of my chair, fighting to keep my frustration in check. "And if they don't pursue it aggressively enough?"

"Then you trust that there are people in this system who care about justice as much as you do, even if they pursue it differently." His tone softened slightly. "Alex, I've seen prosecutors destroy their careers and their cases by going rogue. The system has flaws, but it also has mechanisms for addressing those flaws if you know how to use them."

"The mechanisms seem designed to protect the powerful more than pursue justice," I said, unable to keep the bitterness from my voice. "Thatcher got bail from a colleague. The prosecutors who should have taken this case all developed sudden conflicts of interest. Even Richardson seemed more interested in protecting Thatcher than defending his client. Where were the mechanisms then?"

"Fair point," Callahan conceded. "But that's exactly why we need smart prosecutors who understand how to navigate those obstacles rather than just crash into them."

"Like building relationships with people in other agencies who share your goals. Like documenting everything carefully so that if political pressure derails one investigation, the evidence is preserved for another. Like being patient enough to build cases that will actually result in convictions rather than headlines."

I absorbed what he was saying, recognizing the wisdom even as it frustrated me. "You're asking me to play a longer game."

"I'm asking you to play a *smarter* game. The people you're up against have been playing this game for decades. They understand how to manipulate the system, how to use political pressure and legal technicalities to avoid consequences. If you want to beat them, you need to be more sophisticated than they are."

"That sounds like it could take years."

"Good investigations often do. But they also tend to result in prosecutions that stick." Callahan pulled out another file and set it on his desk. "In the meantime, I have a new assignment for you. Securities fraud case out of Dallas. Complex financial instruments, multiple defendants, the kind of case that requires someone with your analytical skills."

I looked at the file without touching it. "You're trying to keep me busy."

"I'm trying to keep you sharp. And visible in a positive way." His expression became more serious. "Alex, what you did with the Thatcher case was brave, but it also painted a target on your back. You need to rebuild your reputation as a solid, reliable prosecutor before you can afford to take on another high-stakes investigation."

"And if I refuse? If I keep pushing on the Thatcher connections?"

Callahan's expression shifted. "Then you'll probably end up like your mother. Brilliant, dedicated, and ultimately ineffective because you burned too many bridges too quickly."

The comparison stung, but I heard the concern underneath it. "You think my mother made the same mistakes I'm making?"

"I think your mother was ahead of her time in recognizing patterns that others couldn't see. But I also think she underestimated how much institutional support she'd need to expose the kind of corruption she was chasing." Callahan's voice softened. "She was right about almost everything, Alex. But being right isn't enough if you can't survive long enough to prove it."

I reached across the desk and picked up the securities fraud file. "When do you need an answer about this case?"

"Monday morning." Callahan's relief was visible. "Take the weekend to review the materials. It's the kind of complex financial case that could make your reputation if you handle it well."

"And if I don't take it?"

"Then I'll find someone else who's interested in building a career instead of chasing ghosts."

I stood to leave, clutching the file against my chest. At the door, I turned back to face him.

"Can I ask you something?"

He nodded, gesturing for me to continue.

"Do you think Blake Costello killed Melissa Thatcher?"

Callahan was quiet for several seconds, his expression thoughtful. "I think Blake Costello was in that apartment when Melissa Thatcher died. I think he helped cover up what happened afterward. And I think the truth about who struck the fatal blow might be more complicated than either side presented at trial."

"But you don't think he's a murderer."

"I think he's a young man who got caught up in something much bigger and more dangerous than he understood. Whether that makes him a murderer or a victim is a question for philosophers, not prosecutors. Our job is to prove what happened, not to judge the moral weight of people's choices under extreme duress."

Walking back to my office, I carried the weight of the choice I was facing. I could take the securities fraud case and rebuild my career on safe, manageable prosecutions. Or I could continue investigating the network that had killed my mother and Melissa Thatcher, knowing that doing so might cost me everything.

The federal building felt different now, less like a place where justice was served and more like a maze designed to protect powerful people from the consequences of their actions.

In my office, I set the securities fraud file on my desk without opening it. Outside my window, Houston stretched toward the horizon, a city full of secrets and lies that would never be exposed if people like me chose safety over truth.

Blake Costello sat in a federal detention center, awaiting a retrial that might never come. Judge Henry Thatcher was free on bail, protected by lawyers and political connections that reached the highest levels of government.

And somewhere in the shadows, the people who'd killed my mother were watching to see what I would do next.

CHAPTER THIRTY-SIX

Monday morning arrived gray and humid. I'd spent the weekend reviewing the securities fraud case Callahan had given me, trying to focus on complex financial instruments and wire transfers instead of dwelling on the image of Judge Thatcher walking free while Blake Costello sat in a federal detention cell.

The case was exactly what Callahan had promised—intricate, challenging, the kind of prosecution that could build a reputation if handled well. But every time I tried to concentrate on derivative trading schemes and offshore shell companies, my mind drifted back to Melissa's journal entries and the DNA evidence that proved her father had killed her.

I was deep in reviewing SEC filings when Cynthia knocked on my office door.

"Ms. Hayes? There's a young woman here to see you. Says her name is Rebecca Thatcher."

My stomach lurched. I hadn't been expecting a visit from her. "Send her in."

Becca entered my office looking exhausted and drawn, wearing jeans and a Georgetown University sweatshirt that probably belonged to her sister. Her pale eyes were rimmed with red, and she carried herself with the careful composure of someone who'd been crying recently but was determined not to break down in public.

"Becca." Standing, I gestured toward the chair across from my desk. "Please, sit down. How are you holding up?"

She perched on the edge of the chair, her hands clasped tightly in her lap. "I wanted to thank you. For what you did in court. For making sure people knew the truth about what happened to Melissa."

"No need to thank me," I said, sitting back down. "I was just doing my job."

"No, you weren't." Becca's voice was quiet but firm. "You were doing what was right. Everyone else was willing to let Blake take the blame while my father walked away clean."

The matter-of-fact way she said "my father" sent a chill through me. There was no emotion in it, no filial affection or even anger—just cold acknowledgment of a biological relationship stripped of any deeper meaning.

"Becca, I'm sorry about everything you've had to go through. About what's happening to your family."

She shrugged, a gesture that seemed too old for her fifteen years. "He stopped being my family the night he killed my sister."

I absorbed that statement, trying to imagine what it would feel like to discover your father was a murderer. "Where are you staying now?"

"I'm going to go to my aunt in Dallas. She's trying to get custody, but there's a lot of legal stuff to work through." Becca's composure wavered. "My mom is ... she's not handling any of this well. She still believes my father is innocent. Says Blake and everyone else are lying to destroy our family."

I reached across the desk, not quite touching her hands but offering the gesture of comfort. "I'm sorry."

"Don't be. It's better to know the truth, even when it hurts." Becca reached into her backpack and pulled out a small object wrapped in tissue paper. "I came here because I have something for you. Something Melissa wanted someone to have if anything happened to her."

Unwrapping the tissue paper, she revealed a small flash drive. It was unremarkable except for a piece of tape on the side with "M.T." written in careful block letters.

"Melissa gave this to me about a week before she died. She said if anything ever happened to her, I should give it to someone who wouldn't be afraid to look at what was on it." Becca held the flash drive out to me. "She said most people would be too scared or too invested in the system to do anything with it."

I took the drive, its plastic casing cool against my palm. "Did she tell you what was on it?"

"Not exactly. But she said it was everything she'd found about the foundation, about the money transfers, about people who were supposed to protect others but were really just protecting themselves." Becca's voice grew stronger. "She said it was proof that some of the most powerful people in the country were criminals."

"Becca, why didn't you give this to the FBI? Or mention it during your testimony?"

"Because I wasn't sure who to trust. Melissa was terrified in those last weeks, saying she didn't know how high up the corruption went. She was afraid that if she gave her evidence to the wrong people, it would just disappear." Becca met my eyes directly. "But after watching you in court, after seeing how you fought for the truth even when it was dangerous, that you used her journal in a way that respected her memory, I knew you were the right person."

I stared at the flash drive, understanding that this object in my palm could either vindicate everything I'd suspected about the network of corruption, or prove that Melissa's fears had been the product of a stressed student's imagination.

"Do you think he'll ever pay for what he did?" The question came out quietly, but with an intensity that made it clear this was why Becca had really come.

I thought about Judge Thatcher, free on bail posted by a mysterious foundation. About the institutional pressure to handle his case quietly through the Public Integrity Section. About Callahan's warnings about working within the system rather than exposing it.

"Honestly, I don't know." "The system moves slowly when it comes to people like your father. There are protections in place, political considerations, legal technicalities that can delay justice for years."

"But you'll try? You'll look at what's on the drive and decide if it's worth pursuing?"

I could hear Callahan's voice in my head, warning me about the importance of building cases quietly, of working within institutional channels rather than going rogue. The securities fraud file eyed me from my desk, representing the safe path that would rebuild my reputation and keep me out of dangerous territory.

But I could also see Melissa Thatcher, lying dead on her apartment floor. And her sister sitting in front of me, looking at me like I was the last hope she had at believing in a world that had taken so much from her.

"Yes," I said, slipping the flash drive into my desk drawer. "I'll look at it."

Relief flooded Becca's face. "Melissa always said you were supposed to trust the system to deliver justice. But what happens when the system is what you need protection from?"

It was a remarkably sophisticated question from a fifteen-year-old, and it cut to the heart of everything I'd been struggling with since taking the Thatcher case.

"That's when you have to decide whether you're going to work to fix the system or work around it," I said.

"Which are you going to do?"

I thought about my mother, investigating corruption twenty years ago without the institutional support she needed. I thought about Judge Thatcher, using his position to protect criminal networks while murdering his own daughter to silence her. I thought about Blake Costello, sitting in detention while the real killer enjoyed the presumption of innocence.

"I'm going to try to do both," I said. "Fix what can be fixed, work around what can't be."

Becca stood to leave, shouldering her backpack. At the door, she turned back.

"Ms. Hayes? Melissa wrote something in her journal the night before she died." Becca hesitated a moment. I nodded for her to continue. "She said, 'Some people are willing to fight for justice even when justice fights back.' I think she was writing about you. I'm sad she never got the chance to meet you."

The words hit me unexpectedly hard. Melissa and I had been circling the same truths from different angles—she as a daughter discovering her father's corruption, me as a prosecutor chasing my mother's ghost. We could have been allies, could have shared information and strategies. Instead, she'd died alone with her secrets, and I was left to piece together her discoveries from digital fragments.

After Becca left, I sat alone in my office with the flash drive hidden in my desk drawer. Through my window, I could see the federal courthouse where Judge Thatcher had sat every day during the trial, watching us perform exactly as he'd scripted until Blake's confession shattered his carefully constructed narrative.

I thought about Callahan's advice about building relationships with people in other agencies, about documenting evidence carefully, about playing a longer and smarter game. The flash drive might contain exactly the kind of evidence that could expose the network my mother had died investigating, but only if I handled it with the sophistication that she'd lacked.

Pulling out my phone, I scrolled through my contacts until I found Agent Morrison's number. He'd been willing to help authenticate evidence during the trial, and his warning about being careful suggested he understood the dangers better than most.

But before I could call him, I needed to know what was on the drive. I needed to understand what Melissa had discovered and what risks I'd be taking by pursuing it.

I locked my office door and inserted the flash drive into my computer. The screen filled with folder names: Foundation Financials, Shell Companies, Wire Transfers, Judicial Rulings, Communications.

Each folder contained dozens of files—bank records, court documents, emails, financial reports. It would take hours to review everything properly, but even a quick scan revealed patterns that made my pulse quicken.

Money flowing from trafficking organizations through shell companies to charitable foundations. Judicial rulings that protected those same organizations from prosecution. Communications between judges and defense attorneys that suggested coordination rather than adversarial proceedings.

Melissa hadn't just discovered evidence of her father's corruption. She'd uncovered what appeared to be a systematic network of judicial protection for organized crime, exactly the kind of network my mother had been investigating when she disappeared.

And now that evidence was sitting on my computer, downloaded from a flash drive given to me by a fifteen-year-old girl who trusted me to pursue justice even when justice fought back.

Closing the files, I removed the flash drive, my hands trembling slightly as I returned it to my desk drawer. Melissa had been right to be terrified. What she'd discovered could destroy careers, topple judges, and expose corruption within the federal judiciary.

It could also get anyone who possessed it killed.

Outside my office, the normal sounds of a federal prosecutor's office continued—phones ringing, attorneys discussing cases, the mundane business of justice proceeding as if the entire system wasn't potentially compromised.

I looked at the securities fraud case still sitting on my desk, then at the drawer containing Melissa's flash drive. The fraud case suddenly seemed less like a distraction and more like potential cover—complex financial crimes that might intersect with the money laundering operations Melissa had documented. Two paths that might actually be one.

The choice was mine, but the consequences would extend far beyond my own life. If I was wrong about the network, I'd destroy my career pursuing phantoms. If I was right but handled it poorly, I'd end up like my mother—dead before I could expose the truth.

But if I was right and careful enough to survive the investigation, I might finally deliver the justice that had been denied for twenty years.

CHAPTER THIRTY-SEVEN

I STAYED LATE at the office Tuesday evening, poring over the files on Melissa's flash drive until my eyes burned and the cleaning crew had finished their rounds. The evidence was damning—a paper trail connecting Judge Thatcher's foundation to shell companies that laundered money for trafficking organizations, communications between judges discussing "problem cases," financial records showing payments that coincided with favorable rulings.

By the time I finally locked the drive back in my desk drawer and gathered my things, the federal building was nearly empty. My footsteps echoed in the marble corridors as I made my way to the parking garage, the familiar route feeling ominous in the artificial light of the underground structure.

The drive home took longer than usual through Houston's late-evening traffic. I was stopped at a red light on Westheimer when I first noticed the black sedan in my rearview mirror. Three cars back, tinted windows, no front license plate. It could have been coincidence—hundreds of black sedans traveled Houston's streets every day.

But when I turned onto my residential street and the sedan made the same turn, staying exactly three car lengths behind, coincidence became surveillance.

I pulled into my driveway with my heart hammering against my ribs. The sedan drove past my house and continued down the street, but I caught a glimpse of the driver through the windshield—a large man in dark clothing who kept his eyes fixed on my front door as he passed.

I sat in my car for several minutes, watching the street through my mirrors. No sign of the sedan, no movement in the shadows between streetlights. Maybe I was being paranoid. Maybe—

The rap on my driver's side window made me jump. The man from the sedan stood next to my car, having approached on foot while I'd been watching for his vehicle. Up close, he was even more intimidating—dark eyes, broad shoulders, scarred face.

I cracked the window an inch. "Can I help you?"

"Ms. Hayes?" His voice was gravelly, unfamiliar. "Need to have a word with you."

My hand moved toward my purse, searching for pepper spray. "I'm sorry, do I know you?"

"You don't need to know me. You just need to listen." He leaned closer to the window. "Some people think you've been asking the wrong questions, looking at things that don't concern you."

"I don't know what you're talking about."

"Sure you do. Flash drives. Foundation records. Dead judges' daughters who should have minded their own business." His hand moved toward his jacket. "Thing is, smart people learn from other people's mistakes. Your friend Melissa didn't learn fast enough."

The mention of Melissa sent adrenaline surging through my system. I hit the door lock button and kept my window cracked just enough to hear him. "What do you want?"

"Want you to forget whatever that girl gave you. Want you to focus on your nice, safe fraud case and stop digging where you shouldn't be." He placed his palm flat against my window, leaving a perfect handprint on the glass. "People who cooperate tend to have longer, healthier careers. People who don't ..."

He didn't finish the sentence, but his hand completed the gesture toward his jacket. I saw the bulge of a shoulder holster.

"I understand," I said, trying to keep my voice steady.

"Good. Because this is the only warning you get."

He started to turn away from my car, and that's when I made my mistake. Instead of starting the engine and driving away, instead of accepting the threat and living to fight another day, instead of running inside to the safety of my house, I let anger override common sense.

I stepped out of the car and stood tall.

"Is that what you told my mother twenty years ago?" I called after him.

The man stopped walking. When he turned back to face me, his expression had shifted from businesslike to dangerous. "What did you say?"

"Katherine Hayes. Did you give her the same warning before you killed her?"

His hand was inside his jacket now, and I realized I'd just escalated a threat into something much worse. "You really don't know when to shut up, do you?"

The gunshot was deafeningly loud in the quiet residential street. But the bullet didn't come from his weapon—it came from behind him, and it shattered my neighbor's fence post in an explosion of wood splinters.

"Houston PD! Drop your weapon!"

I looked past the man to see my father advancing across our front lawn, service weapon drawn in a perfect Weaver stance, his voice carrying the authority of twenty-five years in law enforcement. He'd emerged from the garage where he must have been working, still wearing his workshop clothes but moving with the controlled precision of an active police officer.

The man's gun was halfway out of his holster when Dad fired again, this time putting a round through the sedan's rear tire.

"Next one goes center mass," Dad called out. "Drop it now!"

The man looked between Dad's gun and his own partially drawn weapon, likely making calculations about angles and reaction time. Whatever he decided, he chose survival over confrontation. He let his gun slide back into the holster and raised his hands.

"Smart choice," Dad said, keeping his weapon trained on the target while moving to position himself between the man and my car. "Alex, get behind me. Stay low."

Dad's voice was ice cold. "Now you're going to walk very slowly to that oak tree and put your hands against it."

Instead of complying, the man bolted toward his sedan. Dad tracked him with the gun for a second, then made the tactical decision not to fire at a fleeing suspect in a residential neighborhood where missed shots could hit houses.

"Dammit." He holstered his weapon and pulled out his cell phone, keeping his eyes on the fleeing figure. "This is Frank Hayes, retired HPD. I need units at my address—" He rattled off our street number. "Armed suspect, fled on foot toward a black sedan, tinted windows, no front plate. Suspect threatened my daughter with a firearm."

I leaned against my car, adrenaline leaving me nauseated and dizzy. The man had reached his vehicle and was speeding away, the flat tire sending up sparks as the rim scraped against asphalt.

"Dad, what were you doing outside?"

"Heard your car pull up, then heard voices. Sounded wrong." He was already moving toward the street, scanning for the sedan's direction of travel. "When I looked out and saw that bastard leaning on your car window, I grabbed my gun and came running."

"You were in the garage?"

"Working on that bookshelf for Mrs. Patterson. Had the garage door cracked for ventilation." Dad's expression was grim. "Good thing, too. Guy was about to escalate this from threats to something worse."

Police sirens grew louder in the distance. Dad shifted back into law enforcement mode, his demeanor becoming professional and controlled.

"How did you know to have your gun?" I asked him.

"Been carrying it for three days, ever since that trial ended and Judge Thatcher posted bail." He was scanning the street, watching for any sign the sedan might return. "Alex, this wasn't random. Professional intimidation, coordinated surveillance. Someone's been watching you."

The reality of that statement hit me hard. They'd known when I'd be coming home, had followed me from the office, had been confident enough to approach me in my own driveway.

"How do you know?"

"Because I know how these people operate. They start with intimidation, escalate to threats, and end with elimination if you don't back down." Dad's expression was grim. "Your mother got the same treatment. The difference is, she didn't have backup when they decided talking wasn't enough."

The first police units arrived with a screech of tires and flashing lights. Dad immediately identified himself and began briefing the responding officers, his voice taking on the professional tone of someone used to giving crime scene reports.

"One suspect, white male, approximately six-two, two hundred pounds, armed with a concealed handgun. Threatened my daughter while she was sitting in her vehicle in our driveway. Vehicle is a black sedan, heading eastbound on our street with a flat right rear tire."

The lead officer, a sergeant who looked young enough to be Dad's son, nodded respectfully. "Mr. Hayes, what's your involvement here?"

"Retired HPD, twenty-five years on the force. Victim's my daughter." Dad gestured toward me. "She's a federal prosecutor working a case that's attracted some unwanted attention."

The officer scribbled some notes then looked back up at me. "What kind of case?"

I thought about Melissa's flash drive, about the evidence of judicial corruption that could reshape the federal court system. About Judge Thatcher, free on bail while his network tried to silence anyone who threatened their operations.

"The kind that makes powerful people nervous," I said.

The sergeant looked between Dad and me, clearly trying to assess how much trouble he was walking into. "Ma'am, are you willing to file a formal complaint?"

"Yes. Assault, terroristic threatening, whatever charges fit."

"Okay. We'll need detailed statements from both of you, and we'll process the vehicle for evidence." He looked at Dad. "Sir, I have to ask—you discharged your weapon. Are you prepared to justify that use of force?"

"Defense of another. Armed suspect threatening my daughter with what appeared to be imminent harm." Dad's answer was textbook perfect. "I fired warning shots to disable his vehicle and create an opportunity for him to surrender."

"Copy that. We'll need your weapon for ballistics testing, standard procedure."

Dad nodded and surrendered his old service weapon to the sergeant. Watching him handle the bureaucracy with practiced ease, I was reminded that he'd spent decades navigating situations exactly like this one.

"Alex," he said as crime scene technicians began photographing the driveway, "we need to talk. About what you're really investigating and what kind of protection you're going to need going forward."

"I can't just hide from these people," I said, watching the technicians dust my car window for the handprint. "If they're willing to send someone to my home, they're desperate. And desperate people make mistakes."

"Desperate people also kill witnesses who won't be intimidated." Dad's expression was grave. "Your mother ignored the warnings. Look how that worked out."

The comparison stung because it was accurate. My mother had been brave, determined, unwilling to back down from dangerous truths. Those same qualities had gotten her killed before she could expose what she'd discovered.

By the time we'd finished giving statements and the officers had canvassed the neighborhood for witnesses, it was nearly midnight. Several neighbors had heard the gunshots, but no one had seen the sedan's license plate clearly enough to provide useful information.

"We'll put out a BOLO for the vehicle," the sergeant said as his unit prepared to leave. "Damaged tire should make it easier to spot. But I have to tell you, professional intimidation like this—the guy's probably already ditched the car and disappeared."

Dad nodded grimly. "They usually do."

After the police left, Dad and I stood in our driveway looking at the scuff marks where the sedan had burned rubber getting away. The suburban street had returned to its normal quiet, but everything felt different now—more vulnerable, less safe.

Inside the house, I told him about Melissa's flash drive, about the evidence of judicial corruption that connected to trafficking networks. About Callahan's warnings and the choice between pursuing dangerous truths or accepting safe assignments.

"So what are you going to do?" Dad asked as we settled at the kitchen table.

"I don't know," I said. "Tonight proved that these people are willing to quickly escalate to violence if I don't back down."

"Tonight also proved that they're scared. People don't send gunmen to threaten prosecutors unless they're desperate to stop an investigation." Dad leaned forward. "The question is whether you're brave enough to keep pushing or smart enough to stay alive."

I looked up at him. "I can't be both?"

"Your mother thought she could be. She was wrong." Dad's voice carried twenty years of grief and regret. "But maybe you can learn from her mistakes. Maybe you can find a way to expose these people without getting yourself killed in the process."

I pushed back from the table and began pacing the kitchen, my mind racing through options and strategies. "They're not going to stop, are they?"

"No. And next time they might not send someone to talk."

I stopped pacing and turned to face him, a decision crystallizing in my mind. "Then I guess I better get to work."

Dad's eyebrows rose. "Meaning?"

"Meaning if they're willing to kill to protect their secrets, those secrets must be worth killing for." I turned back to face him. "Which means Melissa's evidence is exactly as damaging as we thought."

"Alex—"

"Tomorrow I'm calling Agent Morrison. If I'm going to do this, I'm going to do it right." I headed toward the stairs. "I need to get some sleep. Long day ahead."

Dad grumbled but headed towards the front door.

"Where are you going?"

"To change the locks and install a camera."

I chuckled. "So they can review the footage of when I get murdered."

Dad winked. "That's the spirit."

CHAPTER
THIRTY-EIGHT

THE CALL CAME at six-thirty Wednesday morning, jarring me from restless sleep filled with dreams of black sedans and men with guns. I fumbled for my phone, expecting to see Dad's number from downstairs—he'd been checking on me every few hours since last night's incident, his footsteps on the stairs becoming a comforting rhythm through the night.

Instead, the display showed Agent Morrison's contact information.

"Hayes," I answered.

"Alex, it's Morrison," he said with controlled tension, dropping all formality. "Are you somewhere you can talk?"

I sat up in bed, instantly alert. "What's wrong?"

"Judge Henry Thatcher was found dead in his home this morning. Single gunshot wound to the head. Looks like suicide."

I swung my legs over the side of the bed, my bare feet touching the cold floor as I tried to process what he'd just said. Thatcher dead. The man who'd orchestrated his daughter's murder, who'd threatened me in chambers, who'd walked free on bail just days ago.

"Suicide?" The word came out sharp, disbelieving. "You're telling me Judge Thatcher suddenly developed a conscience?"

"That's the preliminary assessment from Houston PD. His housekeeper found him in his study around five AM. Gun in his hand, powder burns consistent with self-inflicted wounds."

I stood and began pacing my bedroom, the floorboards creaking under my feet. "When did this happen?"

"Medical examiner estimates time of death between midnight and two AM. I've got a contact at HPD who keeps me informed about cases involving federal officials."

The timing wasn't coincidental. Thatcher had been killed the same night I'd been threatened, probably while I was giving statements to police officers who had no idea they were investigating a warning delivered by the same network that was eliminating loose ends.

"You don't sound convinced it was suicide," I said.

"I'm not. But the scene's been processed by HPD, and they're not looking for alternative explanations." His voice dropped. "Alex, I need you to stay away from this. Don't go to Thatcher's house, don't contact the family, don't get involved in any way."

A surge of anger rose in my chest. "Morrison, someone threatened me last night, and now the key witness in a judicial corruption case turns up dead. You're telling me I should just pretend those events aren't connected?"

"I'm telling you that Judge Thatcher's death removes a key witness from any potential prosecution of the network you've been investigating. I'm also telling you that people who eliminate witnesses don't usually stop at one."

The phone went dead. Somehow, my refusal to back down last night had triggered a decision to clean house.

I padded downstairs to find Dad already in the kitchen, coffee brewing and the morning news playing quietly on the small TV. He looked up when I entered, taking in my expression.

"What's wrong?"

I filled him in on Morrison's news while pouring myself coffee with hands that weren't quite steady.

"Son of a bitch," he said when I finished. "They killed him to keep him quiet."

"That's what I'm thinking," I said. "But why now? He was already out on bail, already cooperating with his lawyers. What changed?"

"You did. Yesterday's threat was about more than just scaring you off. It was about testing whether Thatcher could still control the situation." Dad's voice was grim. "When you didn't back down, when police got involved and started asking questions, they decided he'd become a liability."

"And they made it look like suicide."

"Classic solution. Removes the witness, ends the investigation, wraps everything up in a neat package that doesn't require uncomfortable questions about judicial corruption."

By the time I reached the federal building, news of Thatcher's death had already spread through the legal community like wildfire. Attorneys gathered in small groups, speaking in hushed tones about the tragedy of a grieving father who couldn't live with his daughter's death or being accused of having caused it. The official narrative was already taking shape: Judge Thatcher, overcome with grief and facing criminal charges, had taken his own life rather than endure the shame of a public trial.

Cynthia was waiting outside my office with a stack of pink message slips and the expression of someone who'd been fielding difficult phone calls all morning.

"Ms. Hayes, Mr. Callahan wants to see you immediately," she said. "Also, there are reporters calling about Judge Thatcher. I told them you had no comment."

"Good. Hold all my calls except family and Agent Morrison."

She nodded, and I continued down the hall.

Callahan's office felt like it had an invisible shield around it—more tense, more guarded. When I arrived, he was on the phone, speaking in careful tones as if managing a crisis.

"No," he said, "we're not making any statements beyond expressing condolences for the family … Yes, I understand the media interest, but this is a personal tragedy, not a DOJ matter …" He glanced up at me and waved me in. "I'll call you back."

He hung up and gestured for me to close the door. When I turned back to face him, his expression was grave.

"Hell of a thing," he said without preamble. "Judge committing suicide while facing trial for his daughter's murder."

I folded my arms. "Is that what we're calling it?"

Callahan's eyes sharpened. "That's what Houston PD is calling it. Single gunshot wound, gun in his hand, powder residue consistent with self-inflicted injury. Classic suicide presentation."

"What about a note?"

"Not everyone leaves notes. Sometimes the guilt and shame become overwhelming, and people make impulsive decisions."

I studied Callahan's face, reading the careful neutrality he'd perfected over years of navigating political minefields. "Nathan, do you believe Judge Thatcher killed himself?"

"I believe the Houston Police Department conducts thorough investigations and reaches conclusions based on evidence." His tone carried a warning. "I also believe that speculating about alternative theories would be inappropriate and potentially harmful to ongoing proceedings."

I all but scoffed. "What ongoing proceedings? If Thatcher's dead, the case against him dies too."

"The case against Blake Costello is still pending retrial. Thatcher's death doesn't change the fact that a jury couldn't reach a unanimous verdict about Blake's guilt or innocence."

"It changes everything about Blake's testimony regarding coercion and threats. If Thatcher's dead—"

"If Thatcher's dead by suicide, it supports Blake's claims that the judge was consumed by guilt over his actions." Callahan leaned forward. "Alex, I'm going to be very clear with you. Judge Thatcher's death ends our involvement in his case. The Public Integrity Section's investigation is closed, the criminal charges are dismissed, and this office moves on to other matters."

"And if he was murdered to prevent him from testifying about the network he was part of?"

"Then that's a matter for homicide investigators, not federal prosecutors." Callahan's voice hardened. "I heard about your incident last night. Armed man threatening you in your driveway, your father firing warning shots to scare him off."

My shoulders tensed at the reminder of how close I'd come to being another casualty. "Morrison told you?"

"Morrison told me, HPD told me, and about six other people called to express concern about your safety." Callahan stood and began pacing behind his desk, his movements agitated. "The timing is unfortunate. Judge Thatcher dies the same night you're threatened by unknown assailants. The media will have a field day connecting those dots."

"Maybe they should connect them," I said. "Maybe—"

"Maybe nothing." Callahan turned back to face me, his expression more serious than I'd ever seen it. "I'm going to give you a direct order here. You will not investigate Judge Thatcher's death. You will not pursue any theories about networks or conspiracies related to his case. You will focus on the securities fraud assignment I gave you and nothing else."

The ultimatum hung in the air between us. I thought about Melissa's flash drive hidden in my desk, about the evidence of systematic corruption that reached into the highest levels of the judiciary. About my mother, who'd been silenced twenty years ago for asking similar questions.

"And if I refuse?"

"Then you'll be looking for a new job. And probably a new career, because word travels fast about prosecutors who can't follow orders."

The threat was clear and unambiguous. Continue investigating, and my career was over. But what good was a career built on looking the other way when powerful people committed murder?

"Yesterday, someone threatened to kill me because of what I've uncovered about judicial corruption. Today, the key witness in that corruption is found dead under suspicious circumstances. You're asking me to pretend those events aren't connected."

"I'm asking you to trust that there are people better positioned than you to handle situations like this. People with resources and authority you don't possess."

"Like who? The Public Integrity Section that just closed their investigation because the target is dead? Local police, who've already decided it was suicide?"

"Judge Thatcher's death is being handled by appropriate authorities." Callahan returned to his desk and pulled out a file folder. "Your job is to prosecute federal crimes, not investigate the deaths of federal judges."

"Even when those deaths themselves might constitute federal crimes?"

"Especially then." He opened the folder and pulled out a document. "This is your formal reassignment to the securities fraud case out of Dallas. You have one week to transition your current caseload and report to the Dallas office for briefings."

I stared at the transfer order, reading it over and over again. They were removing me from Houston, placing me away from Thatcher's death, away from any investigation into the network that might have killed him.

I looked up from the order, not bothering to hide the hurt in my voice. "You're exiling me."

"I'm protecting you. And the integrity of this office." Callahan's expression softened slightly. "Alex, what happened to Judge Thatcher is tragic. But it's also the end of this story. Blake Costello will face retrial, probably plea to a lesser charge, and serve appropriate time for his role in covering up his girlfriend's death."

"And the network Thatcher was part of?" I spread my hands, frustration bleeding into my voice. "The trafficking organizations that used his foundation to launder money? The other judges who protected criminal enterprises in exchange for payments routed through shell companies? The systematic corruption that my mother died trying to expose?"

"Will be investigated by people with the proper authority and resources," Callahan said, his tone laced with finality. "Your job is done."

I picked up the transfer order and read through the bureaucratic language that was effectively ending my involvement in the case that had consumed my life for months. Dallas was three hundred miles away, far enough to keep me out of trouble but close enough to monitor.

"When do I leave?"

"Monday. That gives you the rest of the week to wrap up loose ends." He softened. "Alex, I know this feels like you're being punished for doing your job. But sometimes doing your job means knowing when to step back and let others take over."

I stood to leave, clutching the transfer order. At the door, I turned back.

"Do you think my mother would have taken this transfer?"

Callahan was quiet for a long moment. "Your mother was brilliant, dedicated, and absolutely fearless." He met my eyes directly. "She was also dead at thirty-five because she didn't know when to step back. Don't make her mistakes, Alex."

The weight of his words followed me out of his office and down the corridor. I was so lost in thought that I didn't notice anything amiss until I turned the corner toward my office and stopped dead.

James Holloway sat in my desk chair, perfectly pressed suit, familiar crooked smile, looking like he'd never left D.C. at all. He was reading through the securities fraud case file Callahan had given me, the pages spread across my desk.

"Hello, Alex." He looked up as I stood frozen in my doorway. "We need to talk."

CHAPTER THIRTY-NINE

"James, what are you doing here?" Stepping into my office, I closed the door behind me, my pulse still racing from the shock of finding him there. He was sitting in my chair, studying case files with the same intense focus he brought to everything, his dark suit immaculate despite what must have been an early morning flight.

"Getting you out of here." He stood and gathered the files from my desk with efficient movements, his hands moving with the practiced precision of someone accustomed to handling sensitive documents. "It's not safe to talk in this building. Too many ears, too many people with interests that might not align with yours."

"How did you even—" I started to ask how he'd gotten past building security, but the answer was obvious. James had the kind of federal credentials that opened doors without questions

"Your father called me last night after the police left. Told me about the attack." James's expression was grim, the careful composure he usually maintained showing cracks of worry. "I caught the first flight out of Reagan this morning."

I stared at him. The idea of my father calling James—of the two most important men in my life coordinating behind my back—felt surreal. "Since when do you two have each other's numbers?"

"Since about three months ago. We text regularly." James moved toward the door, clearly expecting me to follow. His overnight bag sat beside my desk, the same leather travel case he'd brought to Houston just weeks ago when he'd delivered his ultimatum about choosing between him and my obsession with the past. "He's worried about you. And after what happened last night, so am I."

"You text with my father?" The revelation felt almost as shocking as finding James in my office. I tried to imagine the two of them exchanging messages, my methodical father and my driven boyfriend comparing notes about my well-being. "About what?"

"About you. Keeping you safe. Whether you're eating enough or sleeping enough or taking care of yourself." He paused at the door, his hand resting on the handle. "Someone has to worry about those things since you won't."

The casual intimacy of it—my father and James forming their own relationship independent of me—left me feeling oddly exposed. I'd been so focused on my investigation that I hadn't noticed the support network forming around me, the people who cared enough to coordinate their concern.

The federal building's lobby was busier than usual, attorneys and clerks moving with the urgent energy of a busy morning. I nodded to colleagues I recognized, trying to project normalcy while James's presence beside me raised questions I wasn't prepared to answer. Outside the building, James guided me toward a black rental car parked in the visitor's section. The Houston heat hit us immediately, an oppressive humidity that made breathing feel like work.

"Where are we going?" I asked him.

"Hotel Zaza. I have a suite." James opened the passenger door for me, the gesture automatic and courteous. "We can talk there without worrying about who's listening."

The drive through downtown Houston took fifteen minutes, James navigating traffic with the casual competence of someone who'd driven in busy cities like D.C. for years. Houston moved around us in its usual rhythm—business people hurrying between buildings, construction crews working on perpetual road improvements, tourists consulting maps and looking overwhelmed by the sprawl. I watched his profile as he drove, noting the tension in his jaw, the way his eyes constantly checked the mirrors.

"James, you're scaring me a little. This level of security precaution …"

"Should have been in place weeks ago." His knuckles were white where they gripped the steering wheel, and I realized he was more worried than he was letting on. "The moment you started investigating connections to federal judges, you should have had protection."

I turned to face him. "Protection from who? The DOJ? The ones transferring me to Dallas to get me away from the case I've blown wide open?"

"From people who understand that networks like this don't just threaten prosecutors." He glanced at me before turning back to the road. "They eliminate prosecutors."

The weight of his words settled within the car's interior, mixing with the artificial coolness of the air conditioning and the faint scent of his cologne. I'd been so focused on the investigation, on following leads and building cases, that I'd somehow managed to minimize the very real physical danger I was in.

Hotel Zaza was exactly the kind of place James would choose—upscale, discreet, the type of establishment that catered to government officials and business executives who valued privacy. The lobby was all sleek lines and modern art, the type of understated luxury that whispered rather than shouted its expense. His suite was on the fifteenth floor, with floor-to-ceiling windows overlooking downtown Houston. The view stretched to the horizon, the city sprawling in all directions under the relentless Texas sun.

"Drink?" James asked, moving to a small bar area stocked with top-shelf liquor.

My stomach churned at the thought. The stress of the past few days had left me feeling constantly nauseated. "It's barely noon."

"It's been that kind of week for me." He poured himself two fingers of bourbon, the amber liquid catching the light from the windows. The smell of good whiskey filled the air as he gestured toward the sitting area. "Your father told me about Judge Thatcher's death. And the timing."

I settled onto the couch, the leather soft and expensive under my body. The suite was decorated in neutral tones with splashes of color from carefully chosen artwork, everything designed to project calm sophistication. "They killed him, James. Made it look like suicide, but they killed him to keep him quiet."

"That's what I'm afraid of." James sat beside me, close enough that I could smell his cologne mixing with the faint scent of bourbon, feel the warmth radiating from his body. "If they're willing to kill a federal judge ..."

"They won't hesitate to kill a federal prosecutor." I finished the thought he was avoiding. "Everyone keeps telling me that."

He looked at me with an expression that was equal parts concern and admiration. "But you're not backing down."

I shook my head. "I can't. Not when I'm this close to exposing the network that killed my mother."

James was quiet for a moment, studying my face with the intensity that had first attracted me to him months ago. His dark eyes took in details I probably wasn't aware of—the exhaustion I'd been carrying, the stress that had been etched into my features over the past weeks.

As though he'd just read my mind, he asked, "When's the last time you slept more than a few hours?"

"I don't know. It's all been such a blur since the trial ended." I leaned back against the couch cushions, suddenly aware of how bone-deep tired I was. The adrenaline that had been carrying me through crisis after crisis was finally wearing off, leaving me feeling hollow and fragile. "Everything's been overwhelming. The hung jury, Thatcher's threats, the attack last night. Us. I feel like I'm drowning."

"You don't have to drown alone." James's voice was gentle, and when I looked at him, the professional concern had shifted to something more personal. "I'm here now."

The space between us seemed to shrink, and I found myself remembering all the reasons I'd fallen for him in the first place. The way he made me feel safe even in the middle of chaos. The strength that radiated from him even when he was being gentle. The intelligence that matched my own, the shared understanding of what it meant to dedicate your life to justice.

"James ..." I wanted to say something about not complicating an already complicated situation. But the words died when he reached to touch my face, his thumb tracing the line of my cheek with a tenderness that made my chest ache.

"I've missed you," he said simply.

The kiss was inevitable, months of distance and tension dissolving into something urgent and necessary. His hands tangled in my hair, pulling me closer, and I tasted the bourbon on his lips mixed with something that was purely him. For a few minutes, there was nothing beyond the hotel suite, nothing beyond the feeling of being held by someone who cared whether I lived or died.

As afternoon sunlight streamed through the windows and I lay against James's chest, my burdens felt marginally lighter. His chest rose and fell steadily beneath my cheek, his hand tracing lazy patterns on my bare shoulder. The city moved on fifteen floors below us, but up here, wrapped in expensive sheets and the scent of his skin, it all felt manageable again.

"Better?" he asked, his voice carrying the satisfied warmth of a man who'd gotten exactly what he'd wanted.

"Better." I turned to look at him, taking in the way the afternoon light caught the silver threads in his dark hair, the contentment in his expression. "But this doesn't solve anything, does it? Tomorrow I still have to decide whether to take the transfer to Dallas or resign and pursue this investigation on my own."

"Actually, there's a third option." James shifted so he could meet my eyes, his expression becoming more serious. "You could come to D.C. with me."

Lifting my head, I propped it in my hand. "Won't that look like I'm running away? Like I'm abandoning my career here because things got difficult?"

"Transfer to the Justice Department. Work on cases that matter without putting yourself in the crosshairs of a network that's already tried to kill you once." His voice took on the persuasive tone I'd heard him use in courtrooms, measured and compelling. "Alex, you're brilliant. Your investigative instincts are better than anyone I've worked with. But you're also isolated here, working without institutional support against people who have unlimited resources."

The offer was tempting in ways I didn't want to admit. Not just the safety it promised, but the chance to work alongside James, to build something together that went beyond stolen weekends and late-night phone calls.

"So I should run away to Washington? Not even consider transferring to Dallas at all?"

"You should recognize that sometimes strategic retreat is the smartest move. Come to D.C., build your reputation, develop relationships with people who can actually help you take down networks like this one." James propped himself up on one elbow, his expression intent. "You could work for the Criminal Division, Public Integrity Section. Cases involving government corruption, organized crime, the kind of work you're already doing but with federal resources behind you."

I sat up, pulling the sheet around me. The hotel room felt different now, less like a refuge and more like a crossroads where I'd have to make decisions that would shape the rest of my life. "James, I can't just abandon this investigation. A young woman is dead, likely by the hands of her father, who's also now dead. Blake Costello might spend years in prison for something he didn't do."

"And if you keep pushing, you'll end up like your mother. Dead before you can expose anything."

The comparison stung, but I heard the fear underneath his words. James had seen what happened to prosecutors who got too close to powerful networks, who pushed too hard without adequate protection. "Is that what this is about? Still trying to protect me?"

"I'm trying to keep you alive long enough to actually make a difference instead of becoming another casualty before the truth even surfaces." James reached for my hand, his fingers intertwining with mine. "Alex, I love you. I can't watch you destroy yourself chasing ghosts."

I couldn't keep the frustration out of my voice. "They're not ghosts. Melissa's flash drive contains evidence of—"

"Evidence that could get you killed before you can use it effectively." James's voice grew more urgent, his grip on my hand tightening. "Come to D.C. We'll figure out how to pursue this investigation properly, with resources and protection."

I chewed on my lip for a moment. "And if the corruption reaches D.C. too? If the network extends into the Justice Department itself?"

"Then we'll deal with that when we get there," he said. "But we'll deal with it together, not with you isolated and exposed in Houston."

I looked out the window at the city where I'd built my career, where I'd uncovered evidence of corruption in an institution that was meant to keep it in check. The skyline stretched endlessly in all directions, a testament to the kind of ambition and determination that had brought me this far. The smart choice was obvious—take James's offer, transfer to D.C., pursue the investigation with institutional support.

But smart choices hadn't exposed Judge Leland's corruption or brought down the trafficking ring that had killed my mother. Sometimes justice required risks that went beyond smart.

"I need time to think about it."

"How much time?"

"The transfer to Dallas is supposed to happen Monday," I said. "That gives me three days to decide."

James nodded, but I could see the frustration in his expression, the way his jaw tightened with the effort of not pushing harder. "Whatever you decide, promise me you won't do anything dangerous without backup. Don't meet with sources alone; don't investigate leads without telling someone where you're going."

I traced the edge of the sheet with my finger, avoiding his eyes. "I promise."

"And promise me you'll consider D.C. Not just as running away, but as a way to pursue justice more effectively."

I looked up at him, seeing the genuine concern mixed with his own desires. "I'll consider it."

James pulled me closer, and I let myself sink into the comfort of him again. The afternoon was fading, painting the city in shades of gold and amber, and I knew that soon I'd have to return to the real world of threats and choices and consequences. But for now, I let myself exist in this moment of safety, wrapped in James's arms and the illusion that love might be enough to protect us both from the storms ahead.

CHAPTER FORTY

Sunday afternoon found me at my kitchen table with Melissa's flash drive, three cups of coffee, and the growing certainty that I was staring at evidence of corruption that reached far beyond Judge Thatcher. James had left for D.C. that morning, promising to call when he landed and urging me one more time to consider the Justice Department transfer.

The files on the drive were meticulously organized—Melissa had approached her research with the same systematic approach I'd seen in her journal entries, each document carefully labeled and sorted. Each folder contained documents that painted a picture of systematic judicial corruption spanning decades.

Shell Company Financial Records: Meridian Holdings, Pacific Trust LLC, Southwestern Capital Group.

Bank statements showing millions of dollars flowing from organizations I recognized from previous trafficking cases. Money that moved through multiple accounts before landing in charitable foundations with names like "Children's Legal Defense Fund" and "Border Security Foundation."

Communications - Judge Network.

Email exchanges between federal judges discussing "problem cases" and "appropriate outcomes." Judge Thatcher corresponding with Judge Kellerman about ensuring certain defendants received "proper consideration" during sentencing. Judge Patterson coordinating with defense attorneys about timing evidentiary hearings to avoid conflicts with "other priorities."

Judicial Rulings - Pattern Analysis.

Spreadsheets documenting rulings that consistently favored defendants connected to trafficking organizations. Cases dismissed on technicalities, evidence excluded on narrow interpretations of Fourth Amendment protections, sentences reduced based on "cooperation" that never led to additional prosecutions.

The scope was staggering. Melissa had uncovered what appeared to be a network of federal judges who'd been systematically protecting organized crime for years, possibly decades. The chess pieces my mother had discovered weren't just symbols—they were an organizational chart.

I was deep in a file containing bank routing numbers when my doorbell rang. Through the window, I could see Erin's car in my driveway, with Lisa's sedan parked behind it.

"Alex!" Erin called through the front door. "We know you're in there. Open up."

I gathered the documents and closed my laptop before answering the door. Erin and Lisa stood on my front porch looking like an intervention committee, both wearing casual clothes and determined expressions.

"Ladies," I greeted. "What brings you by?"

"You do," Lisa said, pushing past me into the house. "When's the last time you left this place?"

"I left yesterday. Went to the office—"

"Besides work," Erin interrupted. "When's the last time you did something normal? Ate a real meal out? Had a conversation about anything other than judicial corruption?"

I considered the question. "Thursday, I think? Had dinner with James."

"Before or after someone tried to kill you in your driveway?" Lisa was already in my kitchen, looking at the coffee cups and scattered papers. "Alex, you're living like a hermit. A paranoid hermit."

"I'm researching—"

"You're obsessing." Erin joined Lisa in the kitchen, both of them surveying my workspace like concerned relatives visiting a shut-in. "Come on. We're taking you out for coffee and normal conversation."

"I can't leave. I'm in the middle of analyzing—"

"The flash drive." Lisa picked up one of the financial documents from the table. "Holy shit, Alex. Is this what I think it is?"

"Bank records showing millions of dollars flowing from trafficking organizations to federal judges through charitable foundations." I closed the folder she was examining. "Along with communications proving coordination between judges and defense attorneys to ensure certain outcomes."

Erin moved closer to the table. "This is evidence of systematic corruption."

"This is evidence that could get Alex killed if the wrong people find out she has it." Lisa set down the document carefully. "Which is exactly why we're taking her out of this house for a few hours of normal human interaction."

"I can't just leave this evidence sitting here—"

"Then bring it." Erin was already gathering files. "We'll go somewhere public, somewhere safe, and you can tell us everything while eating actual food."

Twenty minutes later, we were settled in a corner booth at Catalina Coffee, an out-of-the-way place near Rice University that catered to students and local residents rather than downtown lawyers. Lisa had insisted on the location, claiming we needed somewhere no one from the federal building would think to look.

So much for normal conversation.

"Start from the beginning," Erin said after we'd ordered sandwiches and coffee. "What exactly did Becca give you?"

I pulled out a few of the less sensitive documents from Melissa's research. "Everything her sister had gathered about the Thatcher Family Foundation and its connections to other judicial foundations. Financial records, communications, pattern analysis of court rulings."

"Pattern analysis?" Lisa leaned forward. "What kind of patterns?"

"Systematic protection of defendants connected to trafficking organizations. Cases dismissed, evidence excluded, sentences reduced—all in cases involving the same network my mother was investigating when she died."

Erin studied one of the spreadsheets. "Coordination between multiple federal judges. If this is accurate ..."

"It would explain how trafficking networks have operated with impunity for decades." I pulled out another document. "Look at this—Judge Patterson ruling on a case involving Pacific Trust LLC, the same shell company that was funneling money to Thatcher's foundation."

"Jesus," Lisa whispered. "How many judges are involved?"

"Based on Melissa's research? At least seven in the Fifth Circuit alone. Probably more in other jurisdictions."

We sat in silence for a moment. The coffee shop buzzed with normal Sunday afternoon activity—students studying, couples on dates, families grabbing lunch. Normal people living normal lives, unaware that the federal judiciary was compromised at the highest levels.

"Alex," Erin said finally, "what are you planning to do with this evidence?"

"That's the problem." I gathered the documents back into their folder. "James wants me to transfer to D.C., work with Justice Department resources to build a proper case. Callahan wants me to take the Dallas assignment and forget any of this exists."

"What do you want to do?" Lisa asked.

"I want to expose every one of these corrupt bastards and make sure they spend the rest of their lives in federal prison." I leaned forward, resting my chin against my knuckles. "But I also want to stay alive long enough to see it happen."

"Those goals aren't mutually exclusive," Erin said carefully. "But they might require different approaches than what you've been doing."

"You think I should take James's offer."

"I think you should consider all your options before making a decision that could define the rest of your career. Or end it." Erin's voice carried genuine concern. "What James is offering—Justice Department resources, institutional support, protection—that's not nothing."

"It's also not Houston," I said. "It's not the case that killed Melissa Thatcher and my mother."

"The case will still exist whether you're in Houston or D.C.," Lisa pointed out. "But you might have better tools to pursue it from Washington."

"Or I might disappear into Justice Department bureaucracy while the network covers its tracks and eliminates evidence."

Our sandwiches arrived. I realized I hadn't eaten a real meal in days, subsisting instead on coffee and protein bars. My first bite of the sandwich was filled with flavor against melted cheese and crusty bread.

"Alex," Erin said as we ate, "can I ask you something personal?"

I covered my mouth as I scarfed down another bite and said, "Shoot."

"Are you staying in Houston because you think it's the right choice, or because you're afraid of starting over somewhere else?"

The question caught me off guard. I swallowed and asked, "What do you mean?"

"I mean that sometimes we convince ourselves we're being brave when we're actually being stubborn." She glanced at Lisa who offered an encouraging smile to us both. "Sometimes the courageous choice is accepting help instead of going it alone."

"But sometimes accepting help means compromising your principles."

"Does it? Or does it mean being strategic about how you pursue your principles?" Lisa leaned forward. "Your mother tried to take down this network alone, without institutional support."

I wished people would stop bringing up the death of my mother in this way, but I couldn't argue with the logic. "You both think I should go to D.C."

"We think you should make whatever choice gives you the best chance of actually exposing this corruption instead of becoming another casualty," Erin said. "Whether that's D.C., Dallas, or staying here and working with local FBI resources."

"What about Blake Costello? What about making sure he doesn't rot in prison for something he didn't do?"

"Blake's case will move forward no matter where you are," Lisa said. "And if I know Erin, she'll make sure the right evidence gets presented at any retrial. The testimony from the first trial, the DNA evidence—that's all on record now. Blake's got a much better chance than he did before."

I stared out the window at the Rice University campus, thinking about Melissa walking these same paths just weeks ago, heading to the library to research what she thought was an academic project. How excited she must have been when she first started uncovering connections, before she realized the danger. I thought about my mother, probably feeling that same excitement twenty years earlier, believing that exposing corruption was simply a matter of gathering enough evidence and presenting it to the right people. Neither of them had understood that sometimes the right people were the wrong people, that the system itself could be the enemy.

"I have until Monday morning to decide," I said finally.

"That's tomorrow," Erin pointed out. "So what's it going to be?" Lisa asked. "Dallas, D.C., or resignation?"

I thought about James's offer—not just the professional opportunity, but what it represented. Safety. Resources. The chance to work within the system rather than against it. About Callahan's warning that continuing this investigation would destroy my career, delivered with the weight of someone who'd seen idealistic prosecutors burn out or burn up. About the evidence sitting in my house that could reshape the federal judiciary if handled correctly or get me killed if handled wrong. The flash drive felt heavier than its physical weight, carrying the hopes of two dead women and the fears of everyone still living who knew what it contained.

"I think," I said slowly, "I need to make a phone call."

CHAPTER
FORTY-ONE

THE DRIVE HOME from Catalina Coffee was a blur of conflicting thoughts. Having Erin and Lisa pull me out of my self-imposed isolation had helped clear my head, reminded me that I wasn't just a prosecutor or a target—I was a person with friends who cared whether I lived or died. For the first time in weeks, I'd laughed at something that had nothing to do with the case, had eaten food that I actually tasted instead of just consumed for fuel.

But the lightness evaporated the moment I turned into my driveway.

A small manila envelope sat propped against my front door, identical to the one I'd found weeks earlier. My chest tightened as I approached, keys ready between my knuckles, scanning the street for any sign of watchers.

The envelope was heavier this time. I carried it inside and locked the deadbolt behind me before opening it with trembling fingers.

A chess piece fell onto my kitchen table—not a bishop this time, but a queen. Carved from white marble, more elaborate than the previous pieces, with intricate details that caught the afternoon light streaming through my windows.

The note was typed on the same plain paper as before:
Your next move decides everything.

I set the queen beside the note and stared at both. In chess, the queen was the most powerful piece on the board—able to move in any direction, across any distance, capable of controlling vast sections of the game with a single move.

The message was clear. They knew I was at a decision point. They knew about Dallas, about James's D.C. offer, about the choice I had to make by tomorrow morning.

Walking to my living room window, I looked out at the street where, just days ago, a man with a gun had threatened my life. The same street where I'd grown up feeling safe, where my father still lived, where I'd built what I thought was a normal life.

Nothing about this life was normal anymore. The network had reached into every corner of it—my cases, my office, my home. They'd killed Melissa Thatcher for getting too close to the truth. They'd murdered Judge Thatcher when he'd become a liability. They'd threatened me in my own driveway.

But they'd also just shown me something important: they were still trying to manage me rather than eliminate me. The chess piece wasn't a death threat—it was an acknowledgment that I had power, that my next move mattered enough to influence their strategy.

Picking up my phone, I scrolled to James's contact information. My finger hovered over the call button.

The queen sat on my table, silent and waiting.

If I stayed in Houston, I'd be alone against a network that had infinite resources and no qualms about killing federal prosecutors. If I went to Dallas, I'd be exiled from the case but probably safe.

If I went to D.C., I'd have institutional support, federal resources, and James watching my back. I'd also be walking into the heart of the network's power base, where they could monitor my every move.

But maybe that was exactly where I needed to be. Close enough to strike when the moment was right.

I tapped James's number.

"Alex?" He answered, sounding surprised. "I was hoping you'd call."

"I've made my decision about D.C."

"And?"

I looked at the queen one more time, thinking about strategic positioning and calculated risks. In chess, the queen was powerful but also vulnerable—one wrong move and she could be captured. But played correctly, she could control the entire game. The network thought they were giving me a choice between retreat and surrender. They didn't realize they'd just shown me a third option: advance strategically, gather strength, and strike when they least expected it.

"Book the flight."

CHAPTER FORTY-TWO

MEMORIAL GARDENS CEMETERY stretched across rolling hills west of Houston. Spanish moss draped over oak trees, and weathered headstones marked generations of Texas families. I'd been coming here for twenty years, but it never got easier to see my mother's name carved into gray granite.

Katherine Marie Hayes
1965-2003
Beloved wife and mother
"Justice is truth in action."

The quote from Edmund Burke had been Dad's choice, words that captured the essence of who she'd been better than any flowery sentiment about angels or eternal rest.

I knelt beside the headstone and pulled the two chess pieces from my purse—the white bishop I'd received months ago and the queen from yesterday's envelope. The marble felt warm in my hands despite the cool November air.

My mother's body had never been recovered, so I was really just talking to a stone in the ground. But something about this place, this ritual of visiting, made me feel connected to her in a way that transcended physical presence.

"I'm getting closer, Mom. Not finished, but closer." I placed the bishop next to the headstone, then set the queen beside it. "I know who killed you now. Or at least, I know about the network you were investigating. The judges who've been protecting trafficking organizations for decades."

A breeze rustled through the oak trees, scattering leaves across the cemetery grounds. Somewhere in the distance, a groundskeeper's mower hummed as it worked through the rows of graves.

"I found evidence. Everything you were looking for, everything that got you killed. A young woman named Melissa Thatcher died gathering it, but she made sure it would survive." I touched the edge of the headstone, feeling the rough texture of the carved letters. "Her father was one of the corrupt judges—Judge Henry Thatcher. He's dead now too."

The chess pieces sat side by side on the grass, two white figures that represented years of careful planning and patient corruption. Bishops who moved diagonally, always at angles, never directly. Queens who could strike across the entire board with devastating precision.

"I'm going to Washington, Mom. The Justice Department. I know it sounds like I'm running away, but I think it might be the smartest move." I settled cross-legged on the grass. "James offered me a position. He says I'll have resources there, institutional support. Maybe I can do more good from inside the system than fighting it from the outside."

Footsteps approached across the cemetery grass. I looked up to see Dad walking toward me, carrying a small bouquet of yellow roses—her favorite flowers. He moved slower than he used to, but with the same steady purpose that had defined him for as long as I could remember.

"Thought I might find you here," he said, settling beside me with a slight grunt. "Big day tomorrow."

I picked a blade of grass and smoothed it between my fingers. "Scared as hell, actually."

"Good. Scared keeps you alive." He placed the roses against the headstone, then noticed the chess pieces. "Those from your admirer?"

"The network's way of staying in touch," I told him. "The bishop from months ago, and the queen from yesterday."

"What do you think they mean?"

"That I matter enough to monitor. That my decisions affect their strategy." I picked up the queen and turned it over in my hands. "Maybe that they're not as untouchable as they think they are."

"She'd be proud of you, kiddo. Proud that you're still fighting for justice, even when it's dangerous."

"She'd probably tell me to be smarter about it than she was."

"Probably. Your mother was fearless, but she wasn't always careful." He reached over and squeezed my shoulder. "You've got more sense than she did. More patience."

"I don't feel patient," I said. "I feel like I've been chasing this network my entire adult life."

"Twenty years isn't that long in the grand scheme of things," Dad replied. "Some fights take generations to win."

I looked over at him, noting how life had aged my father. I asked him, "Are you okay with me leaving for D.C.? I know this is sudden—"

He chuckled. "Alex, you're thirty-two years old. You don't need my permission to move to Washington." His voice carried gentle amusement. "Besides, it's not like you're moving to Mars. They have airplanes, phones, all sorts of modern conveniences."

"But you'll be here alone."

"I've got friends, neighbors, the workshop to keep me busy. Mrs. Patterson still needs that bookshelf built." He smiled. "Houston's been my home for forty years. I'm too old to start over in some big city."

"Promise you'll visit?" I asked, needing the reassurance. "When I get settled?"

"Try to stop me. Someone needs to make sure you're eating actual food instead of living on coffee and takeout."

Together, we sat in comfortable silence, watching the late afternoon sunlight filter through the oak trees. Other visitors moved quietly through the cemetery—families placing flowers, elderly couples tending graves, children learning about relatives they'd never met.

"Dad, can I ask you something?"

"Course."

"Do you think she knew?" I rubbed my thumb across my knuckles, an old nervous habit. "When she was investigating this network, do you think Mom knew how dangerous they were?"

Dad considered the question, his weathered expression thoughtful. "I think she knew they were dangerous. I don't think she understood how ruthless they could be." He looked at the headstone. "Your mother believed in institutions, in the idea that good people in positions of power would eventually do the right thing. She didn't account for what happens when the positions of power are held by bad people."

"Is that why you think D.C. is the right move?" I asked. "Because I need to be around good people in positions of power?"

"I think D.C. is the right move because you need allies. Your mother tried to fight this network alone, and it got her killed. You're smarter than that."

I trilled my lips. "I hope so."

"I know so." Dad stood and brushed grass from his jeans. "Come on. Let's get you home. You've got packing to finish."

I picked up the chess pieces and stood, taking one last look at my mother's grave. The roses Dad had brought added color to the gray stone, a splash of life in a place dedicated to memory.

"I'll finish what you started, Mom. Might take longer than either of us wanted, but I'll get there."

As we walked back toward the parking area, Dad put his arm around my shoulders the way he used to when I was small and the world had seemed full of problems too big for me to solve.

He kissed the side of my head as we reached my car. "She knows, kiddo. And she knows you're going to be okay."

Leaning into his embrace, I felt the solid comfort of his presence. Tomorrow I'd board a plane to Washington, leaving behind the city where I'd built my career and the father who'd raised me to believe that justice was worth fighting for.

But I wasn't leaving empty-handed. I carried with me everything my mother had taught me about courage, everything my father had taught me about patience, and everything I'd learned about the cost of pursuing truth in a world designed to hide it.

The network that had killed my mother was still out there, still dangerous, still protecting criminals while wearing the robes of justice.

But for the first time in twenty years, I wasn't fighting them alone.

―――――

The story continues in *The Silent Gavel*

THE ALEX HAYES SERIES

Trial By Fire (Prequel Novella)
Fractured Verdict
11th Hour Witness
Buried Testimony
The Bishop's Recusal
The Silent Gavel

ALSO BY L.T. RYAN

Find All of L.T. Ryan's Books on Amazon Today!

The Jack Noble Series
The Recruit (free)
The First Deception (Prequel 1)
Noble Beginnings
A Deadly Distance
Ripple Effect (Bear Logan)
Thin Line
Noble Intentions
When Dead in Greece
Noble Retribution
Noble Betrayal
Never Go Home
Beyond Betrayal (Clarissa Abbot)
Noble Judgment
Never Cry Mercy

Deadline

End Game

Noble Ultimatum

Noble Legend

Noble Revenge

Never Look Back

Bear Logan Series

Ripple Effect

Blowback

Take Down

Deep State

Bear & Mandy Logan Series

Close to Home

Under the Surface

The Last Stop

Over the Edge

Between the Lies

Caught in the Web

The Marked Daughter

Beneath the Frozen Sky

Rachel Hatch Series

Drift

Downburst

Fever Burn

Smoke Signal

Firewalk

Whitewater

Aftershock

Whirlwind

Tsunami

Fastrope

Sidewinder

Redaction

Mirage

Faultline

Mitch Tanner Series

The Depth of Darkness

Into The Darkness

Deliver Us From Darkness

Cassie Quinn Series

Path of Bones

Whisper of Bones

Symphony of Bones

Etched in Shadow

Concealed in Shadow

Betrayed in Shadow

Born from Ashes

Return to Ashes

Risen from Ashes

Blake Brier Series

Unmasked

Unleashed

Uncharted

Drawpoint

Contrail

Detachment

Clear

Quarry

Dalton Savage Series

Savage Grounds

Scorched Earth

Cold Sky

The Frost Killer

Crimson Moon

Dust Devil

Savage Season

Maddie Castle Series

The Handler

Tracking Justice

Hunting Grounds

Vanished Trails

Smoldering Lies

Field of Bones

Beneath the Grove

Disappearing Act

Affliction Z Series

Affliction Z: Patient Zero

Affliction Z: Abandoned Hope

Affliction Z: Descended in Blood

Affliction Z : Fractured Part 1

Affliction Z: Fractured Part 2 (Fall 2021)

Alex Hayes Series

Trial By Fire (Prequel)

Fractured Verdict

11th Hour Witness

Buried Testimony

The Bishop's Recusal

The Silent Gavel

Stella LaRosa Series

Black Rose

Red Ink

Black Gold

White Lies

Silver Bullet

Avril Dahl Series

Cold Reckoning

Cold Legacy

Cold Mercy

Savannah Shadows Series

Echoes of Guilt

The Silence Before

Dead Air

Receive a free copy of The Recruit. Visit:

https://ltryan.com/jack-noble-newsletter-signup-1

ABOUT THE AUTHORS

L.T. RYAN is a *Wall Street Journal* and *USA Today* bestselling author, renowned for crafting pulse-pounding thrillers that keep readers on the edge of their seats. Known for creating gripping, character-driven stories, Ryan is the author of the *Jack Noble* series, the *Rachel Hatch* series, and more. With a knack for blending action, intrigue, and emotional depth, Ryan's books have captivated millions of fans worldwide.

Whether it's the shadowy world of covert operatives or the relentless pursuit of justice, Ryan's stories feature unforgettable characters and high-stakes plots that resonate with fans of Lee Child, Robert Ludlum, and Michael Connelly.

When not writing, Ryan enjoys crafting new ideas with coauthors, running a thriving publishing company, and connecting with readers. Discover the next story that will keep you turning pages late into the night.

Connect with L.T. Ryan
Sign up for his newsletter to hear the latest goings on and receive some free content
➜ https://ltryan.com/jack-noble-newsletter-signup-1

Join the private readers' group
➜ https://www.facebook.com/groups/1727449564174357

Instagram ➜ @ltryanauthor

Visit the website ➜ https://ltryan.com
Send an email ➜ contact@ltryan.com

LAURA CHASE is a corporate attorney-turned-author who brings her courtroom experience to the page in her gripping legal and psychological thrillers. Chase draws on her real-life experience to draw readers into the high-stakes world of courtroom drama and moral ambiguity.

After earning her JD, Chase clerked for a federal judge and thereafter transitioned to big law, where she honed her skills in high-pressure legal environments. Her passion for exploring the darker side of human nature and the gray areas of justice fuels her writing.

Chase lives with her husband, their two sons, a dog and a cat in Northern Florida. When she's not writing or working, she enjoys spending time with her family, traveling, and bingeing true crime shows.

Connect with Laura:

Sign up for her newsletter: www.laurachaseauthor.com/

Follow her on tiktok: @lawyerlaura

Send an email: info@laurachase.com

Printed in Dunstable, United Kingdom